SKELETON LETTERS

SKELETON LETTERS

Laura Childs

CHIVERS

| British Library Cataloguing in Publication Data available |

This Large Print edition published by AudioGO Ltd, Bath, 2012.
Published by arrangement with The Berkley Publishing Group, a division of Penguin Group (USA) Inc.

U.K.   Hardcover   ISBN   978 1 4458 8472 1
U.K.   Softcover   ISBN   978 1 4458 8473 8

LP

Printed and bound in Great Britain by
MPG Books Group Limited

For Dan

ACKNOWLEDGMENTS

Many thanks to Sam, Tom, Jennie, and Bob, as well as all my readers, scrapbooking friends, bloggers, reviewers, scrapbook magazine editors and writers, and scrapbook store owners.

CHAPTER 1

Carmela Bertrand stepped into the dark interior of St. Tristan's Church and uttered one word. "Spooky." Not only was this historic pile of stones tucked discreetly into New Orleans's freewheeling French Quarter, but it lent a note of Gothic sobriety. Dim overhead lights spilled muddy puddles of light down the center aisle. An ornate wooden altar with a large gold cross and tabernacle loomed at the far end, flanked by two red lamps. Tucked down both sides of the church were small chapels and prayer nooks where flickering vigil lights cast dancing shadows across the faces of painted, peeling statues, giving them an uncanny animated look. All around were the rustlings of unseen people as beads rattled, doors closed softly, and footsteps whispered on slate floors. Choir practice had just concluded, and it felt like the final notes of "Abide with Me" still hung thick in the air.

Blinking rapidly, Carmela fought to adjust her eyes and take in the vaulted arches, dark confessionals, and gigantic pipe organ, which all seemed to impart an air of monastic seclusion and deep solemnity. "It's almost like something out of *Phantom of the Opera*," she murmured to her friend, Ava Gruiex, who was a step behind, juggling a large hand-lettered poster.

"Or *The Hunchback of Notre Dame*," Ava offered. "You remember that poor, twisted creature scrabbling around in the bell tower . . . ?"

"I remember," said Carmela, and wished she hadn't. St. Tristan's had a bell tower, too. A tall, spindly structure with ancient bronze bells that clanged out their soliloquy above the French Quarter three times a day.

"Still," said Ava, gazing about the church with an almost beatific expression on her face, "I love it here. It's particularly meaningful, now that I'm volunteering with the Angel Auxiliary."

Carmela, a youthful blonde of not-quite-thirty, directed a skeptical sideways glance at her best friend, whose va-va-voom figure was sheathed in tight black leather slacks and a plunging yellow T-shirt with sequined court jester motif on the front. She herself was dressed in Republican beige and had worn sensible low-heeled shoes, quite appropriate considering her churchy errand today. But Carmela, who fancied herself conservative and worried that she was plain in a city where moonlight and magnolias were the norm, was really quite lovely in her own right. Her skin glowed with a peaches-and-cream luminosity, blue-gray eyes mirrored the color of the Gulf of Mexico, and she projected an upbeat air of barely contained mirth and energy. And, upon certain occasions, generally a fanciful Mardi Gras ball, Carmela wasn't afraid to fling caution to the wind and jack her five-foot-six-inch frame onto tottering four-inch stilettos to hang out with the tall gals. And the tall guys, naturally.

Still, the fact remained . . . when Ava strutted her stuff with the assurance of a peacock, Carmela sometimes felt like a little brown wren.

Got to ratchet up the sizzle, Carmela told herself. *Buy a Wonderbra or a purple silk teddy. Spritz on a cloud of Chanel No. 5. Keep that boyfriend of mine on his toes. Although maybe I shouldn't be thinking about all this . . . in church.*

"People don't realize," said Ava, dipping two fingers into a marble holy water font, crossing herself, then turning innocent, practically guileless eyes on Carmela, "that I'm a very strict Catholic."

"Really." Carmela's tone was purposefully flat. No question intended, no judgment made. Just a bushel basket full of curiosity. Like . . . had the church elders ever dug into Ava's background? Did they know she was the proprietor of the Juju Voodoo shop? Carmela thought not. But, seriously, what *was* the harm in a voodoo shop owner working as a docent in church? Nothing really. Because Ava was Ava, a retired beauty queen who partied her brains out and was known to enjoy a romantic fling or two. Or eight or nine.

"It's so peaceful in here," said Ava, as they slipped silently up a side aisle and stopped in front of a low wooden table scattered with books, hymnals, and pamphlets. "And I can't thank you enough for hand-lettering this poster." She reached behind the table, slid out a wooden easel, and plunked the poster onto it. "A perfect display," she declared.

Carmela pushed aside a hunk of artfully honeyed blond hair and directed a smile at Ava. "Always glad to help out." She'd been brushing up on her calligraphy like crazy anyway, gearing up for an upcoming seminar at her scrapbook shop, Memory Mine.

Ava set about straightening the little stacks of pamphlets, while Carmela gazed up at a stained-glass window that depicted a tall, stern-looking angel cradling a lamb. What should have been resplendent panes of red, blue, and yellow glass, with thin November sunlight streaming through, only looked dull and muted today. Rain poured down outside, as it had for the past three days, encasing all of New Orleans in a soggy gray amorphous cloud. Even in here, Carmela could hear rain drumming against the roof and gurgling down drain spouts. For a moment, Carmela wondered if, way at the tippy-top of the roofline, St. Tristan's might not have gargoyle drain spouts, much like the great churches of Europe?

And why not? This was an old church built at the turn of the century, not this century, but two gone past, by the hands of the same type of good and God-fearing men who'd supervised the construction of landmark cathedrals and abbeys. Using the tried-and-true Romanesque plan of long nave and short transept, they'd built this fine edifice, established an adjoining graveyard, and buried their noteworthy followers in crypts beneath these very same floors where today's worshippers now walked.

A sudden soft clunk focused Carmela's

eyes on a nearby confessional. Was someone in there? A penitent and priest, conferring over some sins that required forgiveness?

Had those purple velvet draperies stirred just a touch? Or was someone else padding about the church? There was a sense of emptiness in St. Tristan's; the rustlings and bustlings of a few minutes earlier seemed to have faded away. And yet . . .

Carmela touched a hand to Ava's shoulder. "I think we should —"

Like ragged gears scraping against metal, a bloodcurdling scream suddenly ripped through the church. It rose in ghastly screeches, spiraling into high-pitched shrieks.

Ava spun around and caught the eyes of a startled Carmela. Then both women whirled in tight concentric circles, fearful, searching, trying to ascertain where that ungodly scream was coming from.

Ava lifted a hand and pointed across the church. "There!"

Squinting through the darkness, Carmela saw two figures locked in a rough-and-tumble embrace.

"No!" came another piercing scream. Now it was distinctly a woman's scream, a woman who was terrified. "Not the cr—" came her words, and then she broke off in an agonized

14

keening.

Carmela dashed forward a dozen steps, then pulled up quickly. What was going on? Dare she get involved? Was it a robbery of some sort? Was there even anything here to steal?

She was about to leap forward, try to thwart whatever was happening, when Ava suddenly grasped her arm.

"Be careful!" Ava hissed.

Then the woman across the way moaned low and deep.

Ava quickly touched a hand to her mouth. "Oh man, I think she's . . ."

Carmela saw a swirl of brown robe as a cloaked figure forced a smaller figure to its knees. A flash of silver shone in the hooded figure's hands as he swept his arm backward, causing a four-foot-high statue to teeter precariously, then slowly topple from its perch. The statue crashed forward and the woman dropped to the floor like a deadweight as chunks of plaster burst everywhere, knocking over candles, spewing rivulets of hot wax. Then the figure in the hooded robe leaped away and seemed to melt into darkness.

Carmela and Ava dashed between pews toward the small altar, where the woman lay like a tossed and discarded rag doll.

"Call 911!" Carmela shrilled. Ava fumbled frantically in her velvet hobo bag for her cell phone as Carmela sprinted into a turn and smacked her left hip hard against a wooden pillar. Without breaking stride, she careened her way to the wounded woman.

Eyes wide in disbelief, Carmela pulled up short and let loose a startled, "Oh no!"

There, splayed out in front of the small altar like a sacrificial offering, was Byrle Coopersmith, one of her scrapbook regulars!

What? Byrle? Her mind could hardly grasp this horrendous discovery.

Ava skidded to a stop behind Carmela, immediately recognized Byrle, and shrieked at the top of her lungs, "Dear Lord, it's Byrle! It's Byrle!" She gibbered for another couple of seconds, then caught herself and said, in trembling tones, "What *happened?*"

Carmela was already down on her hands and knees. "Knocked unconscious, anyway," she said, tersely. Byrle's head was bleeding profusely, her neck was ringed with purple splotches — almost like fingerprint impressions — and her eyes had rolled so far back in her head that Carmela could see only the whites. Worst of all, Byrle didn't seem to be breathing.

"Do something!" Ava implored. "Maybe . . . chest compressions?"

Carmela nodded with the mechanical movement of a bobblehead doll. She laid her hands flat against Byrle's chest and tried to dredge up every morsel of know-how she had regarding CPR and chest compressions.

"Breathe," Carmela willed, as she pressed her fingers against Byrle's chest, up-down, up-down, working to establish a rhythm, trying to stimulate the poor woman's heart and force some air into her lungs. "Come on, honey, you can do it!" she cried to the woman who was quickly turning a horrible shade of blue. "You *know* you can!"

"Help her!" Ava implored. She squeezed her hands open and shut, as if working in concert with Carmela's efforts.

Carmela's knees scraped against rough stone as she continued to work on Byrle. "Ambulance coming?" she asked. She was filled with panic and starting to tire.

"On its way," said Ava.

"Can you . . . ?" She kept up her constant mouth-to-mouth breathing and repetitive motions of push, push, pump. "Can you . . . spell me for a couple of minutes?" Carmela asked Ava.

"Oooh!" Ava wrapped her arms tightly around herself.

"Never mind," said Carmela, trying to wipe her damp face against her sleeve. She

17

renewed her efforts even as her back muscles burned, and shouted out loud, "Come on, Byrle, *breathe!*"

"Anything?" Ava wailed, as Carmela, resolutely but with hope failing, continued to pump, pump, pump.

"Doggone," Carmela muttered through clenched teeth. Because the poor dear wasn't responding at all.

She was too far gone and, undoubtedly, in the Lord's hands now. As hard as Carmela was trying, she was no miracle worker.

"This is *awful!*" Ava whispered. "Beyond belief!"

Carmela could only nod in agreement. Byrle Coopersmith, their friend and fellow scrapbooker, who'd not long ago bought a pack of pink mulberry paper from her shop, now lay lifeless and cold on the unforgiving stone floor of St. Tristan's.

CHAPTER 2

Carmela stared into the earnest hazel eyes of the young detective who had arrived amid a blat of sirens and a brace of uniformed officers. Yet another shocking intrusion into what had been an oasis of calm and contemplative spirituality.

"Blunt-force trauma," was his quiet pronouncement.

"What?" Carmela asked in a hoarse whisper. Had she really heard Detective Bobby Gallant correctly?

"From the statue," Gallant told her, giving a downward bob of his head. He was young and earnest looking with dark curly hair and hazel eyes. Because of the cool weather he was dressed in a black leather jacket and chinos.

Ava, hovering directly behind Carmela, increased her viselike grip on her friend's shoulder. "The killer smacked Byrle over the head with St. Sebastian," Ava sobbed, trying to be helpful, but failing miserably.

"St. . . . ?" Carmela began, as Ava suddenly released her hold and pointed toward the flagstone floor where shards of plaster lay scattered. The statue, the one Ava had positively ID'd as St. Sebastian, lay facedown amid the rubble. Most of its head was missing. Pulverized from the blow, she supposed.

Byrle's body lay prostrate at the foot of the saint's altar where she'd fallen, looking like some kind of unholy martyr who'd given life and limb for the church. And, in a way, she had.

Carmela let loose a deep and shaky sigh. She knew she had to get a grip and pull it together. After all, she'd been a sort of witness. So maybe she could be of some assistance in the investigation? On the other hand . . .

Making a half-spin so she faced Bobby Gallant, Carmela said, "We need Babcock on this." Her words came out a little more hoarse and a little more demanding than she'd actually intended.

Gallant barely acknowledged her statement concerning his boss. "I'm the one who got the call out," he murmured.

"The thing is," Carmela said, gesturing toward Byrle's lifeless body, "we know her.

She's a friend."

"From Memory Mine," Ava added. "Carmela's scrapbook shop."

"I'm very sorry to hear that," said Gallant. And this time he did sound sorry.

"So we need to do everything in our power," Carmela gulped, "to find whoever did this."

"Which is exactly what I intend to do," said Gallant. He glanced around and noticed a uniformed officer standing off to the side, staring at Byrle's dead body. "Slovey!" he barked. "Get something to cover her up!"

Slovey seemed suddenly unhappy. "What do you want me to use?" he asked.

Color bloomed on Gallant's face. "I don't care," he snapped. "Use your jacket if you have to!"

"This isn't happening," Carmela murmured to Ava. Holding on to each other, they staggered over to the row of church pews that faced the small altar and collapsed together on the hard seat. There, they huddled like lost souls, trying to make sense of it all. At the same time, like some bizarre soap opera, the beginnings of the police investigation played out right before their eyes.

The crime-scene techs arrived, set up enough lights to make it look like a movie set, and began to photograph Byrle's body as well as the damaged saint statue and everything else within a twenty-foot radius.

Uniformed officers were given assignments and hastily dispatched to interview possible witnesses and take statements.

And finally, two EMTs arrived with a clanking gurney to carry Byrle away. Probably, Carmela decided, they were going to transport her to the city morgue. And wasn't that a grim thought!

"Babcock should be here," Ava said in a low voice. "Working this case."

Edgar Babcock, homicide detective first class of the New Orleans Police Department was, to put it rather indelicately, Carmela's main squeeze. As Carmela had wrangled through her divorce from her former husband, Shamus, the two had gazed longingly at each other. When Carmela finally separated from her philandering rat-fink husband, she and Babcock finally started seeing each other. And now that Carmela's divorce was signed, sealed, and delivered, they were most definitely an item.

"Don't worry," said Carmela, "I'm going to call Babcock." She hesitated. "But Gallant does seem to be doing a credible job."

"Credible is only good when it comes to talking heads on TV," said Ava. "For this

22

investigation we need a grade-A detective."

"Sshhh," said Carmela. Gallant was suddenly headed straight toward them.

Stepping lightly, Gallant slid into the pew directly ahead of them, settled onto the creaky seat, and swiveled to face them. Only then did Carmela notice the tiredness and deep concern that was etched in his face.

"Something tells me this isn't the only case you're handling," Carmela said.

Gallant shook his head. "Two drive-bys last night and a floater in the river."

"Tough job," said Ava.

"Tough city," said Gallant.

"What . . . what's happening now?" asked Carmela.

"Well," said Gallant, "we've got the church and outside area pretty much cordoned off, and my officers are interviewing everyone who was hanging around the church. Plus, we're canvassing the neighborhood."

"I think some people left before you got here," said Ava.

Gallant leaned forward. "Did you get a look at them?"

Ava shook her head. "Not really. It was more like hearing them." She looked suddenly thoughtful. "You know how when you're in church you're *aware* of people nearby, you hear their voices and shufflings

23

and such, but you don't really look at them?"

"I suppose," said Gallant. He seemed keenly disappointed that Ava wasn't able to give him a complete description. He directed his gaze at Carmela. "You said earlier that you thought the killer was wearing a brown robe?"

"He definitely was," said Carmela. "Like a monk's robe. Dark brown with a deep cowl and hood."

"With a white rope knotted around his waist," Ava added.

"There's a bunch of those robes hanging in the back room on a row of hooks," Gallant told them.

"That's a problem, then," said Carmela. "It means anybody could have grabbed one and thrown it on."

Gallant shifted on the uncomfortably hard pew. "What's the story with the garden and graveyard outside — all the digging and the stakes and ropes and things? Either of you know?"

"It's an archaeology dig," Ava told him. "Been going on for almost four months now."

"Do you know who's in charge of it?" asked Gallant.

Ava shrugged.

"I'm pretty sure it's the State Archaeology Board," said Carmela. "With assistance from students at Tulane." She paused. "At least that's what the article in the *Times-Picayune* said."

Gallant jotted something in his notebook. "They find anything?"

"Ten feet down," said Ava, "they discovered the ruins of the original church. The one Père Etienne founded back in 1782." Père Etienne had been a Capuchin monk who'd been a much-beloved figure because of his tireless work with the sick and the poor.

Gallant looked mildly interested. "Ruins, huh. Anything else?"

"They also unearthed an antique silver-and-gold crucifix," said Ava, "believed to have been the personal crucifix of Père Etienne."

"Which was stolen during the murder," Carmela said suddenly, almost as an afterthought.

Gallant reared back. "What? A crucifix was stolen?"

"From the saint's altar," said Ava. "Where Byrle was killed."

"I think," said Carmela, "Byrle was struggling with her killer, trying to wrest the crucifix back from him."

"Why didn't you mention this sooner?" Gallant demanded.

"Because," said Carmela, "we thought it was more important for you to dispatch your men immediately to hunt down suspects."

"So a robbery and a murder." Gallant stroked his chin with his hand. "I wonder . . . was this crucifix terribly valuable?"

"Byrle thought so," said Carmela. "After all, she gave her life for it."

CHAPTER 3

The tiny brass bell over the front door *da-ding*ed melodically as Carmela and Ava slipped into Memory Mine. At ten o'clock this Monday morning, Carmela's scrapbook shop already held a half-dozen customers. Eager scrapbookers and crafters busily browsed the floor-to-ceiling wire mesh baskets that held thousands of different papers, perused newly arrived rubber stamps, and sorted through various packages of stickers, brads, beads, tags, and embellishments, to say nothing of embossing powders, ink pads, and spools of ribbon.

The hum of activity was a welcome sight to Carmela, who'd come through a few lean years since that gigantic hiccup known as Hurricane Katrina. Business was good — not great, but with the holidays approaching, she knew sales would soon take a nice jump.

With its warm brick walls, old wooden floors, and charming bay window that looked out onto Governor Nicholls Street, the shop always felt cozy and warm. But this morning, even with customers milling about, her enthusiasm was somewhat dampened.

"What's wrong?" asked Gabby. Gabby Mercer-Morris, Carmela's assistant, was perched behind the front counter sipping gingerly from a cup of take-out café au lait. Normally a cheery, upbeat young woman with brown hair and a luminous complexion who favored preppy-style dressing, Gabby had learned to read the nuances of her boss. And right now, the dour expressions on both Carmela's and Ava's faces clearly scared her to death. "What happened?" she asked again, with some urgency.

"Um . . . ," Carmela began. She really didn't want to upset poor Gabby, who had both squeamish and sensitive tendencies. On the other hand, Gabby was bound to find out about Byrle's murder sooner or later.

"Something happened," said Gabby. She nervously pushed back her hair and turned serious brown eyes on Carmela.

Carmela gave a slow nod.

"Not the dogs . . . ?" said Gabby. Carmela

had two dogs who were the loves of her life: Boo, a girly-girl Shar-Pei, and Poobah, a spunky mutt that her ex-husband Shamus had found wandering the streets. Gabby was almost as in love with the dogs as Carmela was, since her Toyota King husband, Stuart Mercer-Morris, was allergic to dogs. Or so he claimed.

"Pups are fine," Carmela told her.

"Then what?" asked Gabby.

"Over at the church," said Ava. "Just now."

Carmela tried to swallow the lump that felt like a stranglehold in her throat, failed miserably, then managed to croak out, "Byrle."

A frown creased Gabby's normally placid brow. "What about Byrle?" When Carmela hesitated again, Gabby said, in a tremulous voice, "You guys are scaring me."

"Byrle's dead," Ava blurted out.

"What!" Gabby hissed as she stared at them. Color drained from her face and was replaced by a mixture of horror and stunned disbelief. "*Our* Byrle?" She shook her head vigorously, as if in denial. "No, it can't be," she said in a clipped tone. "Byrle was just *in* here two days ago! She asked me to order a package of moss cloth for her!"

"Cancel that order," said a glum Ava.

"Ava!" yelped Carmela. "That's so . . . cold."

Ava bobbed her head and assumed a properly sheepish expression. "Sorry, *cher.* You know I'm not good when it comes to really serious stuff. I get nervous and worked up, and then I go stupid." Ava wrinkled her nose. "And then my mouth starts to work overtime."

Carmela reached an arm around Ava's shoulders and gave her friend a comforting squeeze. "You don't go stupid," she assured her, "you just . . . go to another place in your head."

"That does sound a lot better," Ava admitted.

"Tell me," Gabby said, in a strangled voice. "Tell me what happened."

So Carmela and Ava quickly and quietly related the events of the previous hour.

"I can't believe it," Gabby murmured. "At St. Tristan's? If Byrle was assaulted in some roughneck bar on Bourbon Street I'd believe you, but St. Tristan's? If a person's not safe in a church, where are you safe?"

"Good question," said Ava.

Gabby's shoulders lifted, then relaxed in a deep sigh. "Did you call Babcock?" This question was aimed at Carmela.

"I called him," said Carmela, "and left a

message."

"But he never showed up," said Ava.

"Involved with something else, I guess," said Carmela. "But Bobby Gallant's working the case. I know for a fact that Babcock has total trust in Gallant."

"No," said Gabby, sounding insistent now. "We need Babcock. He's the smartest detective on the force and the only one who can get to the bottom of this."

"Exactly my feeling," said Ava. "Bobby Gallant *seemed* to be doing a pretty fair job. I mean, he was efficient and all, but I didn't get the feeling he was personally *concerned.*"

"Not like Carmela's sweetie would be," said Gabby. She gazed at Carmela. "Maybe you should call him again?"

"I know he'll be in touch," said Carmela. "I hate to bug him too much."

"Well . . . ," said Gabby, who still looked stricken as she continued to digest and process the awful news. "You realize we're going to have to call Baby and Tandy." Baby Fontaine and Tandy Bliss were two of their scrapbooking regulars. They often gathered with Byrle at the big wooden table in the back of the shop — "Craft Central," they'd dubbed it — to scrap the entire day away.

"A bad phone call to make," Carmela

murmured. She knew the two women would be absolutely heartbroken. And though she considered Byrle a friend, she knew that Baby and Byrle had been exceptionally close.

Gabby put some grit in her voice. "I don't want Baby and Tandy hearing about this on the TV news. Or, heaven forbid, in some gossipy Twitter chatter."

"Who's going to make those calls, then?" asked Ava. Clearly, she didn't want to.

"I will," Gabby told her. "I'll go back to the office and call Baby right now."

"But you don't know any details," said Carmela. To be honest, *she* didn't really have any details beyond a few bare-bones facts.

Gabby thought for a moment. "Maybe it's better that way. Just let Baby absorb the awful news. Then, later, when you're able to, or maybe if the killer is apprehended quickly, you can lay out the full story to her."

"Okay," said Carmela, feeling a weight lift from her shoulders. "And you'll call Tandy, too?"

Gabby nodded. "I can do that."

"Sounds good," said Ava.

"It's *not* good," said Gabby. "But it's the best we can manage for right now."

"Thank you," Carmela added, as Gabby walked stiffly away. She ran nervous fingers through her hair, noticed that several women seemed to be glancing at her with expectant looks, and murmured, "Jeez, we're busy."

At which point a customer stepped up to Carmela and asked, "Do you have any leather-bound albums?"

"I can help with that," said Ava, giving a quick smile. "What size were you thinking about?"

"Something small," bubbled the woman. "To showcase photos of my grandkids."

Another woman, a sort of regular named Molly, wanted to decorate a black velvet evening bag. "To make it one of a kind," she told Carmela.

"Do you have a color palette in mind?" Carmela asked.

Molly thought for a moment. "Maybe a dark red and bronzy feel?"

"Over here," said Carmela, making a quick sidestep, "we just happen to have some packages of really adorable silk flowers." She grabbed a couple of plastic packs. "Let's see, we've got purple, gold . . . ah, here's a nice deep red."

"Neat," said Molly, "they even look like camellias."

33

"As for a bronze tie-in," said Carmela, "how about stitching on a couple of these mesh aspen leaves? They have a brushed bronze finish that's low key and rather elegant."

"Perfect," declared Molly. "What else?"

"I think if you applied the flowers and leaves toward the bottom of your velvet bag, you could probably add a bronze-colored tassel as a zipper pull."

"I think you're right," said a delighted Molly.

Carmela gathered up all of Molly's items, wrapped them in blue tissue paper, popped them into a kraft-paper bag, and rang her up at the counter. Then she went to assist another woman who claimed to be in dire need of handmade linen paper as well as some wildlife-inspired rubber stamps.

Carmela and Ava worked for a good twenty minutes, helping customers, and finally clearing out the store for a much-needed break in the action.

Finally Gabby emerged from Carmela's cubbyhole of an office.

"Baby's pretty upset," Gabby told them.

"I can only imagine," said Carmela. Her heart felt as if a lead weight were attached to it.

"And Baby was quite insistent about talking to you," said Gabby.

"Doesn't surprise me," said Carmela. Of course, she'd want all the details.

"Did you speak to Tandy, too?" asked Ava. Gabby nodded.

"Doggone," said Ava, folding her arms and pressing them tight against her body. "I suppose she's real upset, too."

Gabby's eyes fluttered. "You have no idea."

Carmela was suddenly aware that Ava was pale and seemed to be jittering on the balls of her feet. "Are you feeling okay?" she asked Ava.

Ava clutched herself even tighter. "Maybe it's this morning's scare or this cool, drizzly weather we're having . . . but I'm freezing to death."

"Run back and make yourself a cup of tea," Carmela suggested. "There's a pot of hot water in my office along with several tins of fresh tea leaves."

"From that little place in Charleston?"

Carmela nodded. "The Indigo Tea Shop, yes. Really, go fix yourself a cup of Earl Grey. Do you a world of good."

"I think I will," said Ava, skittering away.

"She's really upset," observed Gabby.

"I think we're all a little stunned," agreed Carmela.

The two of them turned in unison then, as the front door opened. But this time it wasn't another eager scrapper coming in for a stencil or package of ephemera. This time it was Edgar Babcock. Tall, rail-thin, with close-cropped ginger-colored hair and blue eyes that were pinpricks of intensity, Babcock exuded a kind of quiet confidence. The kind of effortless calm they dearly needed right now.

"Am I ever glad to see you," exclaimed Gabby. "And, boy, do we ever need your help!" Suddenly looking a little flustered at being so outspoken, Gabby said, "Well, I'll leave you two alone. I know Carmela wants to talk in private."

Eyes focused only on Carmela, Edgar Babcock moved closer and put a hand on her shoulder. "I got your call," he said.

"I wish you could have come to the church!" Carmela said in a rush. Since they'd been snuggle buddies for quite some time now, she felt she had the right to prod him a bit.

"When I found out you'd been a witness, I hurried right over," said Babcock, "but you'd already left." He paused. "You must have had quite a scare."

Carmela tapped him midchest with an index finger. "We need you on this case."

Babcock's jaw tightened and his brows pinched together. "I can't be the lead investigator on *every* murder that takes place in New Orleans," he told her. "If I did that I'd be working 24/7." Indeed, New Orleans had played host to almost 175 murders this past year.

"But this is super important," Carmela told him. "The thing is, we know . . . we *knew* . . . the victim." Feeling hot tears puddle in her eyes, she added, "It was Byrle, one of our scrapbookers."

"Oh," Babcock said, compassion suddenly seeping into his voice. "I didn't realize the victim was a friend of yours. I'm very sorry."

Carmela gave a vigorous nod. "So it'd be nice . . ." She stopped herself and started over. "No, it would be more than nice, I'd be *grateful* if you could kind of oversee the whole investigation."

"I already spoke with Gallant," said Babcock. "When I found out you and Ava were present at St. Tristan's this morning . . . I sort of nudged my way in."

"Oh, that's great," said Carmela, breathing a sigh of relief. Babcock was smart, dogged, and determined. With one of the highest clear rates on the police force.

Ava, who'd fixed herself a fortifying cup of tea, suddenly came breezing toward them. "You're here," she said to Babcock. "Thank goodness. Because this is gonna be a tough one."

"What makes you say that?" he asked, in measured tones.

"No suspects," said Ava, looking wide-eyed. "St. Tristan's was almost empty. Except, of course . . ." She motioned toward Carmela, then touched her own chest. "For the two of us."

Babcock shook his head, looking a little annoyed. "On the contrary," he told her. Reaching into his jacket pocket, he pulled out a black leather notebook and flipped it open. "According to the information Gallant passed on to me, choir practice had just ended, so three or four choir members were still wandering about the premises." He cleared his throat. "A board meeting was set to convene in five minutes and two brothers were in a side room polishing candlesticks."

"Seriously?" said Ava. She looked stunned. "I didn't see those people." She frowned and glanced toward Carmela. "Did you see those people?"

Carmela shook her head no. "Then again," she added, "I wasn't exactly *looking* for anyone. We were talking about . . . um . . . the poster, I suppose."

Babcock held up an index finger and continued. "A couple of docents were also arranging flowers, and a delivery van was parked out back." He snapped his black notebook shut, as if to punctuate his sentence. "And if you add in the dozen or so tourists who were wandering through the garden, graveyard, and archaeology dig out back, that makes for an awful lot of people."

"You mean an awful lot of suspects," said Carmela. She was glad Babcock had decided to take an interest, but worried that so many people had suddenly cropped up. People who, obviously, hadn't been on her radar screen at all.

Babcock gazed at her. "Lots of suspects . . . yes. That's why we have officers conducting interviews and taking sworn statements right now."

"Are all those people suspects?" Ava asked.

"In my book they are," said Babcock.

"That sounds more like Napoleonic law," said Ava. "Guilty until proven innocent."

"Sometimes," said Babcock, the corners of his mouth twitching slightly, "the old laws are the best."

"You don't really believe that, do you?" asked Ava.

Babcock shrugged.

"If there were that many people in the vicinity," said Carmela, "that many witnesses, then it stands to reason a few of them must have seen *something*."

"Maybe somebody else saw Byrle struggling," suggested Ava, "or at least noticed the two of us thundering toward that altar like a herd of cattle."

"It's a possibility," said Babcock.

Ava clenched a fist and declared, "Gonna find that killer and send him to the 'lectric chair! Thank goodness Louisiana is still a progressive state that believes in capital punishment."

"That part's debatable," said Carmela.

"Actually," said Babcock, "the man of the hour, the guy we're trying to track down right now, is the delivery guy. A fellow by the name of Johnny Otis."

"A *delivery* guy?" said Ava.

"What's the deal with Otis?" asked Carmela. Could it be that Babcock had pinpointed Byrle's killer already?

"Of all the names we've collected so far," said Babcock, "he's the only one who has an arrest record."

"For murder?" asked Carmela.

"No," said Babcock, "but he's dabbled in stolen checks and fenced goods."

"Close enough for jazz," said Ava, looking

heartened. "This Johnny Otis is probably your man."

"I also understand a valuable crucifix was stolen?" said Babcock.

Ava seemed suddenly on the verge of tears. "It wasn't just *any* crucifix, it happened to be Père Etienne's gold-and-silver crucifix! It's a rare and precious artifact that was unearthed from the church's archaeology dig something like two months ago." Now her eyes were filled with tears. "And it's been displayed on the saint's altar ever since." Now her chin quivered wildly. "Until . . . this morning, anyway."

"Our theory," said Carmela, jumping in, "is that the silver crucifix attracted the attention of a thief and one thing led to another." She swallowed hard. "In other words, poor Byrle was killed while trying to fight off a theft."

"So grand theft plus murder one," said Ava, wiping at her eyes.

"Your grasp of the legal system is tenuous," Babcock told Ava, "but you do seem to be fairly well versed concerning that particular church."

"Ava's in the Angel Auxiliary," said Carmela.

Babcock looked puzzled. "The what?"

Ava wiped at her eyes again and sniffled.

41

"It's a volunteer group I belong to," she explained, "kind of like museum docents. We help out around the church by guiding visitors on history tours. Sometimes we even handle more mundane things like replacing burned-out candles or helping with floral arrangements. That sort of thing."

"Very commendable," said Babcock. "And what were you two doing there today? This morning?"

"We were delivering a poster I'd hand-lettered," said Carmela. "To promote the Père Etienne Festival that's happening in two weeks."

"If they're even going to *have* it now," Ava said, looking unhappy.

"Okay," said Babcock. He rocked back on his heels, allowing silence to spin out between them.

"Okay?" said Ava. "That's it? You don't want to hear any of our theories?"

"Not particularly," said Babcock.

"But you'll get back to us?" said Carmela.

"Perhaps," said Babcock.

"Excuse me," said Carmela, fighting a rising tide of panic, "but we want to remain an integral part of this investigation!"

"Don't worry," said Babcock, "you were there, so you *are* part of the investigation."

42

CHAPTER 4

"I have to take off, *cher*," said Ava. "We're starting inventory this week and I don't want to stick Miguel with the whole enchilada." Miguel was Ava's crackerjack assistant at Juju Voodoo. "Hey, are you okay?" Carmela was sitting at the front counter, twisting a strand of velvet ribbon through her fingers. She'd added dozens of new spools of ribbon to her inventory recently, since so many scrapbookers were also into card making and other crafts.

"I'm okay," said Carmela. "Are you?"

"I feel a little better now," Ava replied, "now that I know Babcock's on the case. Besides being a sharp dresser, that fellow is one smart cookie."

"Now we just have to wiggle our way into the loop," said Carmela.

"Think we can find a way to do that?" asked Ava. "He did seem a little averse to our getting involved."

Carmela thought for a few seconds. "He's never particularly forthcoming with information."

Ava frowned. "Then we've got a real problem, because Baby's gonna want to know, detail by detail, exactly what's going on."

"You think?"

"Oh, I know," said Ava. "So we should probably noodle this whole thing around. See what we can figure out."

"I think you're right," said Carmela. "So . . . maybe you want to drop by my place tonight?"

Ava brightened. "For dinner?"

"Sure," said Carmela. "Why not?" She knew that at any given time, the contents of Ava's refrigerator were generally limited to cat food, a head of petrified lettuce, and a couple of bottles of premium champagne.

"You're a lifesaver," said Ava, giving her a quick hug.

"I wish," said Carmela.

Gabby hung up the phone, turned to Carmela, and said, "Do you still feel up to having the calligraphy classes?" They'd planned an all-day calligraphy seminar for Wednesday. Carmela was going to teach a few basic points of calligraphy, then demonstrate to

her customers how they could easily incorporate calligraphy into their scrapbook and craft projects.

"I don't really want to cancel," said Carmela.

Gabby shrugged, half in resignation, half in agreement. "You're right, life goes on."

"It has to," said Carmela. "We don't have a choice." She wandered back through the store, straightened a pile of parchment paper, then tried to organize a tangle of fibers. *Of course life goes on,* she thought to herself. She'd learned the lesson about moving forward in the aftermath of Hurricane Katrina. When fate or Mother Nature conspires to stack the deck against you, sometimes the best you can do is smile through the tears, pick up the pieces, and just keep putting one foot in front of the other.

Carmela had witnessed this firsthand and knew that the people who managed to move forward were survivors — and those who couldn't ended up as the walking wounded.

For her, moving ahead was an easy choice — although making it through the rest of the day proved to be a true test of fortitude. And when evening came and Carmela finally ducked through the tunnel-like confines of the porte cochere to enter her

secluded courtyard, she was suddenly aware of just how bone-tired she really was.

"You want your gumbo moderately spiced or kicked up Cajun style?" Carmela asked. She was hunkered in her small kitchen, stirring a bubbling pot of chicken gumbo while a pan of brown sugar bread was hopefully turning golden brown in her oven. Though Carmela was still heartsick from this morning, the mingled cooking aromas filled her apartment and imparted a sense of normalcy and quiet contentment.

Ava, who'd offered several times to assist and had been politely turned down each time, lounged at the nearby dining table, her long legs sprawled out. She was sipping a glass of wine, the last of a bottle of Riesling, and peeling off strips of Liva Lova dog treats to feed to Boo and Poobah.

"Toss in those spices," Ava told Carmela, "and don't hold back on my account. I'm a gal who likes her food, her fellas, and her jazz nice and hot."

"But you don't like being in hot water," said Carmela, attempting a modicum of humor.

"Not usually," said Ava.

A crack of thunder suddenly rattled the rafters, and bright flashes of lightning

pulsed outside. On the roof was the distinct beat of rain.

"Raining cats and dogs out there," said Ava.

"A good night to cozy in," said Carmela, wiping her hands on a dish towel. Carmela's courtyard apartment featured brick walls, leather furniture, and an Aubusson carpet that all lent a warm, lived-in feeling. Of course, Boo and Poobah helped, too. Though tonight they were padding back and forth between Carmela and Ava, making nervous little figure eights, as if they were in a figure-skating competition.

"I keep turning Byrle's murder over and over in my mind," said Ava, looking suddenly morose, "trying to make sense of it."

"Doesn't make *any* sense to me," said Carmela, shaking in an extra measure of chili powder.

Ava grasped a hank of dark curly hair, twirled it around her finger, and said, "Who did Babcock say was at the church again? Around the same time Byrle got murdered?"

Cocking her head, Carmela squinted into the bubbling pot as she tried to recall Babcock's long litany. "Let's see . . . the church choir, board members, tourists, flower arrangers, delivery guy, and candlestick polishers." She hesitated, then added, "And a partridge in a pear tree."

"And Père Etienne's crucifix was stolen," Ava said slowly. "That seems to be the pivotal event."

"I think so, too," said Carmela.

"So who," asked Ava, "would want to steal an antique gold-and-silver crucifix?"

"Lots of people come to mind," said Carmela. "How about a garden-variety thief who might try to sell a valuable artifact to a sleazy antiques dealer? Or some wacky religious zealot? Or even a relic hunter? After all, the historical significance of that crucifix makes it worth more than just the value of the precious metals."

Ava nodded sagely. "When you put it that way, it could even be a vampire hunter."

"I know this is going to come as a real blow to you," said Carmela, as she placed two yellow Fiestaware bowls on the counter, "but there really aren't any vampires."

Ava's perfectly waxed brows shot up as she managed a look of supreme indignation. "Oh no? Tell that to all the vampire wannabes who come swooping down to New Orleans in search of Lestat's grave or wanting to make a pilgrimage to Anne Rice's house. Or . . . or . . ." Ava was wound tight and flying hard. "Or even come to visit the *Cat People* house, not that they were vampires per se."

"I see your point," said Carmela. "Still, the vampire notion seems a bit far-fetched."

"Then what do *you* think?" asked Ava.

"If I had to put money on it, I'd say the crucifix was definitely stolen because of its historical significance."

Ava looked thoughtful as she scratched Boo's tiny triangle-shaped ears. "But wouldn't that kind of rule out the delivery guy? How many delivery guys are, like, knowledgeable about antiquities? I mean, we're not talking Indiana Jones here. Most delivery guys are Guidos, aren't they?"

"Guidos?"

"Tough guys," said Ava. "Guys who like to pump it up at the gym. Not exactly your museum-savvy type."

"You make a very good point," said Carmela. She decided she'd better run that argument past Babcock. It might be important in steering the investigation in a more profitable, probable direction. It could also help insinuate herself into the middle of things.

When the oven bell dinged, Ava jumped in her chair. Then, with a sheepish grin on her face, said, "Ah, time to eat?"

"Almost," said Carmela. She ladled gumbo into the two bowls, placed them on a silver serving tray, then pulled the brown sugar bread from the oven and turned it out onto her cutting board. "Perfect," she said, breathing in the warm, yeasty aroma. Slicing off four generous pieces of bread, she dumped them into a round wicker bread basket and asked, "You want honey butter, too?"

"It's already made? I hope?"

"Natch," said Carmela.

"Let's do it," said Ava.

Carmela carried everything to the table and placed a steaming bowl of gumbo in front of Ava.

Ava grinned, bent forward, and said, "This steam could strip the curl right out of my hair if I'm not careful."

"You're so lucky," said Carmela. "You've got tons of natural curl, while my hair is like . . . I don't know . . . stick-straight opossum hair."

"You've got *great* hair," Ava crooned. "Remember, a caramel-colored bob always looks classy. Like you probably have a closet full of St. John Knits and a couple of Lady Dior handbags."

"Be still my heart," said Carmela. She slid into her chair, then suddenly popped up. "We need a refill on wine."

"Excellent idea," said Ava. "And bring the

rest of the bread. Remember, no carb left behind."

Carmela popped the cork on a bottle of Sauvignon Blanc and carried it to the table, where she poured out a half-glass for Ava. "This is something new," she told her friend.

Ava helped herself to a generous sip. "Mmm."

"You like it?"

"It's good," said Ava. "Is this from . . . ?"

"St. Tammany Vineyard," said Carmela. St. Tammany Vineyard was owned by Quigg Brevard, a previous beau of Carmela's and a dashing restaurateur who owned Bon Tiempe in the Bywater district and Mumbo Gumbo in the French Quarter. "It's called Sauvignon Silver."

"Ah," said Ava, taking another sip and this time savoring it. "Don't you have some sort of wine event coming up?"

Carmela rolled her eyes. "Oh man, do I ever. This Saturday night at the Belle Vie Hotel. A big wine-tasting and press party."

"I thought you didn't do event planning," said Ava, dipping her spoon into the gumbo. "I thought when you took the occasional sidestep outside your scrapbooking world, you only did design work." As she swallowed her first spoonful of gumbo, she quickly fluttered a hand in front of her mouth.

51

"Yowza! This is some kick-butt gumbo!"

"Too spicy for you?"

"Naaah," Ava choked, still fanning.

"Glad to hear it," chuckled Carmela. "And as far as the event planning goes, well, I got suckered in once again."

"Yeah?"

Carmela sighed. "It's the same old story. I started off designing Quigg's logo, which led to designing five different wine labels. And somehow that whole thing snowballed into my planning a red carpet media event."

"Sounds like a powerful amount of work."

Carmela sighed again. "It is."

"So you invited real live media to this big froufrou party? Like guys from radio and TV?" Now Ava was definitely interested.

"Yes, we did," said Carmela. "And it's amazing how many of them actually RSVP'd. My plan of action being to stage a truly elegant wine-tasting event that scores as much free publicity as possible."

"I'll bet you do get a few write-ups," enthused Ava.

"If Quigg's wines and vineyard can get even a small sidebar in the *Times-Picayune* or get picked up as a feature story by one of the local TV stations, it'll really help with the launch of his initial five wines," said Carmela. "Of course, we also invited a whole bunch of local restaurateurs and liquor store owners to the event. If enough of them start stocking his wine, then there's a good chance the St. Tammany brand is off and running." Carmela stopped and took a breath. "It's the old push-pull marketing technique. We push Quigg's wine to the wine shops and restaurants, and then the TV and print media get consumers interested enough so they request it."

"Consumers requesting the wine is the pull?" said Ava.

Carmela hesitated. "I *think* that's right. But you know I was a design major, not a marketing person."

"So . . . can anyone wangle an invite to this fancy shindig?" asked Ava. "And by anyone I mean *moi.*"

"I'd love it if you came," said Carmela.

"And I'm guessing it's formal," said Ava. "Hint, hint."

"So you can dress to the nines or whatever number your little heart desires," said Carmela. "And if you choose to swoop in wearing one of your Goth gowns, that's fine, too." Ava's overstuffed closets contained more black velvet, crepe, and silk than the entire wardrobe department at Paramount.

"Is there going to be a red carpet?" asked Ava, suddenly all a-twitter.

"A small one, with a step-and-repeat background." Carmela could definitely see the wheels turning in Ava's head.

"Then I should wear a gown with an opera cape."

"I think that would be apropos," said Carmela. "For you, anyway." Ava was known to wear a long gown and opera cape at the drop of a hat. To the local pancake house, the hardware store, even scooping up beads at a Mardi Gras parade.

Ava grinned happily. "Dang, this gumbo is good. The bread, too. Really hits the spot on a night like this."

"Still coming down out there," observed Carmela. The thunder had abated somewhat, but rain was beating down and lightning still strobed away.

They finished their gumbo, carried their dishes into the kitchen, and dumped them into the dishwasher. Then, with wineglasses refilled, they retreated to Carmela's living room.

"Cozy in here," said Ava. She plunked herself down on the leather chair with matching ottoman, stuck a tapestry pillow behind her head, and, with a delicious little shiver, stretched all the way out. "Is that a new painting, *cher?*" Ava cocked a forefinger at an oil painting that hung on the nearby dusty redbrick wall. It was a depiction of two shrimp boats in a bayou. Done in rich reds, golds, and yellows, and crackled with age, it gave the impression of shrimpers, their nets up, returning at sunset.

"I picked that up in the scratch-and-dent room at Dulcimer's Antiques," said Carmela, pleased that Ava had noticed her new acquisition. She adored original oil paintings, even the ones where the canvas was worn thin and the paint needed some judicious restoration. This particular seascape also featured a spectacular gold Baroque frame.

"Dulcimer's . . . ," said Ava, searching her brain.

"Place on Royal Street," said Carmela. "Just down from my shop. Owner's a chubby guy with a ponytail. You know, the guy who's always lugging that cutesy little dog around with him?"

Ava snapped her fingers. "Mimi. The pug."

"That's it," said Carmela. She grabbed a lighter, flicked it on, and touched the flame to the wicks of two tall red pillar candles that she'd decorated with Celtic cross charms. "Just in case this crazy storm knocks out our electricity," she told Ava.

"Didn't you get your highboy at Dulcimer's, too?" asked Ava.

55

Carmela turned to admire the fruitwood highboy that held thirty books, part of her prized antique children's book collection, as well as two bronze dog statues. "Mmm, I did. And at a good price, too."

Carmela's apartment was her little oasis of sanity in the French Quarter. Tucked away in a hidden courtyard with bent-over live oak tree and burbling fountain, it rubbed shoulders with elegant old-world hotels, esteemed restaurants, and posh antique shops brimming with oil paintings, family silver, fine furnishings, and the crème de la crème of estate jewelry.

And, as luck would have it, it was located directly across from Ava's voodoo shop. As they say in real estate, location, location, location.

After several years of designing, decorating, and collecting an assemblage of fine things, Carmela's apartment now exuded a lovely belle époque sort of charm. Walls that Carmela had come to think of as museum walls now displayed an ornate, gilded mirror, old etchings of the New Orleans waterfront during the antebellum period, and a heroic piece of wrought iron, probably from some long-ago French Quarter balcony, that served as a bookshelf.

Carmela padded across the room, shuffled

through a stack of CDs, and popped one in the CD player. And just as the mellow strains of Norah Jones filled the room, just when everything was all quiet and relaxing, Boo and Poobah suddenly leaped straight into the air, ears flat against their little heads, and howled at full volume.

So much for peace and contentment.

CHAPTER 5

"Holy shih-tzu!" Ava cried, as Poobah tumbled across her legs like a circus acrobat. "What a racket!" The dogs were barking nonstop, spinning in circles.

Carmela's head periscoped up from where she'd been slumped in a wicker king chair. "Somebody must be out in the courtyard."

"Babcock," said Ava. She gave a knowing grin. It wouldn't be the first time Edgar Babcock had come pussyfooting across the courtyard at night. And since her apartment was tucked in a cozy little garret above the courtyard, Ava had a bird's-eye view of Babcock's comings and goings. Of everyone's comings and goings.

"No," said Carmela, scrambling to her feet, "I don't think so. At least Babcock didn't mention anything about dropping by."

Ava shrugged a tangle of dark hair off her forehead. "Then who?"

Padding to the nearest window, Carmela pushed back filmy draperies and peered through rain-streaked glass into the court-yard. And was pretty sure she recognized the hooded Burberry coat as well as its wearer, who was skipping and dodging across wet flagstones. Then, a sudden flash of lightning illuminated the figure, as well as the live oak tree and pots of bougainvil-leas, giving everything a film noir, color-leached feeling, and Carmela knew for sure who her visitor was.

"It's Baby," Carmela exclaimed, at the exact moment a loud bang sounded at her front door.

Which triggered a second cacophony of barking and howling as the dogs tripped over each other, heading for the door.

"Boo! Poobah!" Carmela commanded in a loud, take-no-prisoners voice. "Sit!" When they hesitated, she yelled, "Do it NOW!"

"Jeez," said Ava, who'd started to get up, "when you yell like that, even I feel com-pelled to sit."

"At least somebody around here minds," Carmela muttered.

Carmela finally corralled the dogs, got their furry little butts plunked squarely on the floor, and pulled open the door.

It was, indeed, Baby Fontaine, one of her

scrapbook regulars and a very dear friend.

But this wasn't the happy-go-lucky Baby who was the matron and self-proclaimed booster of the Garden District, the Baby who giggled and flashed her megawatt smile as she effortlessly hosted elegant parties and gourmet dinners for three hundred. This Baby looked sad, tearful, and practically desperate.

"Oh, sweetie . . . ," said Carmela, sweeping Baby into her arms.

They hugged for a few moments, and then Baby, her voice registering the same pain that was so evident on her face, said, "Carmela, you have to help!"

"Come in," Carmela said in a soft voice. "Take off your coat and we'll talk."

"Oh, I'm dripping wet," Baby said, in an anguished tone. "And, look, I got you all soggy."

"Not a problem," said Carmela, brushing herself off.

Baby slipped out of her raincoat and ran a hand through her pixie-cut blond hair. She was on the far side of fifty, but her tiny figure, smooth complexion, and genteel accent gave her an upbeat, youthful aura. And Baby's good friends, in no hurry to abandon the familiar, endearing moniker that she'd earned back in her sorority days at Tulane, continued to call her Baby.

"You know," said Carmela, leading Baby over to where Ava was now sitting cross-legged, "Babcock is already working on this. Along with Bobby Gallant and a number of other officers. They're taking it very, very seriously."

"Probably the folks at St. Tristan's are, too," added Ava. "Hi, honey." She gave a little wave.

"Hi, Ava," said Baby. She was quick to return Ava's smile but still seemed agitated and sad as she groped her way through the initial throes of mourning. "Yes, I understand all that," she said, settling into a chair. "And I'm grateful the police have put their full weight behind this. But, Carmela, I'd feel a whole lot better if you could sort of nose around, too. I mean . . ." She reached up and gently massaged her temples with her fingertips. "Byrle getting murdered . . . right in the heart of the French Quarter. Inside St. Tristan's!"

"Terrible," agreed Ava.

"It's a nightmare," Baby said in a whispery voice.

Carmela stood up, went to the cupboard, and grabbed another wineglass. When she returned, she held out a half-glass of white wine for Baby. Baby stared at the glass for a

61

few moments, then finally accepted it and took a small sip.

Then Baby's gaze returned to Carmela. "Plus, Byrle is one of us." *Us,* of course, meant a fellow scrapbooker.

"I know all that," said Carmela, "and I've been thinking about this nonstop."

"We both have," said Ava. "It's like I've got theater chase lights in my brain. The notion of Byrle's murder just keeps zooming round and round, faster and faster."

"And I feel that since I was right *there,*" said Carmela, "I should be able to put my finger on something more definite. More . . . concrete."

"But you can't?" Baby's words came out in a plaintive plea.

"Afraid not," said Carmela. "We just didn't see enough." Carmela had racked her brain, trying to recall details. But it was still mostly a bad blur.

"But I thought you two were *eyewitnesses!*" exclaimed Baby. "When Gabby called me this morning, she made it sound like you two saw the whole thing unfold!"

"We were there," Carmela said slowly, "but all we saw was Byrle locked in a life-and-death struggle with some guy wearing a brown hooded robe."

Baby put a hand to her mouth. "Oh dear.

That sounds so utterly *visceral*."

"We've been sitting here trying to figure out the how and the why," said Ava. "Trying to understand just what the heck went down."

"Who would want to murder Byrle?" Baby demanded. "She was one of the dearest, most peaceable souls I've ever known."

"Technically," said Carmela, "it was a homicide, not a murder. Poor Byrle was just in the wrong place at the wrong time. A robbery gone bad."

"Have you ever heard of a robbery gone good?" asked Ava.

"Point well taken," said Carmela. "But seriously, Baby, Ava and I have pretty much bought into the theory that Byrle died trying to thwart the robbery of Père Etienne's crucifix."

"I didn't know about that," said Baby.

Ava nodded. "The crucifix is gone. Just disappeared into thin air." She made a skimming gesture with her hand and said, *"Pfft."*

"That's news to me," said Baby.

"It was rather admirable on Byrle's part," said Ava.

"But still a heinous outcome," said Baby.

"Baby, can I get you something to eat? Gumbo and a slice of bread?" asked Carmela.

Baby loosened the blue silk scarf from around her throat. "Sure, honey, that would be nice. Del's on a business trip, so I've just been rattling around all by myself."

Carmela brought out a tray of food for Baby and restarted her CD, grateful that things had finally settled down to a dull roar.

"What have you heard from Babcock?" Baby asked, between bites.

"He's been a champ," said Carmela. "When he found out Ava and I were at the church this morning, he definitely took an interest."

"And when he found out Byrle was a friend of ours," said Ava, "he promised to jump right on the case."

"That's wonderful!" said Baby.

Carmela gave a strangled smile. Babcock hadn't promised that at all. In fact, he'd been a little noncommittal. But it wouldn't help to assuage Baby's grief if she told her that.

"And Babcock's keeping you in the loop?" Baby asked Carmela.

Again Ava jumped in. "You can count on Carmela to get the straight poop. Right from the horse's mouth."

"Wrong end," Carmela muttered.

But Ava's confidence in Babcock helped relax Baby. That and the wine.

"Besides staying in the loop on the investigation," said Baby, gazing at Carmela, "I have another favor to ask."

"If you want a refund for Wednesday's calligraphy class," said Carmela, "no problem. I understand completely if you're just not up for it."

"No," said Baby, "that's not it at all."

"Then what?" asked Carmela.

Baby fidgeted. "After everything that's happened today, this is going to sound awfully frivolous."

"Come on, honey," urged Ava, "just spit it out. You'll feel better."

Baby took a quick sip of wine and aimed a lopsided smile at Carmela. "You know I'm chairperson of this year's Holidazzle Tour," she began. The Holidazzle Tour was a walking tour of holiday-themed homes in the upscale Garden District.

"Okay," said Carmela.

"And one of my Holidazzle homes just fizzled out on me." Baby squinted, then corrected herself. "Actually, Madge and Bryan LeBeau, the owners of the home, are in the throes of getting a divorce . . ."

"You're saying the dazzle went out of their marriage," said Ava.

"Something like that," said Baby. "Actually, Madge caught Bryan with a . . ." She cleared her throat. ". . . A *girl*friend, but that's beside the point."

"Actually, that's sort of interesting," said Ava.

Baby plunged on ahead. "So I was wondering, Carmela, if you'd agree to decorate your Garden District house for the Holidazzle Tour?"

Carmela didn't hesitate. "Oh no. I couldn't." The Garden District house had been Shamus's home originally and the one she'd finally received in their long, drawn-out divorce settlement. And now that she had it and wasn't even living there, she had to figure out what to do with it. Sell it, keep it, burn it down?

Baby looked disappointed. "You did Holidazzle once before."

"Sure," said Carmela, "but that was different. That was when Shamus and I were still *married.*" She shuddered at the thought of Shamus, who worked a cushy job doing little to nothing as vice president at his family's chain of Crescent City Banks. "Now I'm not even living there."

"So much the better," drawled Baby. "You won't have to worry about hordes of visitors tromping through and disturbing your privacy."

"Baby . . . ," said Carmela, sounding pained.

"It would only be for two weekends," Baby pointed out. Clearly, she didn't want to take no for an answer.

Carmela let loose a deep sigh. Decorate her empty house for the Holidazzle Tour? How would that work, anyway? Could you really make an empty home look all cheery and holiday happy? Or would it just end up looking staged and empty?

"I could help you decorate, *cher*," volunteered Ava. "You know how much I love holidays."

"Thanks a bunch," said Carmela, "but your favorite holiday is Halloween. You're the one who goes all misty eyed over goblins and witches."

Ava gave an energetic nod. "That's all true, but I can work up some Christmassy spirit if I have to."

Carmela looked skeptical. "Not like you do for Halloween."

"How about this," said Ava, "I could *try*."

"See?" said Baby, nodding her approval. "Ava's on board."

"Whoop-de-doo," said Carmela.

"Come on," urged Ava. "Be a sport."

Carmela looked at Ava, then turned her gaze on Baby. She looked so sad and bereft,

67

how could Carmela not say yes?

"Okay, you win," said Carmela. "Yes."

Baby broke out in a wide grin. Good-hearted Carmela, who'd pretty much been on the hook the whole time, had needed only a gentle tug. "And remember," said Baby, "all the proceeds go to charity."

"Which one this year?" asked Ava.

"Rescued sea turtles," said Baby. "All those poor little sweeties who are still being plucked from the oily swamps and wetlands. The loggerheads, hawksbills, and leatherbacks." Baby had a soft spot in her heart for turtles and even had a pet snapping turtle named Sampson who tolerated no one but her.

"Ohhh," said Ava, turning imploring eyes on Carmela. "Turtles. Now you have to do it!"

"Okay, okay," said Carmela. Hard to argue with the both of them. Even harder to argue against charity for turtles.

"Then it's a fait accompli," declared Baby. "Ava will help decorate and I shall list your home on the official Holidazzle Tour program."

Fifteen minutes later, Baby had departed and both Carmela and Ava were beginning to yawn. The day's events had finally caught

68

up to them, frazzling and fraying their nerves.

Ava stood up, stretched her arms above her head, and said in a slightly hopeful tone, "Maybe we should go back to St. Tristan's tomorrow and take a look around."

Carmela stared at Ava. She knew that *take a look around* was code for snooping. "What do you think we're going to find? Some kind of clue? A suspicious person skulking around the back alley?"

Ava shook her head. "Nothing that obvious. But maybe, just maybe, we can pick up a vibe or two."

"Maybe we can pick up a vibe," Carmela repeated. To her way of thinking, it sounded awfully lame.

But Ava was not to be dissuaded. "Come on, Carmela . . . you pretty much promised Baby you'd look into things. You can't back out now."

Carmela pursed her lips and made a face. "Babcock's gonna kill me. He hates it when I get involved."

"Still," said Ava, "a promise is a promise."

CHAPTER 6

As they crept down the narrow back alley in the sputtering rain, St. Tristan's Church looked like a spooky Gothic castle this morning. Its aged gray granite was stained black in several places, while rounded turrets with narrow windows rose up and lent a foreboding atmosphere. To make matters worse, fog had rolled in from the Mississippi to shroud the adjacent graveyard with its tilting, decaying grave markers.

"I forgot how creepy it was back here," said Ava. "I know we're smack-dab in the middle of the French Quarter, but this graveyard and fog make it feel like we're lost in Transylvania." Indeed, the soft rain served to dampen sounds, while the fog gave everything an ethereal, soft-focus appearance.

"We could still try getting in the main entrance," said Carmela.

"With that cop stationed there? No way

would he let us in."

"So we sneak around the back," said Carmela, "seeking alternate means per your plan."

"Look," said Ava, glancing sideways. "The dig is still going on back here."

"Awfully close to the graveyard," said Carmela.

The two of them tiptoed over to a sharply spiked, black, wrought-iron fence.

"Don't say that," said Ava. "It creeps me out."

"It's just a fact," said Carmela. "The graveyard encroached on the site of the old church. On top of the ruins."

"You're telling me they have to move bodies?" asked Ava.

"I guess so," said Carmela.

"Let's not think about it," said Ava, "let's just keep . . . *oof.*" Ava suddenly lurched forward for about the tenth time. "Doggone." She turned and stared peevishly at the cobblestones. "My heels keep catching. And then I look all stupid and ungainly."

"That's because you're wearing four-inch-high stiletto boots," said Carmela. "Honestly, who do you think can walk around in four-inch-high stiletto boots?" She chose not to mention that the boots were also spiked with silver studs and extended well above Ava's knees.

"I usually manage just fine," Ava said pointedly, "as long as I don't have to prance about on cobblestones."

"Oh crap," Carmela breathed, as they rounded the back corner of the church. "The crime-scene tape is still up." Black-and-yellow tape that warned *Crime Scene Do Not Enter* was strung like cobwebs across the back door. The warning tape fluttered and flapped in the chill breeze that swooped and swirled around them.

"But look here," Ava pointed out, "some of it's already been pulled down. So probably a few people have already ventured inside." She reached up and gently peeled away another piece of tape. "Oh boy, some more just came loose!"

"You like to live on the edge, don't you?" Carmela said, under her breath.

"The thing is," Ava reasoned, "now it's not completely verboten to go in the back door. Now it's just a halfhearted warning."

"Clearly," said Carmela, "the police don't want people prowling around this church."

"But we're not just people," said Ava. "We're relevant personnel."

"You think?"

"Sure," said Ava. "We're witnesses. Sort of." She backed up against the rough stone and hugged herself as if trying to keep warm. "Go ahead, try the door. See if it's unlocked."

Carmela reached out a gloved hand, grasped the black metal door handle, and pushed down.

A sharp, dry click rang out.

"Imagine that," said Ava. "It's open. Practically an invitation."

Now Carmela's curiosity got the best of her. "You *are* in the Angel Auxiliary," she reasoned. "So you do have access rights to the church."

"That I do," said Ava. "And you *are* my invited guest."

Carmela took a deep breath and tugged at the heavy wooden door. It hesitated for a split second, and then rusty hinges creaked and the door yawned open to reveal a dark interior.

"Whoa," said Ava. "Dark in there."

"Now you're getting cold feet? Now that we've got access?"

"Not me," said Ava, quickly stepping inside. Carmela followed as the door shut behind them with a loud whoosh, leaving them standing in semidarkness. Stone walls closed in around them, and underneath their nervous feet the cement floor felt hard and pebbled. All around them, the old church seemed to let loose deep, mournful sighs. Maybe the wind? Possibly the old furnace? Suddenly, this little backdoor foray didn't seem like a lighthearted game anymore.

"Have you been back here before?" Carmela asked. She glanced around at putty-colored walls, deciding it all looked rather austere and foreboding, with an unwelcome hint of dungeon tossed in for good measure.

"I *guess* I've been back here," said Ava. "As I recall, it's kind of a twisty-turny labyrinth. Lots of little rooms with nooks and crannies. Kind of like . . . catacombs."

"I wish you hadn't said that," said Carmela. Her breathing was suddenly a little more shallow as her heart pinged with excitement. Or was she picking up something else?

"Let's just wend our way into the main part of the church," suggested Ava. "So we can take another look at that side altar."

"Lead the way," said Carmela.

They crept fifteen feet down a long, dark corridor, Ava walking point, Carmela following closely behind. Their footfalls were soft and dampened in what felt like dead air.

Suddenly, Carmela let loose a low hiss and tugged hard on the back of Ava's sweater.

Ava stopped in her tracks. "What?" she asked in a whisper.

Carmela crooked an index finger and pointed to her left, toward a small, dimly lit room. It was a coatroom, what used to be quaintly referred to as a cloakroom. Only this room held actual cloaks. Or, rather, brown monk's robes that hung in a long row on tarnished metal hooks.

"Jeepers," Ava said, under her breath. "You think maybe the killer grabbed one of those robes yesterday?"

"It's possible," said Carmela. Looking at the robes gave her an unsettled feeling, like seeing a crust of snakeskin that had been hastily shed. Yet the serpent was still wriggling around out there.

"How many robes are hanging in there?"

Carmela did a quick count. "Eleven."

"Think there's one missing?" asked Ava. "Maybe there should be an even dozen? Seems like there *should* be an even dozen."

"No idea," said Carmela. "Can you find out? Ask a docent or something?"

Ava nodded. "I'll try."

They continued down the corridor, passing several closed doors. The air had turned damp and musty and held a noxious touch of ammonia mingled with lemon wood polish. Probably, Carmela decided, the janitor

75

used some crappy lemon-scented oil to keep these old wooden doors and door frames from drying out completely.

"Getting close," Ava told her, then stopped so abruptly that Carmela's forehead bumped against her right shoulder.

"What?" asked Carmela.

Now it was Ava's turn to point.

Carmela slid around Ava and peeked into a small, dimly lit storage room. *A huddle of little people,* was her first reaction. Then, just as quickly, she realized that the room was jam-packed with three- and four-foot-high religious statues. Most of the statues wore solemn, beatific looks on their faces, their painted eyes gazing upward. A few bore horrible stab wounds or crowns of thorns. Obviously, they'd stumbled upon St. Tristan's cache of saint statues.

"Those statues look kind of creepy, don't you think?" asked Ava.

"They're just objects," said Carmela. "Plaster and paint."

"But when they're all jumbled together like that, it kind of looks like they're waiting to be . . . *animated* or something. Like a Chucky doll."

"When you put it that way," said Carmela, staring at the peeling face of a martyred saint, "it is a little weird."

Ava gave a nervous shrug, then whispered, "This way. Almost there."

They made a sharp turn to the left, then a quick turn to the right, and were suddenly directly behind the main altar. And when they crept around the side and into the church proper, they found themselves staring out into the immense darkness.

"Nobody's here," said Ava.

"Just us chickens," said Carmela, trying to be lighthearted yet feeling she'd failed.

"It seems so deserted," said Ava. "Usually there's somebody mumbling away in the confessional or arranging flowers on one of the side altars."

Carmela gazed in the direction of the saint's altar and said, "Let's get on with it."

They slipped through an opening in a wrought-iron railing and hurried down the side aisle. Ten seconds later they were standing at the saint's altar, the site of yesterday's murder.

"Nobody's done a new saint installation yet," Ava pointed out.

"Probably because nobody's been allowed back in here," said Carmela. "But, tell me, what do you mean by 'saint installation'?" Not having been raised a Catholic, Carmela found this all a little foreign.

"Oh," said Ava, "every month or so, a new

saint is put on display."

"Hence the saint's altar," said Carmela. "So it serves as a kind of rotating *Who's Who* in heaven?"

"Something like that," said Ava.

"Okay," said Carmela, knowing what the huddle of saint statues was all about now. "Since we're here, we need to take a quick look around."

But Ava was suddenly jittery. "Sure is deserted," she said, glancing back over her shoulder. "And dark." A single red candle flickered on the main altar; a dim light hung in a flat circular bowl above the saint's altar. The rest of the church — pews, baptismal font, three other side altars, and choir loft — seemed lost in shadows.

"We *think* it's deserted," said Carmela. "But remember yesterday, when we thought the church was empty? There were all those people hanging around the periphery?"

"So you think somebody's hanging around today?"

"Let me put it this way," said Carmela, pulling a small Maglite from her suede shoulder bag, "I think we should look fast and cut bait."

But five minutes of hunting and squinting and scrabbling around on the floor yielded nothing at all.

"No clues," said Ava. "Not a thing."

"I knew this wasn't going to be easy."

"Probably the crime-scene techs got everything there was to get," said Ava.

"Hopefully," said Carmela.

"You think they vacuumed up all the hair and fibers?" asked Ava.

"I'm sure they followed protocol," said Carmela.

"Can you ask Babcock about that?"

"I can try," said Carmela. She glanced around nervously. "Maybe it's time we got out of here."

They padded slowly back to the main altar and slipped behind it, going out through the sacristy, the same way they'd come in.

"I have a question," said Carmela. "If someone had to get out of here fast, how would they do it?"

"You mean like escape?" asked Ava. "Like the killer did yesterday?"

"Yes."

Ava thought for a couple of seconds. "There are only the two entrances that I know of. The main door . . ."

"Which is how we came in yesterday," said Carmela.

"And the back door," said Ava. "Where we sneaked in today."

"Is there a basement?" asked Carmela. "I

mean, we know there's some kind of lower level because the archaeologists were exploring it."

The dig article in the *Times-Picayune* had talked about how archaeologists found the original excavation some twenty feet down.

"Maybe we should take a look?" said Ava.

They crept back down the corridor they'd come through earlier. Only this time they tried every door.

"Everything's locked," said Carmela, as she tried opening each of the doors.

"Gotta give it a shot," said Ava.

The fourth door on the left yielded to their touch.

"This one's open," said Ava.

"The question is," said Carmela, "is it just another room or does it lead somewhere?"

Ava grimaced, then put her shoulder against the door and shoved it open. Much to their surprise, it revealed a narrow flight of stone steps that wound downward. "Shazam," she whispered.

Carmela flicked on her Maglite again and said, "Let's do it."

CHAPTER 7

"What's that musty smell?" asked Ava. Her voice sounded hollow and otherworldly as they wound their way down the stairs.

"No clue," said Carmela. "I'm just focused on trying to stay upright." The steps wound down in a tight spiral, so each was basically a pie-shaped wedge and very tricky to maneuver. You had to practically step sideways.

"But there are lights," said Ava, once they'd finally reached the basement. She pointed at a bare forty-watt bulb that dangled from a low rafter. Some twenty feet beyond them, in the darkness, a second bulb cast a feeble glow.

"So maybe somebody's down here?" Carmela murmured. She glanced at the tumble of junk that surrounded them. There were stacks of broken church pews, wooden boxes, piles of broken bricks, and stacks of old hymnals. In the corner were two headless statues. She decided that, like everyone else in the civilized world, the folks who ran this church had basic hoarding instincts, too.

"It's just junk," said Ava, sounding dismayed.

"But maybe . . . another door?" wondered Carmela. "Or an old coal chute or something?" A coal chute or some other type of basement door certainly could have given the killer a third option for escape.

"What are you suggesting?" asked Ava. "That we explore?" Her enthusiasm was suddenly as dim as the lights.

"Maybe if we wandered around and took a quick peek," said Carmela.

"You twisting my arm?" Ava was somewhat resistant.

"No, but . . ." Carmela stopped and inhaled sharply. She was pretty sure she'd just heard a soft clunk somewhere in front of them. She aimed her flashlight beam into the darkness, but it wasn't powerful enough to pierce the curtain of gloom.

"Somebody's there?" Ava quavered.

"Either that or this church is home to some rather large rodents."

"Ooh," said Ava, "I don't like the sound of that!"

Carmela took a single step forward, moving her beam from side to side. She saw a wooden lectern, a broken wooden cross, and . . . holy smokes! Somebody's face?

She jumped back.

"What?" asked Ava, clutching her.

"Somebody's there."

Ava jittered on the balls of her feet. "Wha-where?"

There was a crunch of gravel, and then a long, angular face wavered in Carmela's weak flashlight beam. And a man in brown robes started toward them.

"Whoa!" said Ava.

"Who are you?" Carmela demanded.

The man continued to move toward them, slowly, silently, almost as if he were floating. His unblinking eyes seemed to pierce right through them.

"Name, please!" said Carmela. She was inches from a full-blown panic attack.

The man slowly raised his right hand. "Peace," he said. "I'm Brother Paul."

"What are you doing down here?" Ava cried, her courage suddenly returning with a vengeance.

"I work here," he told them.

"You *work* here?" said Carmela. *In the basement? Yeah, right.* "Doing what, may I ask?"

But Brother Paul had already slipped past

them, the bottom of his robe gently brushing against their legs as he headed for some other dark corner.

"We're *talking* to you," said Carmela.

Brother Paul stopped in his tracks. Then he turned slowly and gazed back at them. His eyes were pinpricks of light that seemed to throw off bright sparks.

"Were you here yesterday?" Ava asked.

His eyes continued to bore into them.

"Excuse me," said Ava. "Is that a yes or a no?"

"Our friend was murdered here yesterday," said Carmela, in a somewhat more conversational tone. Maybe if she didn't harass him, she'd get an answer? "If you know anything about that, it would be a great help."

Brother Paul ducked his head and turned away, letting one single word float back to them. "Seekers."

"What'd he say?" asked Ava.

"Who are Seekers?" Carmela called after him.

But Brother Paul had already slipped away.

"What a crackpot!" said Ava, when they were finally at the back door again, standing in the small vestibule. "What do you really

84

think Brother Paul was doing creepy-crawling in that basement?"

"Search me," said Carmela. She touched her fingers to the door handle, ready to push it open, when suddenly the door flew open on its own. Then a shadow loomed in the doorway.

"Eek!" Ava let loose a high-pitched squeal, then hastily recovered when she saw who it was. "Oh, Mr. Fried!" She drew a shuddery breath. "It's you. I thought for sure you were . . . um . . . hi there."

A man with a narrow face, his mouth pulled into a surprised O, appeared a little bewildered himself. "Hello, Ava," he stammered out.

"Carmela," said Ava, holding a hand to her throat, trying to recover her composure, "you know Norton Fried, our choir director, don't you?"

"Sure," said Carmela, "I think we met once at a party at the New Orleans Art Institute." She also remembered seeing Fried's name in their annual report, listed as a donor.

"Oh, of course," said Fried. He was slightly prissy with thick glasses that magnified his eyes. "You're Shamus's wife."

"Ex-wife," said Carmela, eager to set the record straight.

Fried snapped his fingers. "In fact, you're going to be part of Open Door this Sunday at the Art Institute. Something to do with children's art, if I recall correctly?"

"That's right," said Carmela. "My friend Jekyl Hardy and I curated a small show of children's art, in conjunction with the Children's Art Association."

"It's going to be a grand day," said Fried, unwinding a black-and-yellow-striped scarf from around his neck. "There's nothing more inspiring than attracting a whole new crowd of people to the museum. Helps to feed the hunger in their souls."

Carmela figured that while they were conversing politely, it wouldn't hurt to slip in a question or two. "I understand," she said, "that you were here yesterday morning." When Fried just stared at her, she added, "Your choir practice had just concluded . . . right before the murder?"

Fried peered sharply at her, a question hovering on his bland face. "I wasn't here — here, if that's what you mean. According to the time line the police gave me, we'd apparently finished choir practice something like ten minutes before poor Mrs. Coopersmith met her untimely end."

"So you were already gone," said Carmela. "Out the door?"

Fried suddenly looked a little less friendly. "Yes, that's correct. Didn't I just say that?"

"I was simply clarifying," said Carmela.

"And your interest is . . . ?" said Fried.

"Byrle was a friend," said Carmela.

"A good friend," added Ava.

"And you two ladies have taken it upon yourselves to investigate her murder," said Fried, in a slightly acerbic tone. "How commendable."

"That's right," said Ava.

"Not exactly," said Carmela.

Fried squinted at them. "Which is it?"

Ava was quick to backtrack. "Really, we're just curious. Because we knew her so well."

Fried pursed his lips and shook his head in disapproval. "You know what they say, don't you?" He let loose a dry chuckle. "Curiosity killed the cat."

"But you know what they say about cats," said Carmela.

Fried lifted his chin ever so slightly. "Pray tell, what is that?"

Carmela offered him a thin smile. "Nine lives."

"Rain let up," said Ava, as they stepped outside.

"Thank goodness," said Carmela, as she pulled her suede jacket closed and buttoned it. "Maybe we'll both enjoy a good spurt of customers today." They hotfooted it down the side alley, came out on Chartres Street, then cut over toward Jackson Square.

Andrew Jackson was balanced astride his fine horse as he had been for the past 158 years, tipping his hat and looking jaunty, while all around his statue, cadres of painters, psychics, cartoonists, street performers, musicians, and panhandlers set up shop for their daily gig. Jackson Square was a crazy quilt of street vendors who plied their trade for eager tourists who flocked to the square each day hoping to get a taste of the *real* French Quarter.

Gazing across Decatur Street, Carmela could see steam rising off the Mississippi and noted that the paddle wheeler *Jeremiah* was taking on a load of passengers.

"This place gets crazier every time I come here," Ava observed.

"But tourists love it," said Carmela. "So much going on."

"Dear ladies," crooned a raven-haired woman in a red frilly blouse and long, purple crinkle skirt, "come see what fate has in store for you." The lady was perched at a card table swagged in black velvet. A small crystal globe sat enticingly before her. A second folding chair sat ready for her first customer of the day.

Ava stopped in her tracks. "Eyyy . . . you're a psychic?"

The woman gave a knowing and sage nod.

"Maybe we should ask her about the murder," said Ava.

Carmela gave a warning look and a quick shake of her head. "Maybe not."

"The murder," said the woman, pouncing immediately. "The one at St. Tristan's Church yesterday?"

"That's the one," said Ava. She pointed a finger at the woman and declared, "You're good."

"Oh please," said Carmela. "She probably read the newspaper when she sipped her morning coffee. Just like everyone else did."

"Still . . . ," said Ava, focusing her attention on the psychic. "Maybe her insight could help us get a leg up."

"You were there?" asked the psychic. "At the murder scene?"

"You see . . . ," began Ava.

"Excuse me," Carmela said to the woman. "But you're the psychic. Why don't you tell us?"

The woman gazed at Carmela for a few moments, and then her eyes seemed to fill with a knowing light. "Yes, you were there yesterday." Her head bobbed eagerly as she stared into her crystal ball. "The two of you saw the murder take place."

"But we didn't . . . ," began Carmela.

The woman held up a finger. "I didn't say you saw the murderer. I said you saw it take place."

"She's right," said Ava, excitedly.

"Okay," said Carmela, "if you can see us witnessing the murder, can you also see the killer?"

The psychic wove her hands slowly above her crystal ball. "Brown," she said.

A little startled, Carmela said, "What else do you see?"

"Profound sadness," said the psychic.

"Pretty close," said Ava. She seemed to run a couple of permutations in her head, then said, "You know, I could use a good psychic at Juju Voodoo. That's my shop, just a few blocks from here. I'm pretty well set for tarot card readers and mediums, but we're skimpy on psychics."

"I could come in a couple of days a week," offered the woman. "Do readings for your customers. Crystal ball, auras, palmistry, whatever you want. I offer quite a repertoire."

"Sounds perfect," said Ava. "Uh . . . what's your name?"

"Madame Eldora Blavatsky," said the woman.

Ava looked surprised. "Seriously? That's your given name?"

"Actually it's Ellie Black," said the woman, "but Eldora is my stage name."

"You worked onstage?" asked a skeptical Carmela.

The woman shrugged. "One of the casinos over in Biloxi. I had a five-day gig."

"Good enough," said Ava. "So . . . you have a business card?" She winked as she flashed a wry grin. "Or should I just send out a few thought waves?"

Eldora snapped open a purple velvet purse and reached in. "I have a card."

CHAPTER 8

"You're here," exclaimed Gabby. She seemed surprised that Carmela had turned up at the shop this morning.

"I told you I'd be here," said Carmela, peeling off her jacket.

"I know," said Gabby, looking concerned, "but I still thought you might take the day off. After . . . you know . . . the stress of what happened yesterday."

"You're probably going to think this is totally whacked," said Carmela, "but Ava and I stopped by St. Tristan's this morning for a quick look-see."

Gabby seemed stunned. "You went back to the murder scene? Why on earth would you do that?"

Carmela gave an embarrassed shrug. "Ava wanted to look for clues."

"Oh." Gabby digested this for a few moments. "Did you find any?"

"No, but we did run into a couple of

people who were there yesterday."

Gabby put her elbows on the front counter and leaned forward with sudden interest. "Like who?"

"Norton Fried, the choir director, for one. He was kind of pussyfooting around."

"Okay," said Gabby.

"According to Babcock, Fried had just concluded choir practice some five minutes before Byrle was killed."

"But you don't think he would . . . I mean . . . isn't Fried a stand-up guy?" asked Gabby. "He's forever being written up in the paper for taking his choir to one or another international chorale."

"I always *thought* he was an okay guy," said Carmela.

"So who else did you run into?"

"Strangely enough," said Carmela, "the one who really got us wondering was the mysterious Brother Paul."

Gabby looked vaguely taken aback. "Who's Brother Paul, and why is he so mysterious?"

"He's some guy who works at St. Tristan's. And he's mysterious because we found him creeping around in the basement."

"You went down in the *basement?*" said Gabby, looking wide-eyed.

Carmela nodded. "We were scoping out

another possible exit. Because, you know, maybe that's how the killer got away."

"Did you find one?"

Carmela shook her head. "Not really. We kind of lost our momentum once we ran into Brother Paul."

"Did you talk to this Brother Paul?"

"Tried to," said Carmela. "But when we threw a couple of questions at him, he mumbled something about Seekers and took off."

"*Seacoast?*" said Gabby.

"I'm pretty sure he said *Seekers,*" said Carmela, enunciating more clearly. "But don't ask me what that means, because I have no earthly clue."

"Maybe he really said *secrets,*" Gabby speculated. "Maybe he was trying to point you toward someone in particular, a suspect maybe, but was too afraid to come right out and say it."

"He didn't seem afraid," said Carmela. "But I want to tell you, when Brother Paul came creeping out of the shadows in that basement, he sure scared the bejeebers out of me!"

Carmela and Gabby spent the next twenty minutes sorting through a new shipment of rubber stamps that had just arrived, all with a sort of Renaissance theme.

"Look at this," said Gabby, holding up a minstrel strumming a lyre. "It's perfect for Mardi Gras."

"Our customers are gonna love this stuff," said Carmela, feeling the first spark of happiness that she'd felt in two days. This was, after all, what it was all about. Preserving photos and memories through scrapbook pages. Creating lovingly crafted handmade goods in an era of foreign-made products and instant gratification.

"Tandy!" said Gabby, looking up as she unwrapped more rubber stamps. "Hello!"

Tandy Bliss, five feet two and 105 pounds soaking wet, walked stolidly into Memory Mine, her scrapbook tote slung over one skinny shoulder. She was followed by another woman, a studious-looking middle-aged blonde, who wore a neat-looking green suit and carried a leather briefcase.

"I heard," said Tandy, greeting Carmela with a big smooch on the cheek and a bear hug that belied her small stature. "I heard you were there." She followed that up with a hug for Gabby.

"You talked to Baby?" Carmela asked.

Tandy bobbed her tight frizzle of red hair. "A couple of times. She called me last night, after she dropped by to see you, and we spoke again this morning. About an hour ago."

"This whole thing about Byrle is so awful," lamented Gabby.

"Agreed," said Tandy, focusing sharp, birdlike eyes on Carmela. "But Baby informed me that Carmela promised to try to pry all the latest case developments out of Detective Babcock."

"*Try* being the operative word," said Carmela. He'd been pretty tight-lipped about the case yesterday, and she didn't foresee Babcock changing his mind.

"In that case," said Tandy, "may I present you with what might just be a secret weapon for your arsenal." She smiled widely, showing her small teeth, then said, "Marilyn?"

The woman in the green suit stepped forward with an expectant look.

"This is Marilyn Casey," said Tandy. "We met a couple of months ago when she spoke at my book club."

"How do," said Marilyn, giving a tentative wave.

"Hi," said Gabby.

"Nice to meet you," said Carmela.

Tandy continued with her introduction. "Marilyn's a local author who's been writing a mystery set in and around the French Quarter. The working title is *Big Easy Dead* and it's loosely based on a particularly grisly murder that took place in the Exeter Hotel." Tandy drew an excited breath. "But now Marilyn's going to expand her story — I think you call that a subplot — and write in Byrle's murder at St. Tristan's, and maybe even the theft of the crucifix!"

Marilyn gave a vigorous nod, like she might be a tad overcaffeinated. "Last night, after I devoured everything I could find on the news, I sat down and wrote almost thirty pages! And this morning there was even more on the television news."

"I guess you're not bothered by writer's block," said Gabby, moving around the counter and edging closer to the little group, the better to hear.

"Not with all the material I have," gushed Marilyn. "Plus the *Times-Picayune* had extensive coverage of the murder in this morning's edition."

"I'm curious," said Carmela, "are you writing fiction or true crime?"

"That's the crazy thing," said Marilyn, taking on a slightly wild-eyed look. "My book started out as fiction, but now it's definitely taken a turn toward true crime!"

"Really," said Carmela. She wasn't sure how she felt about Byrle's murder being part of a book. No, that wasn't quite right.

She knew *exactly* how she felt. She didn't much like it at all. "Is this something you really feel the need to do?" Carmela asked Marilyn. "I mean . . . she's our friend and her murder is still unsolved . . ." She stopped, aware that everyone was suddenly focused on her.

Tandy suddenly looked both puzzled and disappointed. "You're bothered by this?" she asked. "Because, frankly, I thought you'd be thrilled. The fact that Marilyn's writing a book is going to allow her access to police files."

"You really think so?" said Carmela. She didn't think so.

Tandy grabbed Carmela's hand and gave a hard squeeze. "Oh, absolutely, honey. Plus, the *Times-Picayune* is going to do a write-up on the fact that Marilyn's integrating the murder into her book. Oh gosh, we thought you'd totally buy into the idea!" Tandy hesitated. "Now I feel like bringing Marilyn here was a huge boo-boo on my part." Tandy looked ready to cry, and Marilyn just looked embarrassed.

Carmela weighed the idea for another few moments. Maybe she had made a rush to judgment? Marilyn's book might fan the flames and keep everyone on their toes — police, witnesses, and suspects. Plus, if

Marilyn was busy bugging Babcock and the rest of the homicide department for details, wouldn't that be a great smoke screen for her? Leave her free to conduct her own quiet investigation? Yes, it might at that.

"You know what, guys?" said Carmela. "Forget what I just said. I think I'm way guilty of overreacting." She focused her gaze on Marilyn. "It's just that Byrle was such a good friend to us. We're all still a little dazed and confused."

"We sure are," said Tandy. She smiled at Carmela. "So you don't mind about the book?"

"No, I don't," said Carmela. "And you're right; Marilyn's prodding away at the police might be a *good* thing."

"We'd just hope the book would be done tastefully," said Gabby, jumping in.

"Oh, you have my complete assurance on that," said Marilyn. "In fact, I'd be happy to run a few chapters by you. But only if you wanted to read them," she added hastily.

"I'd love to," said Carmela. "When they're ready."

"That sounds more than fair," said Gabby, ever the peacemaker.

"So we're good?" asked Tandy, glancing from Marilyn to Carmela.

"I was way too hasty," Carmela said again. She smiled at Marilyn. "Apologies."

Marilyn held up a hand. "No apology necessary. And I certainly didn't mean to burst in on you and upset the apple cart. Really, I know you all must be absolutely heartbroken, losing a dear friend like that."

"Since we're not busy yet," said Gabby, "and I see Tandy brought along a pan of her famous chocolate streusel bars . . . maybe we could all enjoy one with a cup of tea?"

"Tea would be great," said Carmela, exhaling.

"So you're really okay with Marilyn's book?" Gabby asked, once Tandy and Marilyn had left.

"I guess so," said Carmela. "It was just a little . . . unsettling. That's all."

"But maybe in a good way?" asked Gabby.

"Maybe," said Carmela.

"Anything that pulls attention to a murder case is probably a good thing in the long run," said Gabby.

"I suppose." Carmela spun out a length of ribbon, grabbed a punch, and made two quick holes.

"You okay? You seem to have a lot on your mind."

"I was just thinking about Holidazzle," said Carmela.

"What about Holidazzle?" Gabby asked, eager to change the subject.

"Baby asked me to put the Garden District house on the Holidazzle Tour." For some reason she always referred to it as "*the* Garden District house" instead of "*my* Garden District house." Classic disassociation, probably. Too many bad memories.

"I think that's a splendid idea," said Gabby. "It's a perfectly wonderful home for decorating. Plus it's a good excuse to get you over there and fix in your mind exactly what you want to do with that place. Keep it or sell it." Gabby knew how much Carmela had been struggling with that decision.

"There's only one problem," said Carmela.

"What's that?"

"A home that isn't lived in isn't very holidazzling."

"I don't see that as a huge problem," said Gabby. "We both know who'd be happy to lend an artful hand."

"You mean Ava? She's already thrown in as a volunteer." Carmela chuckled. "Or maybe it's slave labor."

Gabby shook her head. "I'm thinking of

someone else." She gave a slightly mysterious smile. "Who do you know that carries paint chips in his wallet and fabric swatches in his car?"

"Um . . . Jekyl?" said Carmela. Jekyl Hardy, her friend and co-conspirator in the Children's Art Association, was in real life a professional float designer, antiques appraiser, and all-around arbiter of exquisite taste. His palatial apartment in the to-die-for Napoleon Gardens was a belle époque tour de force with mahogany floors, tinkling crystal chandeliers, and dark blue shellacked walls that displayed antique smoked mirrors in gilded frames. Both the living and dining rooms boasted high-backed leather couches as well as overstuffed chairs slipcovered in rich brocades and dark damask fabrics.

"Jekyl would be *my* first choice," said Gabby. "Of course, he's always a little whirlwind with his antiques appraisal business, so there's no telling if he even has time to do it."

"But Jekyl is wild for decorating," said Carmela, liking the idea. "In fact, he once tried to persuade the post office down on Bourbon Street to paint their walls aubergine and then add a crackle glaze."

"I'd say he's your man."

"I'm going to call him."

"Do it now," said Gabby, "before we get too busy."

"You rang?" said a warm baritone voice in Carmela's ear.

Carmela smiled to herself. She could pretty much picture Jekyl sitting at his antique spinet desk. Rail-thin, dressed completely in black, with his long dark hair pulled back in a severe ponytail, the better to accentuate his pale, oval face.

"Jekyl, it's Carmela . . ."

"Oh my *goodness!*" cried Jekyl. "It really is you. I was just sitting here sipping an espresso and scanning the morning paper. How *awful* is it about your friend Byrle!"

"Really awful," agreed Carmela.

"And you were *there!*" said Jekyl. "An actual witness! Seriously, the whole thing gives me the shivers!"

"Ditto," said Carmela.

"So, tell me, have you put on your little Sherlock Holmes cap and resolved to track down the perpetrator?"

"Not exactly," said Carmela, though she knew that he knew she probably would.

"That's quite an understatement coming from you," said Jekyl. "Carmela, dear, I *know* you. You were probably skulking around that church bright and early this morning searching for clues."

Whoa. He really did know her.

"Now that you bring it up . . . ," said Carmela.

"On the other hand," said Jekyl, "you've got your own little direct pipeline to the police. With your own little hip-pocket detective."

"I wish," said Carmela.

"Still," said Jekyl, sympathy evident in his voice, "it's a terrible tragedy." He paused. "Do you know when the funeral is?"

"Baby thought maybe Thursday," said Carmela.

"Well, do let me know, will you?"

"Of course," said Carmela. She cleared her throat. "What I really called about is a little home-decorating advice."

"You're not serious," said Jekyl. "Don't tell me you're finally going to put that white elephant of a house up for sale? Be still my heart."

"It'll go on the market eventually, yes," said Carmela. "But not until after the holidays. You see, Baby twisted my arm and now the Garden District house is officially part of the Holidazzle Tour."

"Ewwww," said Jekyl. "Wherein all the have-nots get to amble through the rich folks' homes and turn pea green with envy?"

"When you put it that way," said Carmela, "it doesn't sound very . . . democratic. Besides, judging from my apartment, which is furnished with the nonpareil of local scratch-and-dent rooms, you know I'm not exactly one of the rich folks."

"No, you just married well and divorced even better," said Jekyl. "Which is what I'd better do one of these days if I want to maintain my luxurious Rolex-Lexus lifestyle."

Carmela chuckled. Jekyl drove a vintage 1978 Jaguar XKE, British racing green. It pretty much coughed and belched its way around town, trailing noxious exhaust fumes. Of course, it wouldn't hurt if Jekyl deigned to change the oil once in a while and didn't have his exhaust pipes bound up with duct tape.

"Okay," said Jekyl, "so I don't drive a Lexus. But my left wrist is adorned with a classic Rolex, thanks to the generosity of my dear departed uncle Aloysius. *Classic* meaning 'old,' of course."

"Back to the house," said Carmela. Sometimes trying to keep Jekyl on task was like herding cats. "Some serious holiday decorating is going to be needed." She paused. "Will you help? Can you help?"

"Of course, I can, lovey," said Jekyl. "In fact, I'm *dying* to get my hands on that mausoleum of yours. Unless, of course, you have your pitty-patty little heart set on . . . oh, horrors! . . . mundane red felt doorknob covers and bilious green Christmas tree skirts. In which case I'm afraid I'd have to take a pass."

"Nothing that conventional," said Carmela. "Fact is, I'd hang twinkle lights from the rafters if you thought it would glam up the old place."

"Still too tacky," purred Jekyl.

"Then how about this," said Carmela. "I'll give you carte blanche. You can bring in live reindeer, ice sculptures, or whatever you want." She paused. "Of course, we'll still need to create some sort of master plan to float past Baby."

"Child's play," said Jekyl. "What say we get together at your white elephant and put our heads together for a group-think. If you're not going to be out clubbing later, maybe we could even get together tonight."

"I can do tonight," said Carmela. "Maybe sevenish?" She glanced up, saw Gabby gesturing. She had another call waiting. "Thanks, Jekyl, I really appreciate it."

"Toodles," said Jekyl.

Carmela immediately punched the second

button. "This is Carmela, how can I help you?" She fully expected the caller to be one of her scrapbook regulars, asking if she could order some rice paper or inquiring about stencil classes. But it wasn't. Not even close.

"Carmela?" said the voice. "Mrs. Bertrand?"

"You were right the first time. Carmela is just fine. And you are . . . ?"

"This is Louise Applegate from the State Archaeology Board."

"Okay," said Carmela.

"I understand you were present at St. Tristan's yesterday when Père Etienne's crucifix was stolen?"

Carmela felt her jaw tighten so hard she was afraid she'd pop a filling. "You mean was I there when my friend Byrle was murdered?" Her tone was cool bordering on icy.

"Excuse me!" came the woman's startled reply. "I certainly didn't mean to imply that Mrs. Coopersmith's death was in any way secondary. Oh my goodness, no. It was a terrible tragedy!"

Great, thought Carmela, *that's the second time today I've jumped down somebody's throat for no reason. Time to do a little deep breathing and calm down! Ohmmm me,*

107

ohmmm my.

"You know what?" said Carmela, deciding to come clean. "This isn't the first conversation I've had today that sent me off the deep end, and it probably won't be the last. So apologies for overreacting and, uh, could we please start fresh?"

There was a long pause and then Louise Applegate said, "Absolutely. I was just calling to see if I could steal a few moments of your time. But if this is a *bad* time, and it seems like it might be, then perhaps . . ."

"No," said Carmela, "it's okay. Now I'm just moderately freaked out."

"That's understandable," said Applegate. "I just wanted to have a short conversation with you and get some facts straight."

"I take it," said Carmela, "your archaeology office has some questions?"

"Yes, we do," replied the woman, sounding relieved.

"And your office is where?" Carmela asked.

"We're at Marais and Pauger," responded Applegate.

"Just a few blocks away," Carmela murmured. She glanced at her watch. "If you wanted to drop by my shop around four o'clock or so, that would work for me. You know where we are? Memory Mine on

Governor Nicholls Street?"

"Of course," said Applegate. "See you then."

Carmela hung up the phone, took a deep breath, and spun her chair around.

"Hi," came a deep voice.

"Eeeyh!" Carmela jerked upright as if a red-hot wire had been run up the inside of her leg.

Quigg Brevard held both hands in front of himself in an appeasing gesture. "Sorry, sorry, I didn't mean to scare you like that."

"Well, you did," said Carmela, sounding as cranky as she felt unsettled. Honestly, what was it in men's DNA that caused them to sneak up and surprise women like that? Didn't they know women *hated* to be spooked? Obviously they didn't. Or maybe . . . maybe they just didn't care. Maybe it was done in sport.

Quigg took a tentative step into her office. He was a truly handsome man; his olive complexion set off dark, snapping eyes and a sensuous mouth. With his broad shoulders and big-cat way of moving, he could almost take your breath away. Almost.

"What do you want?" Carmela asked, still feeling crabby.

"Just checking in," said Quigg. "As you recall, we have our big media event this

Saturday night."

"Yes, yes," said Carmela, giving a sort of offhand wave. "I'm well aware of that."

"So is everyone we invited," said Quigg. He grinned and showed a row of even white teeth, like Chiclets. "Can you believe we have over one hundred people coming?"

"Sounds right," said Carmela. She'd designed the invitations, after all, and sent them out to the media as well as a restaurateur and bottle shop list they'd developed together.

"Well, it's darned exciting," said Quigg. He'd launched two restaurants in the last couple of years and had enjoyed a whirlwind of success that included rave reviews and a backlog of reservations. But launching St. Tammany Vineyard was a tricky proposition. These days a vintner didn't just compete with California and European wines. Now there were more than three thousand commercial wineries, with at least one in each of the fifty states. And good wines were being imported from South Africa, Australia, and even Argentina.

"I hope you didn't bet the farm on this vineyard venture," said Carmela. Success in one arena didn't necessarily guarantee success in another.

Quigg gave a laconic shrug that said, of

course he had. "Go big or go home," he told her. "That's what I always say."

"And I prefer to think big but take smaller steps."

"Same goal, different philosophies," said Quigg. His brows arched. "So you've got everything squared away with the folks at the Belle Vie Hotel?" He'd wanted to hold the wine tasting and launch party at one of his own restaurants, but Carmela had convinced him that the rather grand Marquis Ballroom at the Belle Vie would be an even more impressive venue. She sincerely hoped she was right.

"I've got a final meeting with the catering manager Thursday afternoon," Carmela told him. "After that, we cross our fingers and cast our fate to the wind."

"I'm all for that," said Quigg.

"Oh," said Carmela. "You remember you wanted to know about swag bags?"

Quigg nodded. "Yeah?" He'd wanted to give something to each guest to take home with them, a kind of remembrance of the event. Carmela had told him she'd design something only if she had time.

"Well, I came up with this." Carmela turned back to her desk, grabbed a tubular cardboard wine carrier, and handed it to him.

"A cardboard wine carrier," said Quigg. He juggled it in his hands, not all that impressed with its basic brown kraft-paper look.

"That was my template," Carmela told him. She reached back and grabbed her finished piece. "And this is what it looks like when you apply design principles and glitz it up."

"Wow!" said Quigg. Carmela had covered the cardboard tube with shiny tortoiseshell-printed paper, then added embossed gold metallic bands at the top and bottom. A polymer clay medallion of a Bacchus face was adorned with gold leaf and stuck on the very top. A parchment tag with gold lettering was attached with gold thread.

Quigg cradled the elegant wine container in his hands. "This is sexy!"

"Glad you approve," said Carmela, handing him a small brochure. "And this promo piece gets rolled up and popped inside along with a bottle of your wine."

"What is it?" asked Quigg.

"A three-fold brochure that basically describes your different varieties of wine. So when it's all put together we end up with a combination swag bag and PR kit."

"It's so professional and artistic looking," said Quigg, tapping the tortoiseshell paper with his thumbnail. "I'm stunned."

"If it's okay with you," said Carmela, "I'll e-mail the artwork to my service bureau and have everything printed out."

"Just like that?"

"Your people will have to do some final wrapping and gluing on Friday, but it shouldn't be a big deal," Carmela told him.

Quigg was still grinning, still turning the wine container over in his hands. "I knew I could count on you," he told her.

"No problem," said Carmela, plucking the wine container from his hands as she stood up.

"You're really great, you know?"

Something in his tone put Carmela on alert.

"Are you . . . still dating that beat cop?" Quigg asked. He moved a step closer to her, the better to crowd her.

"Homicide detective," said Carmela, correcting him. "And, yes, we're still seeing each other." She took a half-step back, then felt her hip press tightly against the edge of her desk.

"Too bad," said Quigg, giving a regretful shake of his head.

"Why's that?" asked Carmela, pretty much knowing what he was going to say.

"I always figured you and I would get

together," said Quigg, giving her a deep, soulful look.

"We did get together," Carmela reminded him. "As I recall, it wasn't exactly love at first sight." *Or even second or third sight.*

Quigg slapped a hand over his heart as if to register deep and profound shock. "Am I that big a jerk?" he asked.

Carmela smiled. "Yes. Sometimes you are."

CHAPTER 9

"We really should put our heads together," Carmela told Gabby. "Since we've got our calligraphy seminar tomorrow."

Gabby set down a holiday card she'd been working on, dabbing bronze ink on the edges of the blue card stock. "I am feeling a slight flutter of worry," she admitted, "wondering if you . . ."

"Had it all figured out?" asked Carmela.

Gabby nodded. "Do you?"

Carmela cocked her head and gazed at the front window, which held a display of silver-and-gold angels, made from an assemblage of Paperclay, papier-mâché, and filmy ribbons. "I *think* I do. Still, we should run through our projects and make sure we're both on the same page."

"That's funny," said Gabby. "*Same page,* seeing as how it's calligraphy."

"And tricky calligraphy at that," said Carmela. "Skeleton letters." She thought

115

for a moment. "You've got the paper and pens set aside?"

Gabby nodded. She'd put in the order a month ago. "And we're still going to have the two sessions, morning and afternoon?"

"Right, but most people signed up for both."

"You mean Baby and Tandy signed up for both," said Gabby. "Like they always do."

"They're hardcore crafters," agreed Carmela. No matter what type of seminar they held at Memory Mine — Paper Moon, Memory Boxes, Card Making, or Collages — Baby and Tandy were always front and center.

"What I want to do in the morning session," said Carmela, "is focus on teaching basic calligraphy letters. Then, in the afternoon, we'll show them how to incorporate calligraphy into scrapbooking, cards, and decoupage."

"Sounds like you've got the crafts part pretty much figured out," said Gabby.

"Pretty much," said Carmela.

"If you make a list of materials, I'll start pulling paper and things right now."

"A sensible plan," said Carmela, as two women who were sort of regulars pushed their way into her shop. While Gabby helped one woman sort through packets of charms,

Carmela helped the other woman, an older lady with spiky white hair who went by the name of Ricky.

"You're so good at paper crafts," said Ricky, "are you as talented at needle crafts?"

"No, I'm not," said Carmela. "For some reason, I've never been very skillful at sewing."

"The thing is," said Ricky, looking hopeful, "I'm trying to make fabric-covered buttons."

"Oh," said Carmela, "I do know how to do that."

"Really?"

"It's actually pretty simple," said Carmela. "Want me to show you?"

Ricky nodded.

"First of all," said Carmela, "you have to use a button with a shank." Carmela reached over and grabbed a stray button, then placed it on a square of paper for demonstration purposes.

"Okay," said Ricky.

"You lay the button on your fabric," Carmela told her, "then draw a circle around it, allowing for a little extra fabric. You cut out your fabric circle, then take a needle and thread and do a running stitch around the edge of the circle. Once you have that done, just place your button in the middle of your fabric circle and pull the string. You'll have to, you know, kind of ease the folds around the edge of the button and smooth it in back. But when it all looks right, just pull your thread tight and tie a knot."

"You make it sound so easy," said Ricky.

"Crafting doesn't always have to be tricky," said Carmela. She took her demo button and placed it in Ricky's hand. "Here. Take this home and give it a try."

"I will," said Ricky, looking inspired.

Ten minutes later, Louise Applegate, the woman who was overseeing the dig at St. Tristan's, dropped by.

Applegate didn't look like an archaeologist. In fact, with her warm smile, sunny blond hair, and wrist full of gold bangles, she looked more like a housewife. But she was wearing khaki, a nicely tailored skirt and jacket with the requisite epaulets. Not exactly field gear, but it did project a certain note of archaeological authenticity.

"Thanks for seeing me on such short notice," said Applegate, after they'd made their introductions.

Leading her back to her office, Carmela said, "Sorry I was so testy on the phone earlier."

Applegate waved a manicured hand. "It's completely understandable, considering what you've been through. Must have been awful for you, finding your friend like that."

Seeing my friend die, thought Carmela.

"So," said Carmela, settling into her leather swivel chair, "your being here obviously has something to do with the dig that's going on at St. Tristan's. And . . . yesterday's murder?"

"That's right," said Applegate. "Our archaeologists were the ones who excavated the churchyard and discovered the old foundation along with a number of antiquities."

"One of the antiquities being Père Etienne's crucifix?" said Carmela.

"We haven't verified his ownership one hundred percent," said Applegate, "but my gut tells me it did belong to the good padre. There are also a number of old records that reference the crucifix and, of course, his grave is close by."

"How do I fit into all of this?" asked Carmela.

Applegate licked her lips and leaned forward slightly. "You were there."

Carmela grimaced. "People keep saying that."

"And according to the police report . . ."

"You read the police report?" Carmela blurted out.

"Yes, in fact I was given a portion of it."

"May I see it?"

"Well, that would be somewhat irregular . . . ," began Applegate.

Carmela settled back in her chair, rested her hands casually in her lap, and gave a helpless shrug. Body language that indicated this conversation was all but over.

Sensing that the door might slam abruptly in her face, Applegate said, in a hasty tone, "In your case, I could probably make an exception."

"Excellent," said Carmela, leaning forward as Applegate dug into her briefcase.

"But please don't tell anyone," said Applegate, handing Carmela a sheaf of papers.

"My lips are sealed," Carmela assured her, as she set about taking a quick scan of the papers. By the second page, Carmela was completely unnerved. It was one thing to read about a murder in the newspaper, and another to witness a murder with your own eyes. But to read about it in factual, non-emotional, cut-and-dried police lingo chilled her to the bone.

"This report makes it sound so impersonal," Carmela murmured.

"I'm sorry, this must be very difficult for

you," said Applegate, sensing that Carmela needed some soothing.

Carmela handed the report back to her. "What could you possibly want from me? It seems like you have a serious amount of information right here."

Applegate put her hands on her knees and leaned forward slightly. "We've had . . . how shall I phrase this? . . . other items go missing."

"You mean from the St. Tristan's site?" asked Carmela. "Or from other digs?"

"Both," said Applegate. "It seems that whenever we unearth a tasty item, then get the metallurgic report back attesting to its authenticity, we have . . . how shall I phrase this? . . . another theft."

"You're thinking an inside job?" Carmela asked. If so, this information could put a whole new spin on things.

"It's crossed my mind," said Applegate, giving a little frown.

"Again, what do you want from me?"

"Really," said Applegate, "I'm just trying to get an *impression* of what you might have seen."

"I didn't see much," said Carmela.

"Man? Woman?" asked Applegate.

"It's in the report," Carmela said. She leaned back in her chair and gave a couple of nervous bounces. "But I'm pretty sure it was a man."

"Why do you say that?"

"Just the way he moved. A certain . . . strength. A sureness. And he seemed taller than Byrle. Huskier."

"But the assailant was wearing a robe," said Applegate.

"That tosses a wrench into things," Carmela admitted. "A monk's robe does add a good deal of volume." *And maybe hides a smaller figure?*

"Anything else come to mind?" asked Applegate. "Anything you recall, any feeling you had?"

Carmela let her mind wander back to St. Tristan's, and the vision of Byrle's struggle suddenly played in her head like a bad YouTube video. "Just that the whole thing felt incredibly vicious," Carmela finally said.

The two of them sat there for a few moments, the murder hanging in the air between them like some kind of shared bad dream. Then Applegate rose from her chair and said, "You've been a big help."

No, I haven't, thought Carmela.

"Do the police know about the other missing items?" Carmela asked.

"They do. Although I can't say they've taken our reports all that seriously."

122

"Which is why," said Carmela, "you're talking to me?"

Applegate stuck out a hand. "Thanks again. I appreciate your input."

"Oh, that's cool," said Gabby, peering over Carmela's shoulder at the repeated image on her iMac screen. "What is it?"

"A step-and-repeat," said Carmela, continuing to click away.

"A step and what?"

"You know, when you see celebrities on those red carpet preshows?" said Carmela. "And there's a backdrop that says *Bulgari* or *Tiffany* or *Mercedes-Benz*?"

Gabby nodded. "Sure."

"That backdrop's called a step-and-repeat."

"So kind of a sponsor's backdrop. For name recognition and to make sure their logo gets seen in photographs and stuff."

"Marketing buzz," said Carmela.

"How do you know all this stuff?" asked Gabby.

Carmela shrugged. "I don't know. Just picked it up, I guess. Probably from watching too much junk TV. *TMZ, The Daily Ten, E News Entertainment.*"

"You really watch that stuff?"

"Sometimes," said Carmela. "If it doesn't

burn my eyeballs too badly."

Gabby grinned. "My guilty pleasures, along with Belgian chocolate, are those *Real Housewives* shows. I'm wild over the housewives from New Jersey; those ladies are pistols!"

"Maybe you'll get lucky and they'll have a casting call for New Orleans housewives," laughed Carmela. "You could end up a reality TV star."

"Oh no, I could never do that," said Gabby. "Stuart would never . . . he would never allow it."

"Sweetie," said Carmela, "you can't go through life worrying what Stuart does or doesn't approve of. Life's too short."

"But he's my husband," said Gabby, suddenly looking very wifely and demure.

"My point exactly. If I'd have allowed Shamus's opinion to color my entire world, I can't imagine what would have happened to me. Heck, we probably wouldn't be standing in this shop right now."

Gabby sighed. "You realize, Carmela, not all women are as brave as you are. A lot of women would *love* to dip their toe in entrepreneurial waters and start their own business, but they just can't work up the courage. Or someone close to them is a naysayer, so they fret and fritter and never make their move."

"Worrying about other people's negative opinions is generally a huge waste of time," said Carmela. "Since most naysayers tend to be dunderheads. Case in point . . ." She grinned. "Shamus."

"That's what kills me about you," said Gabby. "You're fearless to the core and outspoken without being a diva."

"Yeah?" Gabby's words tickled her.

"And," added Gabby, "you have a keen sense of justice."

"A sense of justice?" said Carmela, giving a little start. She threw a crooked look at Gabby, as if she didn't believe her. "You think so?"

"Absolutely," said Gabby. "That's why you're such a champion of underdogs."

"Maybe *some* underdogs," said Carmela, as she opened her e-mail and added her step-and-repeat design as an attachment.

Gabby tapped her foot quietly behind Carmela. "So," she continued, "you *are* going to start looking into things, aren't you? I mean, concerning Byrle?"

Carmela hit Send, sending her design winging its electronic way to Inky's Print Shop.

"I'm afraid," said Carmela, "I've already started."

CHAPTER 10

Evening draped across the Garden District like a dark blue cashmere blanket. Stately live oaks festooned with Spanish moss and Gothic-looking wrought-iron fences were but dark smudges, while lights sparkled brightly inside enormous mansions. Here was antebellum Louisiana at its finest. Big homes, big money, big names. Novelist Truman Capote and French Impressionist Edgar Degas had both called the Garden District home. Jefferson Davis, president of the Confederate States of America, had died here. And though many of the old homes exuded a faint patina of age, they were still quite magnificent.

Carmela stood in the foyer of her old brick mansion, while Ava and Jekyl quickly shucked their jackets and wandered into the parlor. She lagged behind, feeling slightly hesitant. There were ghosts here, after all. Not ethereal phantasm-ectoplasm ghosts, but ghosts of people and spirits of past lives. Memories.

"First floor only, correct?" asked Jekyl. He spun around, touching an index finger to his lips. This was a man who'd adopted the Vampire Lestat as his ideal and always dressed in black, the better to set off his pale skin and long, dark hair.

Carmela ventured in a few steps, noting the musty odor and the creaking wooden floors. "That's right," she told him. "So, for the Holidazzle Tour, we're really just talking about the front verandah, living room, dining room, and sunroom." She gestured toward the back of the house. "The kitchen we'll lock off."

"Still," said Jekyl, giving everything his keen-eyed appraisal, "this is a whale of a house. High ceilings, large-scale rooms, oversized furnishings."

"I'm afraid so," said Carmela. It had been too much house for her when she'd been married to Shamus and they'd resided here. Too much work even with a cleaning lady and gardener. Now it just felt like a gigantic, creaking dinosaur.

But Ava had other ideas. "We should move in here," she announced, suddenly. "It's so big and grand and . . ." She spun around happily in the center of the living room, arms extended. "We should move in and open a house of ill repute or something." She ended her spin in a ballerina pose, arms across her chest, head tilted like a coquette.

Her idea was preposterous, but Jekyl giggled anyway. "And I presume you'd be the madam?"

Ava looked infinitely pleased. "Why, of course." She glanced at Carmela and smiled. "And Carmela would be our . . . business manager. 'Cause she's so smart with facts and figures."

"Thanks a lot," said Carmela. "You're front of house, I'm behind-the-scenes ugly stepsister bean counter."

"Aw, I didn't mean it like that," said Ava. "You could be a sexy bean counter, *cher.*"

Carmela shook her head. "Never mind, it's not going to happen. This is only your weird little fantasy."

"And fantasies rarely come true," added Jekyl.

Ava gave a pussycat grin. "Sometimes they do."

"I just decided," said Carmela, "that once the holidays are over I'm definitely going to sell this place. Lock, stock, and barrel."

"I suppose it is time," Ava agreed. She was contrite now, after her little faux pas.

"You know," said Jekyl, glancing around, a

look of interest animating his angular face, "there's a way you could sort of . . . mmm . . . maximize your investment here."

"What are you talking about?" asked Carmela.

"For one thing," said Jekyl, "you could sell off some of this furniture."

Carmela let loose a disdainful hoot. "This dowdy stuff? Who'd even *want* it?" She glanced at the frayed damask sofa where Shamus's heels had dug in nervously and repeatedly as he'd watched New Orleans Saints football on TV. "I was thinking of calling the Salvation Army to see if they'd deign to come over and cart it all away."

Jekyl regarded her with interest. "You just don't like these pieces because they belonged to Shamus."

"No," said Carmela, letting her true feelings emerge, "I detest them because them belonged to Glory." Glory was Shamus's big sister. The controlling, parsimonious moneybags of the Meechum family. Glory Meechum was also mean as cat pee and had despised Carmela from the get-go. She'd thrown a fit at their rehearsal dinner, which probably should have been a red flag right there. And crazy Glory had even tried to stop their wedding. Then, more recently, she'd opposed their divorce. Go figure.

"Glory's a good reason to toss it all in a Dumpster," said Ava, giving a disdainful sniff.

"You're both wrong," said Jekyl, running a hand across his sleek head. "This stuff is worth money."

"Say what?" said Ava.

"Seriously?" said Carmela. Now he had her attention.

"I'm an antiques appraiser by trade," said Jekyl. "But just because I don't handle this particular type of furniture doesn't mean I don't know market value. Fact is, I could hook you up with a couple of dealers who would take this stuff on commission and probably help you net a tidy sum."

"How tidy?" asked Carmela.

"That brocade love seat is probably worth twelve hundred," said Jekyl. "And that pecan dining room table should easily go for at least four grand."

"That's tidy," agreed Ava.

"You see," said Jekyl, pointing, "you've also got a lawyer's bookcase and a Sheraton-style table."

"Huh," said Carmela. It still looked like junk to her.

Now Jekyl cast an almost-admiring glance around the room. "And that fireplace and marble mantel would photograph beautifully," he added.

"Photographs?" said Carmela, perplexed now.

"If you're going to sell this place you'll need good, professional photos," Jekyl explained. "To use on the real estate agent's Web site as well as in a folder to pass out to prospective buyers." Jekyl scratched his head. "Which gives me a gem of an idea . . ."

"What?" asked Ava.

"Let me make a call and get back to you," said Jekyl.

Ava looked perplexed. "I thought we were here to talk about holiday décor."

"Right we are," said Jekyl, "so let's stay on task."

"Where's the best place to start?" asked Carmela, gazing at an oil painting of Great-Granddaddy Meechum, the cantankerous old chap who'd sired the whole miserable clan.

"First things first," said Jekyl. "We should choose a color palette."

"Agreed," said Carmela. It was the same technique she used in scrapbooking. Select a couple of key colors, say purple and pink, then build around them with coordinating paper, inks, ribbon, and anything else that added to the richness of the design.

Jekyl's eyes became Kabuki dancer slits.

"I'm envisioning crystal, white, and ice blue." He waved his hands in front of his face, fingers spread out, then flung his arms out to the side. "Think snow queen!"

"I love it!" declared Ava.

"Really?" said Carmela. Snow queen? Could something like that be worked into a legitimate theme? On the other hand, this was from a man who'd worked wonders with the sets and backdrops for *Ballet Dracula,* incorporating dark, brooding mountains with English drawing room scenes.

But all Jekyl needed was Ava's enthusiastic approval to send him spiraling off on his tangent. "I see gigantic wreaths, swags of garland, and an enormous Christmas tree — all flocked white and hung with crystal and blue ornaments. Crystal candle holders with tall white tapers." He touched his index finger to his lips again, thinking. "And for the pièce de résistance, white plumed birds. An entire *flock* of them!"

"It's showy," said Carmela, "I'll give you that." Obviously there'd be no potted poinsettias or traditional green wreaths for her. Jekyl had been struck with a searing vision, and when Jekyl gazed deep into the depths of the universe and plucked out a shining star, everyone better watch out!

Ava was nodding along. "I can see it

before my eyes, plain as day."

Not exactly plain, thought Carmela. *More like froufrous and swirls of whipped cream.*

"You like?" asked Jekyl, draping a conspiratorial arm around Carmela's shoulders.

Carmela had committed her home to Baby and knew she had to do *something.* So . . .

"I like it," said Carmela, mustering up a modicum of enthusiasm.

"Excellent," declared Jekyl. "I'll start hunting down the birds and swags and icicles from my various vendors." He scowled. "It's going to be awfully tight, but hopefully we can squeak in a rush order."

"Hopefully," murmured Carmela. She didn't know how much this was going to set her back financially, but it had to be significant. Maybe she could ask Shamus to chip in? She chuckled to herself. Maybe she could ask Shamus to bite off a piece of the moon for her.

Locking the front door and tumbling down the front steps, the three of them rushed out into what had become a cool, velvet-dark night. All around them, glowing yellow beams of light peeked from the tall, shuttered windows of neighboring homes.

"Bye-bye, sweeties," crooned Jekyl, crooking himself forward to administer extravagant air kisses to each of them.

"Bye-bye," said Ava.

"Thanks so much," said Carmela, as Jekyl dashed for his car. She and Ava headed in the opposite direction to her Mercedes, which was parked maybe thirty feet or so down the block. In fact, she'd parked directly in front of . . .

"Oh crap," Carmela muttered, under her breath, "there's Rain Monroe." Rain Monroe was a socialite who'd married, obtained an expedient divorce, and recently bought a home two doors down from Carmela's Garden District property. She'd just pulled into her short driveway and climbed out of her silver Bentley.

"Ooh, I just *hate* her," Ava seethed, when she noticed Rain. Rain had once flirted outrageously with a man Ava had been semi-in-love-with. The dispute was long over, of course, but Ava never forgot where she buried the hatchet.

"Maybe she won't notice us," Carmela whispered.

"Well, if it isn't Carmela," Rain called out in a loud, flat voice, as she sauntered toward them. She wore an expensive, tightly tailored gray suit with a fur scarf flung casually about her thin shoulders.

"Hello, Rain," said Carmela.

"I see you were involved in a bit of trouble again," said Rain, working her thin lips into a mirthless smile.

"Excuse me?" said Carmela. Rain was pretentious and arrogant, and for some reason — maybe because of Ava? — Carmela seemed to have gotten on her bad side. Whenever they bumped into each other they were like two pit vipers hissing and thrashing at each other.

"I'm talking about the incident at St. Tristan's," said Rain.

"That's what you call it?" said Carmela. "An *incident?*" She took a step toward Rain. "You make it sound like somebody spilled hot candle wax when what really happened was cold-blooded murder."

"Murder of a dear friend of ours," Ava added, baring her teeth.

Rain looked peeved. "Well . . . yes. It was a hideous situation."

"*Really* hideous for Byrle," said Carmela.

"You realize," said Rain, "I'm on the board of directors at St. Tristan's." This was delivered in a superior, gloating tone.

"I didn't know that," said Carmela. *And I really don't care.*

"That's right," continued Rain. "In fact, we were forced to call an emergency meeting last night."

136

"For what purpose?" asked Carmela. She could almost feel waves of heat emanating from Ava and fervently hoped her friend would contain her fierce temper.

"Crisis management," said Rain. She hawked out the word *crisis* as if it were particularly distasteful. "With the media frenzy and all. But, quite frankly, I'd be happy if it all just went away." She threw a vengeful smile at Ava. "After all, we don't want anything to ruin the upcoming anniversary festivities for Père Etienne."

"The two are hardly connected," said Carmela.

"Hardly," seethed Ava, as Carmela reached out and grabbed her arm.

Rain shot another disdainful glance at Ava, then focused her attention back on Carmela. "You're moving back? Back into the neighborhood?"

Carmela shrugged. "I own the house, so I haven't technically left."

Rain offered a thin smile. "And I understand you're finally divorced from, uh, what's-his-name?"

Carmela nodded. "Shamus. Yes, our divorce is final. Has been for a while."

"Good for you," said Rain. "Probably for the best." She spun on her stiletto heels, threw up a single hand, and waved a hasty

137

good-bye.

Forty seconds later, Jekyl came putt-putting up to them in his Jaguar. He rolled down the passenger-side window and leaned toward them. "Hobnobbing with the neighbors?"

Carmela shrugged. "Such as they are."

"Rain Monroe is a total bee-yatch," said Ava.

Jekyl glanced in the direction of Rain's house. "Rain's hobby is to verbally *Taser* people."

Ava sighed. "She was positively awful to us. But Carmela kept pinching my arm, not wanting me to say anything back."

"If it's any consolation," Jekyl told Ava, "I don't get along with her, either."

"Nobody does," said Ava.

"But did you know," said Jekyl, "that Rain Monroe is on the mayor's Cultural Advisory Board?"

"So what?" said Carmela. "She's an indolent rich person who sits on a lot of boards. Until they figure out she's a know-it-all, do-nothing airhead and then bounce her."

Jekyl made a face. "I agree . . . partially. Rain wouldn't know culture if it reared up and bit her in her skinny backside. Unfortunately, the woman has her sticky little manicured fingers in lots of different pots.

And, right now, she holds the purse strings on who gets arts funding."

"That's not good," said Ava.

"I should say not," said Jekyl. "You remember that wonderful children's theater company? The one that was made up of some of the kids from the Bywater?"

Carmela and Ava both nodded.

"The Oliphant Theater," said Carmela.

"Well, it's gone now," said Jekyl. "Poof! Its funding completely pulled. And, wouldn't you know, Rain was the nasty little darling who dropped the hammer."

CHAPTER 11

"Let's stop by Royal and Romeo's," Ava suggested, as they breezed down Chestnut Street, "and get something to eat." Royal and Romeo's was a neighborhood joint on the first floor of a green stucco apartment building that served great po'boy sandwiches, stuffed artichokes, alligator soup, and a smattering of local jazz. It was a smoky, easygoing place that was pure New Orleans. The kind you'd stumble into only if you were a local.

"Last time I ordered their alligator soup," said Carmela, "I had heartburn for a week."

"Why do you think they invented beer?" asked Ava, then giggled madly as she answered her own question. "To cool things down and quell the pain!"

But when they pulled up in front of the little honky-tonk, the neon beer signs were dim and a hand-lettered *Closed for Vacation* sign was tacked to the screen door.

"On vacation!" said an outraged Ava. "How *could* they? Just when I had a power-ful hankering for stuffed artichoke."

"Someplace else?" asked Carmela.

Ava pondered this for a moment. "There's a new place I heard about, over on Magazine Street . . ."

"Let's do it," said Carmela. She knew that Ava prided herself on keeping up with all the hot spots.

"I hope they have stuffed artichokes," said Ava.

"And beer," added Carmela.

"Purgatoria?" said Carmela, as they pushed open a set of heavy wooden double doors.

"This is it," said Ava. "Cool name, huh?"

They stepped into a dark, cavernous room with wood-paneled walls, an enormous black metal chandelier, and an old marble baptismal font that was now being used as a hostess stand.

"Are you sure this is a restaurant? Or some kind of nightclub?" asked Carmela. "Because this place looks a little crazy to me." Fact was, it reminded her of the interior of a church — and that conjured up some awfully frightening memories from just two days ago.

"Yeah," said Ava, smiling and gazing

around, "it does look a little churchy." She pointed a thumb at a gargoyle statue that perched on a tall stand. "Except for that guy. You'd never find *that* critter in any self-respecting church."

"Two for dinner?" asked the hostess. She was a tall lady with long, dark hair, wearing a long black Morticia Addams–style dress.

"Two," said Ava. "And by the way, that's a great Goth dress you're wearing."

"Thank you," said the hostess as she led them across threadbare Oriental carpets to a tall, narrow booth padded in black leather.

Carmela and Ava slid in and got comfortable as the hostess handed them oversized menus bound in red leather.

"Somebody likes leather," said Ava. She sounded pleased.

"Maybe the owner's got a thing for it," said Carmela, knowing full well this was a city where leather-and-bondage balls were routine during Halloween and Mardi Gras. "Who is the owner, anyway?"

Ava lifted her shoulders. "No clue. I only know about this place because I saw a snippet in the restaurant section of *New Orleans Scene.*"

"What'd it say?" asked Carmela. "The snippet."

"Oh," said Ava, "just that Purgatoria's a

new fine dining place with an emphasis on local seafood."

"And an emphasis on religious icons, too," said Carmela. She'd just spotted what had to be one-half of an old wooden pulpit, snugged up against one wall.

"Do you think most of this stuff is from Pier One or some prop house?" asked Ava.

"I don't know," said Carmela, "some of it looks awfully authentic." A gold Byzantine double-headed eagle flag that hung from the ceiling looked positively papal.

"Come to think of it," said Ava, "that article did mention that you have to walk through a confessional to get to the ladies' room."

"That's a little quirky," said Carmela. Although she'd once visited a gay bar where you had to walk through a roomful of drag queens to get to the ladies' room.

Ava grimaced. "I wouldn't know whether to genuflect or brush my hair. Also, going to confession is not one of my favorite pastimes."

Carmela chuckled. "I suppose not. Seeing as how your romantic inclinations are —"

"Ladies," a male voice boomed at their elbow, "may I extend a warm welcome to Purgatoria."

Ava fluttered her eyes at the tall, broad-

143

shouldered man standing next to their booth. He was fifty-something, wore what was probably a bespoke suit, and had just the right amount of silver in his hair. "Well, hello there," she said, her shoulders moving back a notch.

"Careful," Carmela said under her breath. "Confession?"

Turns out the man was Drew Gaspar, the rather charming owner.

"This week is our quiet opening," Gaspar explained to them, "and we're still training kitchen staff, so I hope you'll be patient with us. But I promise we'll do our very best to delight you. And I'd be more than happy to tell you about our two daily specials."

"Do tell," said Ava.

"Sautéed gulf shrimp," said Gaspar, "pulled fresh from Breton Sound and done in beurre blanc sauce with sun-dried tomatoes, shallots, and roasted mirlitons."

"Sounds fabulous," said Carmela.

"Our second special is seared yellowfin tuna," continued Gaspar. "Served on spinach and almond pilaf and glazed with a brandy-apricot sauce." He smiled at their reactions. "Obviously, our saucier is up to speed."

"Obviously," said Ava, dimpling.

Gaspar gestured at the oversized menus.

"Of course, we also have many more creative dishes on our extensive menu."

Carmela opened her menu and scanned the offerings.

"May I point out a few of our entrées that are particularly noteworthy?" Gaspar asked.

"I wish you would," said Carmela, "because your Gothic typeface is very difficult to read."

The smile faded on Gaspar's face, and he suddenly looked pained. "You really think so?"

Ava was quick to agree. "Sorry, hon, but this script is headache inducing."

Gaspar shook his head. "Doggone twenty-two-year-old graphic designer. He told me it was the perfect typeface."

"Well, it's really not," said Carmela. "In fact, rule number one for any piece of printed material is readability. After that you worry about creative topspin."

"Are you a designer?" Gaspar asked.

"Used to be," said Carmela. "Package goods, brochures, print ads, that sort of thing. Now I run a scrapbook shop over in the French Quarter."

"Carmela's just being modest," said Ava, eager to put in a plug for her best friend. "She's *still* a whiz-bang designer. I don't know if you've ever seen the menus she created for Mumbo Gumbo, but they're fantastic. Lots of fun, bouncy type . . . but *readable.* Plus she just designed a whole bunch of super gorgeous wine labels."

Really?" Gaspar was suitably impressed. "For which winery?"

"St. Tammany Vineyard," said Carmela. "It's a new venture by Quigg Brevard?"

"Oh sure," said Gaspar, "I know Quigg. In fact, I'm supposed to attend his press event this Saturday night."

"Which Carmela completely planned and organized," said Ava, neatly jumping in again.

Gaspar fixed a speculative gaze on Carmela. "You do menus *and* press events?"

"Only as an occasional sideline," said Carmela. She sensed a job offer coming and wanted to downplay her status as freelance designer.

"Still," said Gaspar, "you're obviously a very talented lady. Maybe I should give you a crack at redoing my menu."

"I'm awfully backed up . . . ," Carmela began.

But Ava leaned forward, a big old grin plastered across her face, and said, "She'd *love* to. She's tickled you asked."

"Wonderful!" exclaimed Gaspar. "In that case dinner's on me tonight."

"Oh no," said Carmela.

"You're too kind!" gushed Ava.

Carmela demurred a second time, but when the dust settled and it was clear that Gaspar was picking up the tab, she opted for a shrimp and heirloom tomato salad with goat cheese, while Ava went for the coconut shrimp stir-fry with shiitake mushrooms. They washed it down with a half-bottle of wine that was sent to their table. Again, compliments of the house.

"Good," said, Ava, scraping up the last bits with her fork.

"Your coconut shrimp hit the spot?" asked Carmela. "You're not disappointed they didn't have stuffed artichokes on the menu?"

"I'm good," enthused Ava. "Better than good. The food here is fantastic! In fact, I'll bet this place gives Commander's Palace, Antoine's, and some of those other fat cat restaurants a real run for their money."

"Maybe," said Carmela, not quite buying into that idea. New Orleans was a fine dining town, and eateries like Commander's Palace, Antoine's, Broussard's, and Brennan's had stood as the old guard for decades. As good as the food was at Purgatoria, it would be difficult for Gaspar to compete with world-famous restaurants

147

with well-earned pedigrees.

Ava dug in her bag, a navy-blue Chanel look-alike, and pulled out a Chanel lip gloss, the real thing. "Gaspar's very charming," she said. "Almost European."

"*Charming* is one word, *obsequious* is another."

"How old do you think is too old?" Ava asked, as she swirled Rose Sand gloss across her full lips.

"Too old for what?" asked Carmela. "Too old to compete on *American Idol*? Too old to wear a ponytail?"

"I'm talking dateability," said Ava. "What's your top line on men?"

"Oh . . . ," said Carmela. She shrugged. She'd never given it that much thought. "Maybe . . . fifty?"

"How old do you think Drew Gaspar is?"

Carmela raised her eyebrows and gazed at Ava. "Fifty?"

"So I just made it under the proverbial wire," said Ava.

Carmela reached across the table and put her hand on top of Ava's. "Honey, you don't even know if the man is single."

"Oh, he's single," said Ava. "My single-guy radar rarely malfunctions. I can generally spot a single, dateable guy at a thousand paces."

"I suppose," said Carmela. They'd once gone to the Gumbo Festival in Bridge City and unattached, single guys smelling of Axe and Paco Rabanne had buzzed around Ava all day. She'd come home with something like fifteen invitations for dates.

"Besides," said Ava, letting loose a deep sigh, "I've got to think about settling down one of these years. Fact is, I'm aging right before my very own eyes." She sighed deeply. "I sincerely hope all those mad scientists who are fudging around with DNA and stem cells will hurry up and unlock the secret of perpetual youth. Invent a face cream or a version of Mr. Peabody's Wayback Machine or something."

"You're not exactly Dorian Gray," said Carmela. "And you could console yourself with the fact that you're not quite thirty."

"Still," said Ava, "time marches on, and eventually it's going to march right across my poor face."

"We should leave a good tip," said Carmela, eager to change the subject. Whenever Ava fretted about getting old, she turned a little morose.

"And we should go thank our generous host," said Ava.

"My pleasure," said Gaspar, who, rather

149

than offering a handshake, seemed to delight in kissing the backs of their hands. "Come back soon." He focused on Carmela. "And you, dear lady, we must certainly talk."

"Wonderful," said a less-than-thrilled Carmela.

"And you," Gaspar said to Ava, his eyes roving up and down her statuesque figure, "I really admire your style."

"Ava's got personal style like nobody else," said Carmela. After all, who else could pull off thigh-high boots with such graceful aplomb? Nobody she knew.

"I sure do, sugar," grinned Ava.

"I actually have another enterprise I'm involved in," Gaspar said, in a confidential tone. "I can't let the cat out of the bag yet, because I don't want my idea swirling around in the ozone where somebody else could pick it off . . . but I just might call upon *you* for a little project, as well."

"Aren't you the mysterious one," cooed Ava.

When Carmela pushed open her door and turned on the light, Babcock was sitting in the dark waiting for her.

"Why didn't you turn the lights on?" she asked, dropping her jacket and bag, then stepping over to give him a kiss.

"You've been out investigating," he said, without preamble.

"No," Carmela said, trying to look wide-eyed and innocent, deciding she probably just looked wide-eyed. "I wouldn't do that."

Babcock's handsome face crinkled into an indulgent smile. "Of course you would."

"Really," said Carmela, reaching forward to snap on the lamp, illuminating them both in a warm puddle of light. "I had a meeting with Ava and Jekyl over at the Garden District house. Some . . . business. And then Ava and I stopped to get a bite to eat."

"You're not thinking of moving back into that place, are you?" Now Babcock looked a little nervous. Carmela figured it was because he probably didn't want to sniff around another man's turf. Even if it was lost-in-the-divorce turf.

Carmela sidled closer to him. "What if I did decide to move?" she asked, playfully. "Is the Garden District not convenient enough for you?"

He grabbed her hand. "I'd miss your little pied-à-terre right here."

"So would I," agreed Carmela, scrunching down next to him. "No, we were over there because Baby asked me to decorate the place for the Holidazzle Tour."

"Seriously?"

151

Carmela nodded.

Now Babcock threw her a questioning look. "I thought you didn't go in for all that Garden District society stuff."

"I usually don't," said Carmela. "But we're talking about Baby, one of my dearest friends. She asked for a favor and I said yes. Simple as that."

"Mmm," said Babcock. He hunched his shoulders forward, suddenly looking like he was drained of energy.

"Hard day at the office, dear?"

Babcock offered a halfhearted wave. "Eeh."

"That's an *mmm* and an *eeh*," said Carmela. "You're just bubbling with conversation."

"Hungry," said Babcock, stretching out his long legs and dangling his left hand over the edge of the chair. Boo promptly sniffed it, then positioned herself beneath his splayed-out fingers, the better to catch a good ear scratch.

"I'll fix you something to eat," said Carmela. "What would you like?" She quickly ran through her list of leftovers in her head, then said, "Jambalaya? Maybe a sandwich?"

"Sandwich would be great," murmured Babcock.

"Done," said Carmela.

She puttered in her kitchen for eight minutes tops and came up with a sort of Big Easy Reuben — corned beef, Swiss cheese, horseradish, and Thousand Island dressing on rye. She plated it, added a dill pickle spear as well as a pickled onion from a jar she'd picked up at the farmers' market last week, and carried it all over to Babcock.

He seemed surprised. "Oh man," he said, as he pulled himself up. "I didn't expect you'd go to so much trouble." He swiped the sandwich off its plate and propelled it toward his mouth in one swift move.

"No trouble," said Carmela. She sat at his feet, watching him eat for a couple of minutes, passing him a paper napkin when Thousand Island dressing threatened to drip onto her leather chair.

"Good," said Babcock, as he chewed. "What is it exactly?"

"Big Easy Reuben," Carmela told him.

Babcock looked puzzled, though he continued to munch with gusto. "Never heard of that. Where'd you get the recipe? Which restaurant?"

"I made it up myself," said Carmela.

"Just now?"

"Well . . . ten minutes ago."

"Good," Babcock said again, as he continued to eat.

"So," Carmela said, when the lines that were etched into his face seemed to finally relax, when he began to lose his hungry, haunted look. "How goes the investigation?"

Babcock finished a last little bit of crust, then fastidiously wiped his mouth with the napkin. "We made some progress."

"Really?" This was the kind of news she wanted to hear.

"We picked up that delivery guy, Johnny Otis, today and are holding him for questioning."

"Can you do that? I mean, just hold him, without any concrete evidence?"

Babcock gave a thin smile. "I can do anything I want."

"Somehow I doubt that."

"You'd be surprised."

Carmela studied him carefully. Was he a tougher, flintier guy than she'd ever imagined? Maybe so. Just because she'd never seen the full-court-press law enforcement side of him didn't mean it wasn't there. "Why did you single out Johnny Otis?"

Babcock put one arm behind his head and wriggled his shoulders. "Proximity, mostly. Otis was in the area and he gave a fair amount of back talk to the officers who questioned him." He let loose a discreet burp. "Plus Otis has a record."

"You mentioned that before."

"Nothing dramatic. Mostly breaking and entering."

"Not murder," said Carmela.

"For your information," said Babcock, "Mrs. Coopersmith wasn't murdered. At least I don't believe it was premeditated."

"So her death was technically a homicide?"

Babcock's nod was imperceptible.

"But your hunch about Otis is based on the fact that he's a burglary guy."

"Right."

"The thing is," said Carmela, "nobody broke into St. Tristan's. The church was already open."

"A B&E generally involves burglary. Stolen goods."

"Ah, there was that," said Carmela. "Père Etienne's crucifix is definitely missing." She waited a couple of beats, then said, "Have you come up with anything on that yet?"

"No," said Babcock. Now he was the one who waited a couple of beats before he asked, "Have you?"

CHAPTER 12

Tandy flashed a broad grin at Carmela as she cruised into Memory Mine. "We wanted to get here early," she explained.

"This one called me at six thirty this morning!" exclaimed Baby, jerking her thumb at Tandy. "I was like . . . still in REM sleep."

"Too excited," said Tandy. "I just couldn't wait."

"To do calligraphy?" asked Carmela. Her class didn't kick off until nine o'clock and here were Baby, Tandy, and two other women already seated at the big craft table, a half hour early, with Gabby hovering nearby.

"That and I thought there might be an update," said Tandy, peering at Carmela sharply. "On . . . you know."

"We should really discuss that later," Baby said, in a quiet tone. Then she smiled serenely and seemed to refocus. "Can you believe it? Tandy even made early-morning forays to both Café du Monde and Duvall's Bakery."

"And look at the goodies I brought back!" Tandy exclaimed. She jumped up from her chair, almost knocking it over, and thrust a take-out cup of café au lait into Carmela's hand. Then she reached out and pushed an enormous white bakery box across the table. "Surprise!"

"French almond croissants," said Gabby. "As well as those delightful little Doberge bites and date bars." She seemed as excited about the eats as she was about today's class.

"Wow," said Carmela, taking a sip of her coffee.

"Dig in," enthused Tandy.

Baby lifted her Gucci tote bag onto the table and pulled out a plastic storage container. "And just in case we don't have enough of the sweet stuff, I brought along some fresh-baked chocolate streusel bars."

"We have enough bakery for twenty people," Gabby laughed.

"So what?" said Tandy, slyly dipping her hand into the container and pulling out a chocolate streusel bar. "A person can never ingest too much sugar."

"Or chocolate," said Baby.

"You think?" said Carmela. "Then how come nutritionists always caution against eating sugar? It's always held up as something that's positively toxic."

Tandy wrinkled her nose in dismay. "That's because they're wet blankets. Honestly, a day without sugar is like a day without . . ."

"Scrapbooking!" cried Baby.

"Exactly," said Tandy. Plunking her skinny bottom down on the chair next to Baby, she placed her elbows solidly on the table and proceeded to munch her bar.

Fifteen minutes later the table was completely filled with a dozen paying customers. An electric buzz filled the air as scrappers and would-be calligraphers waited with anticipation. Although when Carmela and Gabby conferred at the flat file, Gabby whispered to Carmela that it seemed more like a sugar buzz.

"Okay," said Carmela, raising her voice as she stepped to the head of the table. "Time to kick this class into high gear. Let's clear off the food debris and make our worktable as tidy as possible. Tandy, can you gather up the used coffee cups?"

Tandy nodded as she sprang from her chair, definitely a little sugar-buzzed.

"Thank you," said Carmela. "And Gabby,

you go ahead and pass out the pens and graph paper."

There was an urgent scuffle then, as everyone seemed to shift into serious craft mode.

"First things first," said Carmela, as all eyes turned toward her. "We're not going to take up pen and ink today, because that's awfully tricky and messy for beginners."

There were audible sighs of relief.

"The fact is," said Carmela, "there are lots of great calligraphy pens readily available. Sharpie, Speedball, and Bic Sheaffer all make excellent calligraphy pens. We stock them all, so be sure to try out the various brands to find the one that's most comfortable for you." She lifted a large cardboard poster that displayed basic alphabet letters onto the table. "And these are the letters we'll be practicing. The skeleton letters."

"So they're like writing architecture?" asked Tandy, squinting at the poster.

"Very close to it," said Carmela. "These letters appear fairly simple and pretty much are. They're the basic forms you need to master for calligraphy. Then, once you feel comfortable rendering rudimentary skeleton letters, we'll move on to more complex forms of calligraphy. Depending on how it goes, we might try copperplate, rustica, or even Carolingian."

One of the women raised a tentative hand. "So how do we begin? Just practice our *ABC*s?"

"You can do that," said Carmela, as she walked around the table passing out mini versions of her alphabet template to everyone, "or you can get creative and start thinking about some of the ways you might actually use calligraphy."

"What do you mean by that?" asked Baby.

"Once you master the basic skeleton letters," said Carmela, "and are able to enhance them with a few swirls and flourishes, you can incorporate calligraphy into all sorts of things. Think about lettering on a scrapbook page or making your own greeting cards, maps, or place cards. When your lettering gets good enough, you can move on to certificates and awards, or even make your own gift wrap."

Gabby grabbed a sample of Carmela's work and popped it down in the center of the table. "This is a little placard that Carmela created last week. It's a verse from a Shakespeare sonnet, hand-lettered onto bamboo paper, then mounted on chipboard. You can see she deckled the edges, then smoothed on a little gold leaf."

The sample was met with murmurs of

"Fantastic" and "Beautiful."

"*Oof,*" said Tandy, scowling down at her paper, "I think I already made a mess."

"Don't worry," said Carmela. "Your first couple of attempts are going to be a little shaky, but keep practicing. Keep your letters within the grid lines on the paper and try to master the basic skeleton formation. Then you can move on and enhance it."

"My pen's not doing what I want it to," complained one woman.

"Okay," said Carmela, "here's an important trick. For thick strokes, apply pressure to the tip of your pen. For thin strokes, simply ease up and go lightly."

"Good advice," said Baby, as she rendered a lovely letter *B*.

"Also," said Carmela, "it's better to draw thick strokes with a downward motion of your pen and thin strokes by moving your pen upward."

"Now I get it," said Tandy, looking pleased.

"And don't expect to make a letter all in one single stroke," said Carmela. "In fact, it's better to go slowly and even lift your pen a couple of times."

Carmela and Gabby went around the table, giving pointers here, encouragement there. When all her crafters were working away diligently, Carmela slipped into her back office. She had a small project she wanted to finish up, an example of one of the projects she was going to have her crafters work on.

Last week she'd decoupaged a few images of roses, ballerinas, and a piece of opera music onto a small, round cardboard box. When the glue had dried, she'd shellacked the sides and top and glued a string of pearls around the top edge. Now she was hard at work, lettering the phrase *You are the wind beneath my wings* onto parchment paper. This would be artfully torn out, then decoupaged onto the cover of the box. And she'd probably line it with a crumpled piece of silk. Hopefully, the little jewel box would serve as inspiration for her class today.

"Carmela," said Gabby. She was standing in the doorway, looking pleased.

Carmela finished the final letter on her verse and lifted her head. "Yes?"

"They're all doing rather brilliantly."

"You think they're ready to tackle a project?"

Gabby gave an emphatic nod. "I think they are."

Carmela grabbed her decoupaged box and lettered phrase and headed back out to the table, eager to see how the class had done.

"Look what we've been busy doing!" boasted Tandy, holding up a sheet of beautifully rendered letters.

"Perfect," said Carmela. She circled the table, checking everyone's progress.

"Did we do good?" asked one of the women.

"Better than good," Carmela told her. "You're ready to integrate your calligraphy into a real live project."

"Oh goody," said Tandy. "What do you have in mind?"

"Let's start with something fairly simple," suggested Carmela. "Maybe a hand-lettered quote or poem, some lettering on a picture frame, or a sentiment lettered and decoupaged onto a small wooden box." She set her little box on the table, showed them what she'd done so far, and explained exactly how she'd finish it up.

"That's what I want to make," declared Tandy.

"Me, too," came a chorus of enthusiastic voices.

"It just so happens," said Gabby, stepping in, "that we have a baker's dozen of small boxes." She scattered them on the table — square boxes, round boxes, even a couple of hex-shaped boxes — and let each woman choose her favorite.

163

"If you want to wander through the shop and select paper, charms, beads, fibers, or whatever," said Carmela, "please help yourself. And whatever items you choose today for your jewel box project, remember, it's all included in the price of today's seminar."

That brought another round of smiles, and a gaggle of women suddenly leaped to their feet and began combing through the shop like they were on a treasure hunt, searching for the perfect paper, ribbon, charms, and adornments.

"What are you two going to do?" Carmela asked Baby and Tandy. They'd remained seated at the table.

"We were thinking of making a shadow box in memory of Byrle," said Tandy. She squinted at Carmela. "What do you think of that?"

"I think it's a lovely sentiment," said Carmela. She reached up and grabbed a twelve-by-fourteen-inch shadow box from a top shelf. "Will this one work?"

"Perfect," said Baby, accepting it gingerly. "Oh, and it's even got a glass front."

"Have you thought about what you'd put in it?" asked Carmela.

Tandy nodded. "Baby's going to select an appropriate poem and do the calligraphy and I'm going to gather up some dried flowers, a bit of lace, velvet paper for a backdrop, and a crucifix."

"We thought we might put in a string of pearls, too," said Baby. "Byrle always loved her pearls."

"If you want," said Carmela, "I could help you ghost some sort of image onto a piece of vellum."

"I like that," said Baby.

"Were you going to, um, display it tomorrow at the funeral?" asked Carmela. Byrle's funeral was scheduled for ten o'clock tomorrow at St. Tristan's.

"I don't know," said Baby. "Maybe. If we get it done today."

"Know what I think?" said Tandy. "I think it's kind of creepy that Byrle's funeral is being held in the same place she was murdered."

"It's where she went to church," Baby said in a quiet voice. "Where her family still attends church."

"Still," said Tandy, pushing her red half-glasses up onto her nose and giving a shudder, "I think it's weird."

"Think of it as being appropriate," said Baby, "in a dust-to-dust sort of way."

"Maybe," said a still skeptical Tandy.

"I understand you're going to do a reading at the funeral tomorrow?" Carmela asked Baby.

Baby bit her lip and nodded, as tears sprang to her eyes. "A poem by Emily Dickinson."

"And there'll be others, too?" asked Carmela. "People who'll do testimonials or readings?"

"That's right," said Baby, "two other folks are lined up to give tributes. One is her sister, Stella Marie Deveroux from Baton Rouge, and the other is a cousin, I think."

"I could design a program if you'd like," Carmela offered.

Baby looked sad but thrilled. "Would you really do that?"

"Of course," said Carmela. "You know I'd be happy to. Well, not *happy,* because she's . . ."

Baby reached for Carmela's hand and gripped it. "I know, dear," she said, in a mournful voice. "I know."

Carmela cruised her shop then, helping customers select paper and various items to decorate their jewel boxes. One woman, Sylvie Webber, seemed to be stuck.

"Do you think I could use this Japanese wrapping paper?" Sylvie asked. She held a rolled sheet of burnished brown paper covered with cream-colored Japanese kanji in her hand.

"I think it would make a lovely background," Carmela told her.

But Sylvie was still undecided. "But then what? How do I carry out the Asian theme?"

"How about adding stickers or stamps with cranes on them?" Carmela suggested. "Cranes being an auspicious symbol in Japan."

"Perfect," said Sylvie. "And maybe some beads?"

"I have some gold lantern beads," said Carmela, "as well as some lovely silk tassels."

"Do you think I could try doing some Japanese calligraphy?" asked Sylvie.

"I don't see why not," said Carmela. "You might find out you're very good at it!"

Carmela moved to the front counter, where she sifted through a basket filled with beads and charms, looking for something else Sylvie could use. When she glanced up, Baby was staring at her, an inquisitive look on her face.

"Do you know?" Baby asked in hushed tones, "is there anything new on the investigation?"

"Not really," said Carmela. She felt guilty about holding back information about

167

Johnny Otis's arrest from Baby, but she didn't want to betray any confidences with Babcock, either.

"I've been asking around," said Baby. "Talking to people I know on various boards and committees . . . people associated with St. Tristan's. And there's one name that keeps coming up."

"Who?" asked Carmela, pretty much expecting Baby to spit out the name Johnny Otis.

"Paul Lupori," said Baby. "Brother Paul, to be exact."

"Oh my gosh," Carmela exclaimed, putting a hand to her head and pushing back a tangle of hair, "I met him! He was the guy creeping around the basement of St. Tristan's yesterday when Ava and I went back to check things out."

Baby gazed at her in surprise. "There you go! I heard that Brother Paul had recently begun an affiliation with St. Tristan's. Running some sort of program, though I'm not sure what it is exactly."

"So . . . why does his name keep coming up?" asked Carmela. "Among the people you talked to."

"Here's the thing," said Baby, lowering her voice. "Apparently Brother Paul had been working over at St. Cecilia's and some

168

money went missing. A lot of money."

"Okay," said Carmela.

"And now," said Baby, "just as Brother Paul begins an affiliation with St. Tristan's, a valuable crucifix is stolen and poor Byrle ends up dead. Does that sound a little fishy to you?"

"Maybe," said Carmela. Brother Paul had *seemed* harmless enough. But since Baby had information concerning stolen money, it did cast him in a different light.

"So what I'm wondering," continued Baby, "is if you could dream up some sort of excuse to talk to him. See what you can find out."

"Are you serious?" Carmela's voice rose in a squawk. "Talk to Brother Paul? What would I say to him? What on earth would be my excuse?"

Baby shook her head. "I have no idea. But I'm positive you'll come up with something." A smile crept onto her face. "After all, investigating is pretty much your area of expertise."

After checking on the rest of her crafters, Carmela ducked back into her office to fix a cup of Darjeeling tea. She took a couple of fortifying sips and decided, then and there, to call Babcock. Go right to the horse's mouth, so to speak, concerning the mysterious Brother Paul.

"What do you know about Brother Paul?" Carmela asked Babcock, once she had him on the line.

"What!" Babcock screeched. "Why would you bring *that* name up?

Carmela moved the receiver away from her ear and said, "I didn't."

"Yes, you did," fumed Babcock. He sounded harried, and Carmela could hear horns honking in the background. Probably Babcock was out driving around, trying to talk, trying to listen, trying to maneuver around potholes and juggle a cup of black coffee at the same time.

"Technically, it was Baby who mentioned Brother Paul's name to me," said Carmela. "It seems he got into some sort of trouble when he was working over at, um . . ."

"Over at St. Cecilia's," said Babcock. "Yes, yes, I've heard the whole sad tale."

"Really? From him? From Brother Paul?"

"Yes, from him," said Babcock, still sounding crabby.

"So is it?" asked Carmela

"Is it what?" asked Babcock.

"A sad tale," said Carmela. She paused. "Do we have a bad connection or something? Because this conversation suddenly

170

sounds very long distance."

"That's because you're doing it again," said Babcock.

"Excuse me?"

"You're snooping," Babcock told her. "Butting in where you don't belong."

Carmela took a sip of tea and said, "Oh, I *belong,* detective. Because I was *there.* Much to my abject horror, I had a front-row seat for the big bad show at St. Tristan's this past Monday. Which makes me a very interested party." She counted silently from one to ten, then said, in a more conversational tone, "So now I'd like you to tell me everything you know about Brother Paul."

"You're incorrigible," said Babcock.

"Speak," said Carmela.

"There's not much to tell," said Babcock. "Brother Paul runs a place called Storyville Outreach Center over on Basin Street. Apparently, he lives there, too."

"Storyville," said Carmela. "Interesting." Storyville was the old name for the infamous red-light district that was closed down by the federal government during World War I. "What do you know about this . . . what did you call it? Outreach center?"

"I know that Brother Paul preaches a little gospel and serves food to the local down-and-outers."

"So it's basically a soup kitchen?"

"Pretty much," said Babcock, "with a few prayers thrown in for good measure. Apparently Brother Paul scrounges donations from grocery stores, local food companies, and a few sympathetic restaurants. I already checked it out with the state's Charity Review Council. Brother Paul's Storyville Outreach Center is aboveboard and seems to be charitable."

"Is Brother Paul a suspect?" asked Carmela. She had to know.

"Not as this point," said Babcock.

"Why not?"

"Not a speck of evidence," said Babcock. "Also no motive or reliable eyewitnesses."

"Hmm," said Carmela, not liking the emphasis he'd put on the word *reliable.* In fact, Brother Paul suddenly sounded like the perfect suspect to her.

"So," said Babcock, "that means I don't want you badgering the man." He paused. "Do you hear me, my dear? I don't want you running around, asking questions, and poking your nose where it doesn't belong."

"Sure," said Carmela. "No needless running around." As far as asking questions and poking her nose into places, there was no way she'd agree to *that.*

"Good," said Babcock, sounding distracted now. "I'll call you later."

Carmela hung up the phone, took a sip of tea that had grown lukewarm and a little puckery, and thought to herself, *Is Brother Paul really on the up-and-up?* After all, appearances could be so deceiving. Case in point, Rain Monroe. The woman displayed all the trappings of an upscale society matron, but beneath that high-gloss exterior beat the heart of a viper.

"I'm taking orders for a run to the Pirate's Alley Deli," said Gabby, interrupting Carmela's dark thoughts. Gabby hunkered in the doorway, pad and pencil in hand. "You want something for lunch? A po'boy or a muffuletta?"

"Sure," said Carmela, her brain still whirring.

"Po'boy?" asked Gabby. "Your fave?" Carmela's fave was deep-fried soft-shell crab with cole slaw, pickles, and mayo on a grilled bun. Not the most heart-healthy New Orleans dish, but certainly not as bad as good old artery-clogging étouffée.

"The po'boy sounds great," said Carmela.

"You say that," said Gabby, "but I'm sensing a certain lack of enthusiasm."

"It's just that I . . . well . . . I'm in the middle of something."

"If I could do a brain scan on you," joked Gabby.

"You really wouldn't want to," said Carmela. "Say, could you ask Baby to come back here?"

"Sure," said Gabby, a puzzled look on her face.

A couple of minutes later, Baby was perched in the director's chair across from Carmela, listening attentively as Carmela related the details of her conversation with Babcock.

"Storyville Outreach Center?" said Baby. She patted the tips of one manicured hand against the side of her smooth cheek.

"That's what he said."

"Carmela," said an excited Baby, "you've got to go over there! Take a look around. See what Brother Paul is really up to!"

"Maybe he's up to gospel music and serving dinner, just like Babcock said."

"And maybe it's something else," said Baby. She furrowed her brow, looking worried.

"If I go cowboying in there," said Carmela, "what's my story?" What she really meant was, *What's my cover?*

Baby thought for a few moments, then said, "Tell Brother Paul that you want to volunteer!"

174

"Not very likely," murmured Carmela.

"Don't sell yourself short," said Baby. "He might buy it." She reached over and grabbed Carmela's hand, clutching it tightly in her own. "Please, honey, just go over and look around. See if his place really is on the up-and-up. See if he's running a for-real charity or a scam." Baby drew a deep breath. "See if he sets off any bells or whistles with your inner truth detector."

What she really means, thought Carmela, *is my bullshit detector.*

CHAPTER 13

Just as Carmela had started her group on their afternoon project, the front door flew open. A swirl of colorful leaves rushed in along with a glut of cool air. On the tail of it, dressed in impeccable brown tweeds, came the tall, broad-shouldered form of Drew Gaspar.

"Close the door! Close the door!" shrilled Gabby, as she rushed to the front of the shop, arms akimbo. "Our papers are flying everywhere!" she scolded.

"Ooh, sorry, sorry," said Gaspar. He hastily reversed course and pulled the door shut tight, then turned around with an embarrassed smile on his face.

"That's better," said Gabby, in a sharp bark.

Now Gaspar just looked flustered, as if he'd stumbled into the ladies' lingerie department instead of a scrapbook shop.

Carmela's heels rang out like castanets as

she hurried to greet him. "Mr. Gaspar, I had no idea you were going to drop by."

"Apologies," said Gaspar, fluttering his hands and furrowing his brow. "I was in the neighborhood and thought I'd pop in. From the looks of things, you're quite busy."

"We're always busy here," Tandy called loudly from the back of the shop. "So don't mind us chickens."

"It's my calligraphy class," Carmela explained to him. "Really an all-day seminar."

"And are we ever having fun," Tandy called out again.

"As you can see," said Carmela, unable to suppress a grin, "we have some very enthusiastic participants."

"Calligraphy," said Gaspar, seizing upon the word. "The very subject we were discussing last night."

We weren't really discussing it, thought Carmela. *You were.*

Gaspar gestured toward the back of the room, where Carmela's crafters were working away. "May I? Take a peek, I mean?" His unease seemed to have vanished.

"I suppose," said Carmela, as Gaspar bounded through the shop, brushing past floor-to-ceiling racks of paper and shelves stocked with ribbons and albums.

"Welcome," called out Baby, as Carmela

177

hastened to make quick introductions.

Then Tandy, never shy about anything, had to show him her project.

"Really quite fantastic," Gaspar marveled. "But I'm interrupting your class. Please forgive me, dear ladies."

"Don't worry," Carmela told him, "they're well into their next craft project."

"Then perhaps we could chat," said Gaspar. "About that menu design?"

Carmela dutifully took Gaspar into her office and sat him down.

"So creative," he said, glancing at her walls, where various papers and sketches were tacked up. "There's nothing more stimulating than being in the presence of a person with a true creative bent."

Carmela let that comment roll past her.

"You were primarily interested in a new menu, I believe," said Carmela, taking the lead. She rolled her chair back, pulled open one of her flat files, and grabbed one of the menus she'd designed for Mumbo Gumbo. Passing it to Gaspar, she said, "This is the menu I designed for Quigg."

Gaspar patted his jacket pocket for a pair of glasses, found them, slipped them onto his nose, and perused the menu she'd handed him. "Wonderful work!" he proclaimed after a few moments.

Carmela tried not to giggle. It was fun, colorful, and serviceable, but it was never going to be a finalist for a CLIO or CAA award.

"It's cheeky," Gaspar declared. "You're a cheeky designer. And you love to play with type and color."

Carmela squinted at Gaspar. If he had that much aptitude for design, how come he hadn't been a good judge of his own menu?

"I still do the odd design project," Carmela told him, "but these days I spend much more time doing commercial scrapbooks."

Gaspar raised a single eyebrow. "Commercial scrapbook? That's something I'm not familiar with."

Carmela pulled out a scrapbook she'd recently created for Lotus Floral and handed it to him. "It's like an expanded brochure," she explained. "This particular florist wanted customers to get an idea of what kind of unique bouquets, centerpieces, and wedding flowers they could do. So we took pictures, mounted them on colorful scrapbook paper, and did hand-lettered captions."

"This is gorgeous," said Gaspar. He'd turned to a page that featured a photo of a bride and groom standing in a courtyard festooned with flowers. "I meant the scrapbook," he said. "Though the floral designs are lovely, too."

Carmela glanced out the door of her office. She was starting to wonder if inviting Gaspar into her office had been a good idea, after all.

Gabby noticed Carmela's worried look and said, "Don't worry, Carmela, I can honcho this next project."

"I love your idea of a commercial scrapbook," said Gaspar. "I can see where it could be useful in promoting special events — business dinners, meetings, wedding receptions."

Carmela nodded, although she couldn't imagine any girl having her wedding reception in a place where an army of gargoyles scowled down at her guests.

"But my immediate need is a new menu," said Gaspar. "Will you help?"

"Your menu presentation is fine as is," said Carmela. "With the leather folders. It's the type that's problematic."

"It would seem so," said Gaspar.

"Why don't you let me noodle around some ideas," said Carmela. "Maybe work up a couple of samples."

"You're a lifesaver," said Gaspar.

"Not really," said Carmela. She was luke-warm about this project at best.

"Another quick question," said Gaspar. "Your lovely friend . . ."

"Ava," supplied Carmela.

"Has she ever done any modeling?"

Carmela thought for a few seconds. The two of them *had* modeled in a Moda Chadron show a while back. Though that little episode had ended in complete disaster. So maybe she should play it straight and tell the truth? On the other hand . . .

"It's really just a yes-or-no question," laughed Gaspar.

"Yes," said Carmela, "she has."

"I suspected as much," said Gaspar. "Do you have her current address?"

Carmela pulled open a desk drawer and reached in. "Actually, I have one of Ava's business cards." She handed him a black-and-red card that said *Juju Voodoo* in fat, funky letters.

"Very nice," said Gaspar. "Your design?"

"That's right," said Carmela.

"I have something very special in the works," said Gaspar, giving her a wide grin that displayed lots of teeth, "but I want to make sure everything is in place first."

"Sounds mysterious," said Carmela.

"Believe me," said Gaspar, "it is."

■ ■ ■ ■

"A new design project?" asked Gabby, once Gaspar had left, and Carmela had determined that her customers were still happily toying with lettering and paper and design ideas.

"Something like that," said Carmela, as they walked together toward the front counter.

"It's always nice to pick up a design project, isn't it?" said Gabby. She slipped behind the counter and grabbed a packet of colored tags. "What's his business exactly?"

"He runs a restaurant called Purgatoria," said Carmela. "It's a new place over on Magazine Street. Ava and I dropped in for dinner last night, which is how we became acquainted."

"Purgatoria," said Gabby, tilting her head. "That's a funny name for a restaurant."

"If you saw it, you'd understand the name," said Carmela. "It's a kind of crazy-quilt place filled with old church pews and statues and . . ." She stopped abruptly as Gabby's eyes suddenly went round as saucers. "What's wrong?"

"Church stuff?" said Gabby, her voice rising a few octaves. "He likes *church* stuff?"

"Well . . . yes," said Carmela. "He's got quite the collection of candlesticks and crosses and . . ."

"Think, Carmela!" hissed Gabby. "What if he's the guy who snatched the crucifix!"

"I can't imagine . . . ," began Carmela. Then stopped. Because all of a sudden, like a whoosh of noxious air, she *could* imagine it.

"Carmela?" said Tandy. Carmela was hunched over the front counter, still thinking about Gaspar. Was he some kind of wacko collector? Had the menu design been a ruse to get close to her? Was she clutching at straws?

Carmela shook her head to clear it and said, "What, honey?"

"Do you have any really sheer gossamer ribbon?"

"Let me check," said Carmela. "I know we've got some pink chiffon, but I . . ."

The front door suddenly flew open again and Carmela spun around, figuring that Drew Gaspar, for whatever annoying reason, had returned. But it was Marilyn Casey, Tandy's writer friend, who came hustling in.

"Hey, Marilyn!" said Tandy. She opened her arms, swept her friend into them, and proceeded to administer a quick string of air kisses. "What brings you here?" Not letting Marilyn get a word in, she added, "You just missed Carmela's calligraphy seminar, you know." Tandy glanced at her watch. "Well, we've got like another hour and a half to go, but I don't think . . ." Tandy waved a hand in front of her face. "Here I am, jabbering away like a dingbat." She gave a feigned shrug of dismay and said to Marilyn, "How are you, hon?"

Now it was Marilyn Casey's turn to vent. "If you really want to know, I'm about to go plumb crazy! I've made so many notes and written down so many ideas, I don't know where I'm going anymore!"

Tandy took a step back. "That's good for a writer, huh?"

"I don't know," said Marilyn. "Maybe." She looked both excited and frustrated.

"How can we help?" asked Carmela. Probably, Marilyn had a good reason for stopping by today, right?

"Notebooks," said Marilyn, holding up her hand, as if asking for permission to speak. "I need at least two more notebooks." Her eyes lasered across the displays at the front of the store, but didn't find what she was looking for. She looked fretful, producing a set of deep, vertical furrows right between her brows. "You carry that sort of thing, right?"

"We sure do," said Carmela. She led Marilyn back to a pecan highboy that had been shoehorned between the paper baskets and the flat files, and said, "We've got tablets, spirals, leather bound, and, let's see, even some notebooks with recycled paper." She pulled a couple of notebooks down and handed them to Marilyn. "These have lined paper, I think that's what you probably want. Oh, and if you're interested in decorating the covers with fabric or paper, we also stock plain chipboard notebooks."

Marilyn balanced a notebook in each hand as if she were carefully weighing the merits of each one. Finally she held one out and said, "This orange spiral is perfect. I'll take two."

"Good choice," said Carmela. The orange spiral notebooks were her personal favorite, too. "Anything else? Pens? Maybe a Rapidograph?"

Marilyn blinked at her. "What's a Rapidograph?"

"They're neat little pens," said Carmela, grabbing one from a display. She pulled the cap off and said, "See? It's a pen with an extremely fine tip. Artists and designers use them mostly, but if I'm writing a longer piece, I use a Rapidograph because it practically flies across the page."

"That's for me," Marilyn enthused. "Two of those, please."

Carmela popped everything into a brown paper bag with handles, slapped on a colorful crack-and-peel Memory Mine label, and asked, "Anything else?"

Marilyn sidled up to the counter. "Do you know anything more?" she asked in a low voice. "About the murder investigation?"

"Not really," said Carmela.

"Because," continued Marilyn, "I heard you were very close to one of the detectives." She gave a sheepish shrug and said, "At least that's what Tandy told me."

"I'm close to him," said Carmela, "but that doesn't mean I'm close to the investigation."

"Too bad," said Marilyn.

Carmela tapped an index finger against the bag. "Too bad is right," she agreed. "But maybe . . ."

"What?" asked Marilyn, leaning in closer.

"I might have something in the next day or two. There's something . . . someone . . . I want to check out."

"Really?" said Marilyn. She seemed incredulous.

"Baby . . . Baby Fontaine . . . asked me to

kind of look into things. Since Byrle was a really dear friend of hers."

"And you do this kind of thing?" asked Marilyn. "Investigate?"

Carmela gave a reluctant nod. "It would appear so."

"Then you're the lady in the middle of it all," breathed Marilyn. "Seeing as how you were also a kind of witness."

"Not much of a witness," Carmela admitted. "I didn't even get a look at the killer's face."

"Because he wore some kind of cloak."

"That's right," said Carmela.

"Still," said Marilyn, "it's wonderful you're trying to untangle this thing. As a kind of . . . good citizen Samaritan." Marilyn's eyes sparkled with enthusiasm. "Kudos to you, girl. Go for it."

"And if I find out anything," said Carmela, "I will let you know."

"Bless you," said Marilyn.

Carmela was about to wander back to her crafters when Ava called.

"Carmela!" Ava sobbed. "You're not going to believe what just happened!" There were more heartrending sobs, then she gasped out, "They just told me . . . oh, I can't even . . ."

"Ava? What's wrong?"

"Everything!" came Ava's anguished voice.

Carmela had no clue what Ava was upset about, but immediately asked, "Are you in any physical danger?"

"No," Ava gasped again. "It's just that . . ."

"Drew Gaspar didn't drop by, did he?" asked Carmela. For some reason, an image of Gaspar had suddenly popped into her head. Gaspar pressuring Ava for . . . something.

There were a few seconds of silence, and then Ava said, "No. But I really need to . . ."

"Hang on, honey, I'm coming right over," said Carmela. "I'll be there in five minutes."

"Hurry!" sobbed Ava.

Carmela ducked out the back door, breezed down the cobblestone back alley that was already garbed in twilight, and flew the two blocks to Ava's shop. For some reason she kept thinking about Drew Gaspar. A little smarmy, a little bit slithery.

Carmela pulled the front door of Juju Voodoo open forcefully as she plowed her way in. Her caramel-colored hair was tousled from the wind, and her cheeks were flushed from her half-walk, half-run over. "What's wrong?" she demanded of Ava, who was standing behind her counter, looking angry and stunned.

"You're not going to believe this!" Ava wailed.

Carmela put a hand on her chest, trying to still her thready breathing. "Try me."

Turned out, Gaspar hadn't dropped by to see Ava at all. But someone had delivered a bombshell.

"I've been kicked off the Angel Auxiliary at St. Tristan's!" said Ava, looking positively stricken.

"You *what?*" Carmela blinked, even as she warned herself not to get too upset. After all, she'd just broken a land speed record for this?

"It's so unfair," Ava moaned.

Carmela gazed across a shop counter that was piled high with a jumble of shrunken heads, plastic skulls, voodoo potions, and evil eye necklaces, and said, without batting an eye, "You're right, it's terribly unfair."

Ava sniffled into a rumpled hanky. "From what Camille told me, it was all Rain Monroe's idea. Rain spearheaded the movement against me!"

"Who's Camille?" asked Carmela. Best to get the players straight in her head before she tried to sort things out.

"Camille's the head of the Angel Auxiliary," said Ava. "She called me, like, five minutes ago." Ava sniffled. "Well, maybe ten

189

minutes ago now."

"Okay," said Carmela.

Ava continued to leak tears. "Camille promised to plead my case in front of the board of directors, but . . ." Ava just shrugged and looked lost. "Who knows?"

"And you say this was Rain's idea?" It sounded like the kind of sheer nastiness Rain Monroe delighted in perpetrating.

"Yes!" Ava wailed. "She must really hate me!"

Carmela fumed inwardly. She knew how much Ava loved her work at St. Tristan's. And wondered what had prompted Rain's nasty maneuver. Was the board worried that Ava was somehow connected to Byrle's murder? Was the board genuinely disturbed that Ava owned a voodoo shop? Was Rain Monroe just a rabid nutcase? Or, Carmela wondered, had she herself provoked Rain, and firing Ava was just petty retribution?

"You know what?" said Carmela, forcing herself to sound upbeat. "This is all going to work out."

Ava picked up a beige linen voodoo doll marked with various body parts. "You think?" She toyed with a long red pin.

Carmela gave a warm smile. "Sure I do." *Maybe I do.*

Ava still didn't look convinced. "But what

190

can we . . . ?"

"Don't worry about it," Carmela told her. "I'll figure something out. I'll speak to the board or have Babcock explain about the investigation or whatever." She squared her shoulders and said, "I'll go talk to Rain myself if I have to."

"You'd do that for me?" Ava gave her a look filled with puppy-dog adoration.

"Of course, I would. I can be very persuasive when I want to be."

Ava gave a final sniffle, picked up a can of Diet Coke and took a sip, then said, "Thanks. I feel better now."

"Sure you do."

"This thing just came zooming out of left field."

"Bad new . . . tough news . . . is always like that," said Carmela. "You never get a chance to prepare yourself for the big disappointments in life. You just get . . . gobsmacked."

"And just when things were going so well." Ava glanced back toward her reading room, where a customer, a woman in an expensive-looking camel-colored suit and cape, was just getting up to leave.

Carmela caught her drift. "You hired Madame Blavatsky?"

"I sure did," said Ava. "And I have to say,

my customers adore her. She's a very gifted psychic."

"Maybe we should go back and take a little sip of psychic energy," joked Carmela. "It might be better than chugging a can of Red Bull."

They walked past life-sized skeletons, shelves of saint candles, colorful bags of love charms, voodoo jewelry, and potions in purple bottles.

"Sorry the shop is such a mess," Ava apologized. "We're hot and heavy into inventory. Everything's all moved around."

To Carmela, Ava's place didn't look one bit different. It was always a mishmash of skull earrings, candles, potions, evil eye necklaces, T-shirts, and various Halloween items. Which, of course, was its charm. Today, for instance, a large furry bat with a six-foot wingspan peered from dark rafters overhead.

Madame Blavatsky gave a welcoming smile as they entered the little octagonal reading room. She was sitting at a small, round table with her trusty crystal ball, and was all glitzed up in a shimmery silver blouse, floor-length midnight-blue skirt with silver threads running through it, and a couple of dozen chunky silver bracelets and rings flashing on her hands. Carmela managed a peep at the madame's shoes. Yup, those were silver, too.

"How's it going?" Carmela asked, trying for low-key friendly.

"Very well," said Madame Blavatsky. Her fingers skittered over her crystal ball, then closed around it. "You're interested in a reading?"

"Maybe," Carmela hedged. Truth be told, she wasn't a big believer in tarot, the *I Ching,* and the like. Wasn't any sort of believer in prognostication.

"You want to know what's going to happen tonight?" Madame Blavatsky asked. "When you go talk to that man?"

Her words stopped Carmela dead in her tracks. "Um . . . what?"

"The little adventure you have planned for tonight," said Madame Blavatsky. "You want to peer into the future? Try to pierce the veil of space and time?"

"Well . . . sure," said Carmela. "Why not?" She let loose a low chuckle, but the hair on the back of her neck was standing straight up and prickling like crazy. She wanted to yell out loud to herself, *Calm down, there's no reason to get nervous. No spirits or otherworldly beings are at work here. This all falls into the category of stupid parlor trick.* Although, for some reason, she wasn't quite believing any of that at the moment.

"Oh," Madame Blavatsky said to Ava, seeing the confusion on her face. "She hasn't told you yet."

Ava turned dark, questioning eyes on Carmela and said, "Told me what?"

CHAPTER 14

Rain pelted down in juicy splotches as Carmela navigated her car through the dark city. Overhead lights and neon signs cast test patterns of light on her windshield. Ava sat cross-legged in the passenger seat, the defroster swirling her hair into a tangled Medusa-do as it worked overtime to keep the windows defogged.

"When were you going to tell me about this mysterious foray to visit Brother Paul?" asked Ava.

"I was going to tell you after you calmed down," said Carmela. "After you got over your initial shock of being booted out of the Angel Auxiliary."

But Ava was still smarting and filled with emotion. "It felt awful," she said, wringing her hands, "almost like I'd been fired from a job. And, you know, I've never been fired from anything in my whole entire life!"

"Never?"

"Well, once I worked at the corn factory over in Hamilton. After about two hours of chucking cobs into the husker I realized it wasn't the career path I wanted to pursue. Still, when I left, it was by mutual agreement."

"You agreed you didn't want to work there anymore," said Carmela.

Ava giggled. "And they agreed I wasn't very good at chucking cobs."

"I can understand that," said Carmela, as they splashed through an enormous puddle.

"This much rain is just plain crazy," said Ava, peering out. Lookit, your wipers can barely keep up."

"It's a deluge, all right," said Carmela. "Thank goodness we're past hurricane season."

"Seeing this much rain just brings back bad memories," said Ava, suddenly looking morose again.

Carmela squinted through her windshield as she negotiated a turn onto St. Bernard. "Of Katrina, yeah." The entire city had been smacked down by the hurricane. And Carmela, doing her very small part in the recovery, had spent months and months helping customers dry out and salvage soggy photos and important documents.

"I hope this rain isn't heralding some kind

of bad luck," commented Ava.

"Have you been listening to Madame Blavatsky's predictions?"

"I'm, like, being serious here," said Ava. "The lady is relevant. She possesses some very keen insights."

Carmela wasn't buying it. "You think?"

"Oh yeah, she's definitely in touch with the great beyond. She knew you were going to ask me to help spy on Brother Paul tonight."

"Maybe she didn't divine it," said Carmela. "Maybe you just happened to mention that we'd run into him and she made a lucky guess. Sometimes luck is a dandy stand-in for intuition."

"Maybe," said Ava, scratching her head. "But I'll tell you one thing. My customers love her. Missy Lafourche has been in three times this week alone."

"Good for business," Carmela murmured. "I don't know how good it is for Missy."

"Some people just like to know what's around the next corner," said Ava.

"And I'm happy just to see what's directly in front of me," said Carmela.

They whooshed down Paris, past a row of wrought-iron gaslights strung out like glowing rosary beads. Carmela didn't know if it was an optical illusion caused by the rain and fog, but it felt like she was entering some ethereal magical realm.

And that lasted for about three more minutes, until she turned into the parking lot of the Storyville Outreach Center. She slowed to a halt as a large, ramshackle building that had once been a warehouse loomed in front of them. A few rusted and pock-marked cars sat willy-nilly in a muddy parking lot. Rain continued to pound down.

"This is it?" said Ava. Her upper lip was curled in disgust, distaste evident in her voice. "It looks awful. Like a cootie factory."

"It's a soup kitchen," said Carmela, un-snapping her seat belt. "It's not supposed to replicate a plush dining alcove at Antoine's. Stands to reason a place that feeds the homeless is going to look a little rough around the edges."

"But if it looks this nasty," said Ava, pulling herself out of the car, "how bad is it going to smell?"

Turned out, not so great.

Pushing their way through the double doors of Storyville Outreach, they were met with the mingled odor of wet clothes, burned coffee, and beef stew. Luckily, the stew was the more prevalent top note.

"I guess they're just serving dinner," said Ava. All around them, men and women were picking their way toward long trestle tables. They looked tired, downcast, and weather-beaten.

"Hungry?" said Carmela.

Ava gave a tight shake of her head. "Not really."

"Oh hey," said Carmela, noticing Brother Paul acknowledge their grand entrance. "Looks like we've been spotted."

"What do you think gave it away that we're not exactly in the homeless category?" asked Ava. "Your Louis Vuitton bag or my Ralph Lauren jacket?"

"Hard to say," said Carmela, as Brother Paul's wary eyes continued to home in on them from across the room. Then he whispered something to an assistant and headed directly for them.

"Peace be with you," said Brother Paul, as he greeted them. Tonight he was dressed civilian style. Black long-sleeved shirt, baggy blue jeans, ragged tennis shoes. His thin gray hair was combed straight back, and his dark eyes remained as piercing as ever.

"You remember us?" asked Carmela.

Brother Paul tilted his head sideways, as if he were deep in thought.

"We met the other day," said Carmela. "In the basement of St. Tristan's Church."

"And that must be why you were sent to

me," murmured Brother Paul. "To help serve in our ministry."

His words lit up Ava. "Serve?" she squawked. "You mean . . . serve dinner?" She uttered the word *dinner* as if she'd been asked to dish up dog poop.

Brother Paul gestured toward the rows of tables. "I have a hungry and weary flock tonight."

"Wait a minute," said Ava. She put a hand on her hip and twisted her body. "You want us to be, like, waitresses?" She looked horrified.

The beginnings of a smile flitted across Brother Paul's stern face. "No, no," he told her. "First we say a few prayers of thanksgiving, then our flock will proceed through our rather democratic cafeteria line."

"Maybe we could make this little venture reciprocal," said Carmela, eager to lob a few questions at Brother Paul. "We help you, then you help us."

"Perhaps so," said Brother Paul. He crooked an index finger and they followed him as he threaded his way through an orderly layout of tables, then through a swinging door and into a large industrial kitchen.

"Whoa," said Ava. "Big place." Storyville Outreach may have looked shabby from the

200

outside, but the kitchen, with its second-hand stainless steel restaurant counters and shelves, fairly gleamed. Enormous silver pans bubbled atop two large industrial stoves and at least a dozen people, all garbed in white, bustled to and fro in the hot, steamy environment.

A volunteer named Ruth led them into a back room where they donned long white aprons, plastic hairnets, and plastic gloves.

"Look at this crappy outfit," Ava complained, spinning around with her arms outstretched. "It's like wearing a hazmat suit. Are we supposed to serve dinner or swab out the containment core of a nuclear reactor?"

"Just think of this as quid pro quo," said Carmela, as they walked out into the busy kitchen. "We help in the kitchen, then Brother Paul sits down with us and answers a few questions."

"If he keeps his word," said Ava, bending over to sniff one of the pans that sat atop the stove. "Agh!" She straightened up. "This stuff smells like dog food!"

"I think it's really, um, beans?" said Carmela.

"Awful," said Ava.

"Still," said Carmela, grabbing a long-handled spoon and dipping it into the beans for a taste, "if you were homeless and hadn't eaten for a day or two . . ." She tasted the beans, then made a face. Way too bland.

"You know what your problem is?" said Ava. "You're too kindhearted and always see the upside of things."

Carmela chuckled. "And that's a *bad* thing?"

"No, I suppose not." Ava glanced at the beans. "Maybe . . . you should work some of your kitchen magic?"

"Worth a try," said Carmela. She scouted around the kitchen, found the walk-in pantry, and proceeded to grab salt, pepper, brown sugar, and a large bottle of hot sauce off the shelves. She carried it all back to the pot of beans, then added ingredients, stirred, tasted, and judiciously added some more.

"Better now?" asked Ava.

Carmela nodded. "Lots more savory." She dipped a clean spoon into the beans. "Care to taste?"

Ava held up a hand. "Pass."

"You ladies gonna eat those beans or serve 'em?" asked Ruth, though she said it with a good-natured smile.

"Let's do it," said Carmela. She and Ava grabbed pot holders, hoisted the pot of beans off the stove, and lugged it over to the cafeteria line.

"Good job," said Ruth. She held up an ice-cream scoop. "Who wants to do the honors?"

"Me," said Ava. She dipped the scoop into the pot and, as the first folks began shuffling through the cafeteria line, proceeded to dole out big helpings of beans.

Most of the men and a scattering of women went through the line silently. A few murmured hoarse thank-yous. To Carmela, who'd always been a champion of underdogs, it was heartbreaking. Especially in a city that thrived on parties and wild celebrations, and touted the good life with the motto *Laissez les bons temps rouler.* Let the good times roll.

But not so many good times here.

After fifteen minutes or so, Carmela took over serving, while Ava took a well-deserved break. As Carmela scooped beans, she noticed Ava sidling up to another volunteer, a man with a thatch of unruly blond hair who wore a white chef's jacket. She grinned. A leopard didn't change its spots, even in a homeless shelter. And Ava was definitely on the prowl.

Five minutes later, the line dwindling, Ava came back over to see how Carmela was doing. "Everything cool?" she asked.

Carmela nodded. "Looks like we're ready to wrap it up."

Ava gave a self-satisfied smile. "Did you see that guy I was talking to?"

"The one with the Chia Pet hair?" asked Carmela.

Ava giggled. "Ned's just a little avant-garde. Besides, he's the executive director of this place."

"No kidding?"

"Oh yeah," said Ava, "he was telling me all about it. Basically, he spends most of his day as a big-time fund-raiser. Writing grants, schmoozing donors, that type of thing. He's the one who really keeps the doors open."

"That's wonderful," said Carmela. She was always impressed by smart business-people who, instead of working plush jobs at big corporations, chose to bring their skills into the nonprofit sector. There had to be a special place in heaven for people like that.

"Anyway," said Ava, "I'm ready to hang it up. And I'm not just talking about my apron."

But once they'd changed back into civilian clothing, Brother Paul was busy out front, leading his flock in prayer. So Carmela and Ava took seats at the back of the room and bowed their heads, prepared to wait.

Finally, some twenty minutes later, the prayer session concluded with a hymn, a shaky, slightly off-key rendition of "Rock of Ages."

Before the last note had died, Carmela sprang out of her chair and buttonholed Brother Paul. "We need to talk," she told him, in no uncertain terms.

"What is it you want from me?" Brother Paul asked. Now he just looked tired.

"Information," said Carmela. "Specifically about the rather cryptic words you spoke to us yesterday at St. Tristan's."

"Which words were those?" asked Brother Paul. Now he seemed to be purposefully obtuse.

"Seekers," said Carmela. "When we told you we were looking into the murder of our friend Byrle, you referred to the Seekers." She paused. "I want to know exactly what you meant."

"They exist," said Brother Paul.

"Is this a group that's somehow affiliated with St. Tristan's?" asked Ava.

Brother Paul let loose a low snort.

"Then who are the Seekers?" asked Carmela. "Please tell us."

"Sounds like a sixties Motown group,"

said Ava. She took a step backward, bumped into someone directly behind her, and turned to apologize. Then her eyes lit up as she recognized Ned, the executive director. "Leaving so soon?" she asked. He'd changed into jeans and a blue plaid shirt.

"Duty calls," said Ned, giving her a longing gaze. "But do come back and visit us again, won't you?"

"I might just do that," Ava told him. She spun back around, grinned at Carmela and Brother Paul, and said, "Nice guy, your executive director."

"You mean Roach?" said Brother Paul. "He's one of our flock."

"What?" Ava screeched. "What do you mean?" Her mouth opened and closed a few times, and then she stammered out, "His name is *Roach* and he's *homeless?*"

Brother Paul nodded. "Temporarily between dwellings, as we like to say."

Ava looked stunned. "Well . . . dang."

Brother Paul seemed to be enjoying her discomfiture. "You never can tell about people," he said.

"I guess not," said Ava.

"Getting back to the Seekers," said Carmela. She wasn't impressed by Brother Paul's slightly snide attitude that had just been revealed.

"Ah, yes." Brother Paul crossed his arms and looked properly attuned once more. "The Seekers are a somewhat reclusive group."

"I take it they're some kind of religious organization?" said Carmela.

"They claim to be," said Brother Paul. "The group holds their meetings at a make-shift church just off Trempeleau Road, south of here. South of the village of Mayport."

"Excuse me," said Carmela. "Are you implying they're some sort of cult?"

Brother Paul's eyes seemed to gleam. "Their leader is a man by the name of Reverend Frank Crowley. But, I daresay, his title was purchased via the Internet."

"This is all very interesting," said Carmela, "but why would you think these people, the Seekers, are even remotely involved?"

"Because of the silver-and-gold crucifix," said Brother Paul. "The Seekers' basic coda is based on Judas's betrayal of Christ."

"Excuse me?" said Carmela, trying to pull together a connection.

Brother Paul's voice was low and gravelly. "For thirty pieces of silver."

Chapter 15

The last vestiges of rain swirled in the downspouts outside Carmela's apartment. This Thursday morning's walk with Boo and Poobah had been slow and damp as the dogs picked their way miserably down the alley, trying to avoid puddles, phobic about getting their tidy little paws wet. And now Carmela was running late.

Knock knock.

"That you?" Carmela called from the bedroom. She was struggling to zip her black skirt, wondering what the problem was. *Too much bread pudding with brandy sauce? Overdoing it on the cheese and crab étouffée? Naw, that couldn't be it.*

"It's me!" Ava called, as she let herself in. Carmela heard woofs and snorts, a sure sign the dogs were giving a proper greeting to their aunt Ava.

"Be right out." Carmela finally got the zipper to close, patted her tummy, and made a solemn vow. *As soon as this rain lets up, we're going to do a whole lot more walking.*

"What are you wearing, *cher?*" Ava called.

"Black suit," Carmela shouted back. At one time she'd considered the black wool Liz Claiborne outfit her power suit, but now it was just her funeral suit. "You?"

"I'm wearing my funeral suit, too," yelled Ava.

Carmela dipped her hand into a small woven basket that held a nest of necklaces and fished out a single strand of pearls. She clipped them around her neck, then stared into the large, round mirror above her vanity. Did she look properly sedate? Yes. Yes, of course. Hair combed into a conservative bob, lipstick just a dash of pinky-peachy gloss, black wool suit with cuffed white blouse. On the other hand, she knew that New Orleans was a city that adored jazz funerals, jazzed-up funeral processions, and elaborate post-funeral luncheons at Brennan's. So . . . whatever.

"Hold everything," Carmela exclaimed, as she emerged from her bedroom and got her first glance at Ava, "*that's* what you consider a funeral suit?" Ava was wearing a black wool jacket over black leather pants. A red lacy camisole peeped from beneath the jacket. "It looks a trifle duded up to me."

Or tarted up.

"It's supposed to," said Ava, putting a hand on her hip and striking a flirty pose. "This happens to be a particularly trend-conscious look for a funeral. And mark my words, it's going to catch on."

Carmela shrugged. "Sure. If you say so."

"We gonna hotfoot it over to St. Tristan's?" asked Ava. "Or drive?"

Carmela peered out the window. The rain seemed to have let up for now. "Let's walk. But we better hurry." They hustled outside, jamming back eager dog paws as they gingerly pulled the door shut, then hurried across the courtyard and into the street.

"You think any more about what Brother Paul said last night?" asked Ava. "About the silver?" Ava was also wearing black leather boots with playful little gold spurs decorating the heels.

"I pretty much dreamed about it," said Carmela. She'd been plagued with confusing, stressful dreams all night in which men in brown hooded robes whispered through deserted churches.

"Correct me if I'm wrong," said Ava, "but Brother Paul seemed to imply that the silver cross stolen from St. Tristan's was probably coveted by the Seekers."

"That's pretty much what I took away

from it."

Ava looked angry. "He made it sound like there was some kind of cult that targeted the church. I seriously doubt that would happen!"

"How would we know?" asked Carmela. "Since we don't even know who these Seekers are."

"You think they have, like, spies?" asked Ava. "Or scouts looking for silver religious objects?"

"Search me," said Carmela.

"Oh man," said Ava, when they got within a block of St. Tristan's. "Look at all the big black limos."

"But no hearse," said Carmela. According to her family's wishes, Byrle's body had been cremated.

"I think this whole thing is a little weird," muttered Ava. "Having Byrle's funeral in the exact spot where she was killed."

"Tandy said the same thing," said Carmela. "But Baby explained it as a dust-to-dust kind of thing."

"Still," said Ava, giving a little shudder, "the whole notion kind of creeps me out."

They each grabbed a program — the one Carmela had designed and that Baby had taken to a printer — and slipped down the center aisle, taking seats just this side of the midway point. Carmela figured it would put them in the middle of the action, with a good bird's-eye view of all the mourners. She didn't know what she was looking for, of course, but she had a creeping feeling that she'd know it if she saw it. If that made any sense at all.

Ava studied the cover of her program, then said, "I love what you designed."

"Thank you," said Carmela. She'd ended up using a stamp of an angel against the background of a Romanesque medieval church, then incorporated a loose freehand sketch of a heart.

"Lots of people here," Ava said, twisting her neck back and forth. She was tapping her foot and getting a little restless.

"Nice she had so many friends," Carmela whispered back.

"They're not all friends," said Ava, a certain gritty tone coloring her voice. "Some of the people here are board members and such."

"Interesting," said Carmela. She wondered if the church was worried about getting slapped with some kind of wrongful-death lawsuit. Could happen.

"No, not that interesting," said Ava. She was still clearly upset at being deposed from the Angel Auxiliary.

A few minutes later the big pipe organ rumbled to life with a swell of notes. Then the choir chimed in with "How Great Thou Art." Everyone scrambled to their feet and grabbed hymnals so they could sing along. Except for Carmela and Ava. Carmela wanted to observe, while Ava preferred to stage a sort of protest sit-in.

As the notes faded away, Byrle's sister stepped slowly down the center aisle, carrying the ashes in a tall bronze urn. When she got to the low wooden railing that separated the sanctuary from the congregation, she stopped, then placed the urn on a small table covered with a lacy white cloth. A bell tinkled and a priest in black vestments came out to conduct the burial mass.

That was all it took for Ava. She bowed her head, made the sign of the cross, and was suddenly deeply devotional.

Carmela touched her shoulder to Ava's shoulder. "You okay?"

Ava gave a vigorous bob of her head. "It's just so darned sad," she whispered.

Carmela couldn't agree more. Byrle Coopersmith had been a bright button of joy in their scrapbook shop. She always had a kind word for everyone and possessed an enthusiastic spark for scrapping and crafting.

Which made Carmela all the more interested in following up on her investigation. The question, of course, was what to do next. Try to pry more information from Babcock? That was like trying to unlock a rusty old lock.

On the other hand, Brother Paul, with all his mysterious hints and innuendos, had pretty much handed them a clue.

The Seekers.

Was it a clue worth following up on? Good question.

Whatever strange group the Seekers were — religious cult, biker club, or book club — Carmela was slowly developing an itch to find out more.

Of course, Brother Paul might just be sending them on a wild-goose chase. There was always that. But why would he do that? What would be the point? To direct suspicion away from himself? She supposed there was that possibility.

Midway through the service, Baby walked primly up to the front of the church and did her reading. In her gray wool suit she looked fragile and small, though her cultured voice rang out through the church with great feeling.

The service continued and then, seemingly all too soon, the giant organ rumbled to life again and the choir sang the closing hymn, "Amazing Grace."

Everyone clambered to their feet, while Carmela turned around and peered up into the choir loft. Norton Fried was standing there, his back to the mourners, hands cutting through the air with broad, sweeping gestures.

And Carmela thought, *Norton Fried. Up there in your little perch. I wonder.*

Ugly purple-and-gray clouds threatened to unleash a downpour. But for some reason, the rain held off. Encouraged by this small respite in the weather, many of the mourners congregated on the sidewalk outside St. Tristan's, chatting among themselves.

"Do you suppose we should go say something to Byrle's sister?" asked Ava. "Or her husband?"

Carmela hung back. "I don't know. I've never really met them." She glanced at the people milling about, her eyes bouncing from person to person. What she was really hoping for was . . .

"You're checking everybody out, aren't you, *cher?*" said Ava. "Looking for suspects." She grabbed Carmela's hand. "Good for you!"

"I'm not sure there are any suspects to be

215

found here," said Carmela, "but yes, I'm trying to get a fix on somebody . . . anybody."

"What about Rain Monroe over there?" said Ava. "She was hanging around the church that day, though I don't know what her beef would have been with Byrle."

Carmela spun on her heels. She hadn't noticed Rain Monroe inside the church, but now Rain was standing with Baby, talking excitedly and making broad hand gestures. "What's she all wound up about?" Carmela wondered.

"Don't know," said Ava. "Maybe we should wander over and see what we can see?"

"Will you promise to behave?" Carmela asked Ava. Ava could be a real pill when she wanted to be.

Ava looked supremely injured. "Me?" She touched a hand to her chest. "I'm always on my best behavior."

"Here's the thing," said Carmela, trying not to sound as if she were lecturing. "If we're going to resolve this Angel Auxiliary thing, you're going to have to play it cool."

"Okay," Ava agreed. "I can stay frosty."

But before they made their move toward Baby, Marilyn Casey intercepted them.

"Carmela!" cried Marilyn. "I thought I

might find you here."

"Hello, Marilyn." said Carmela. She figured the woman had probably been hunkered in the back of the church, taking frantic notes.

After a quick introduction of Ava, Ava smiled warmly and said, "Oh sure, Tandy told me about you. You're in her . . ."

"Book club," finished Marilyn.

"But now Marilyn's an author," said Carmela. "Writing a French Quarter mystery."

"I think," said Marilyn, "I'm still technically a writer." The corners of her mouth twitched and she gave a wry smile. "Author status is probably conferred *after* a person gets published."

"I never thought of it that way," said Ava. "But you may be right."

"You hear anything more?" Marilyn asked, focusing her gaze on Carmela.

Carmela shook her head. "Not really."

"Wait a minute," said Ava, suddenly snapping her fingers, "you're the one writing the *murder* mystery. And" — Ava glanced sideways at Carmela, looking for confirmation — "incorporating some of the facts about Byrle?"

"Trying to work it in," admitted Marilyn, "but there's not a lot of information that's

217

come out yet."

"No," said Ava. "There's darn little. But . . . you never know." Marilyn nodded and started to slide away from them. "But hey," Ava called after her, "if we hear anything we'll cut you in."

"Appreciate that," Marilyn called back.

"Her book could be a good thing," said Ava, as they headed to greet Baby.

"You think so?"

"Sure," said Ava. "Marilyn starts asking questions, snooping around the French Quarter and all, she just might shake something loose."

"Carmela!" cried Baby. She threw her arms around Carmela, giving her a big embrace followed by a hard but friendly squeeze. Ava and Rain stood rigidly to one side, eyeing each other with frosty disdain. In fact, Rain looked like she was about ready to spit a rat.

"Your reading of Emily Dickinson was wonderful," Carmela told Baby, as her friend loosened her grip.

Baby raised a manicured hand to the pink Chanel scarf that floated airily about her neck. "Really? Because I was so doggone *nervous* standing up there. I suppose partly because we were in church . . . and also because so many people showed up."

"A full house," Rain said, through tightly clenched lips.

"You know," said Baby, reaching out to touch Carmela's elbow again, "we were just talking about you."

Carmela glanced over at Rain. "Really? I'm a hot topic of conversation?"

"I was just telling Rain," continued Baby, "that it would be marvelous to invite you to our cultural advisory meeting."

"Marvelous," echoed Rain, though she didn't look one bit interested.

But Carmela wasn't sure what Baby was talking about.

"Oh," said Baby, seeing the confusion on Carmela's face. "You don't know." A little pussycat grin lit her face. "Of course, you don't know, since I only found out last night myself." Now she fairly beamed. "The thing is, I've been nominated to the mayor's Cultural Advisory Board."

"Congratulations," said Ava. "It's great to know that finally, someone with actual culture will be doing the advising."

"I'm not sure about that," laughed Baby, "which is why I was hoping Carmela could join us." She hesitated. "Could you? Tomorrow night at my house?"

"She'd *love* to come," piped up Ava.

"Wouldn't you, Carmela?"

"If you think I would be of help," said Carmela, "then sure. I'll be happy to join you."

"Then it's settled," said Baby. She put a hand gently on Ava's shoulder. "And you come, too, sweetie. For fun."

Ava aimed a mirthless smile at Rain, showing her eye-teeth in the process. "I wouldn't miss it for the world!"

Carmela had just buttonholed Norton Fried, the choir director, when she suddenly became aware of Babcock circling the outer fringes of the mourners' group.

"Excuse me?" said Carmela, blinking at Fried. "What did you say?"

Fried assumed a put-upon expression and repeated his words: "I said I'm worried that no one suspect sticks out."

"That worries me, too," said Carmela. "Because, personally, I think three or four good suspects have emerged. So it's difficult to narrow it down to just one."

Fried reared back as if he'd been slapped in the face. "Are you *serious?* You're telling me there are actual suspects? I didn't realize there were *any* besides that awful delivery driver." His brows beetled together and he leaned forward as if inviting Carmela to share a confidence. "Can you give me any names?"

Carmela shook her head slowly, as if the whole notion saddened her deeply. "I think that might be awfully premature," she told him. "And, really, it's just personal speculation on my part." She gazed over Fried's left shoulder and saw that Babcock had edged closer, a bemused expression dancing across his handsome face.

"I understand," said Fried, looking grim. "You wouldn't want to cast aspersions on someone who was entirely innocent."

"Excuse me," said Carmela, slipping past Fried and hurrying to join Edgar Babcock. "Hey, you," she said, touching a hand to his lapel. Of course, if she'd had her druthers, she would have planted a big old smackeroo right on his face.

Babcock smiled at her. "Hey, yourself."

"You were here?" she asked. "At the service?"

Babcock shrugged. "Sitting in the back, tucked artfully behind a pillar."

"Did any fresh ideas percolate?"

"Nope."

"So you're not really any closer?" she asked. "You haven't settled on any particular suspect or suspects?"

Now Babcock assumed a grumpy expression. "We pretty much had to kick the delivery guy loose."

"Why? I thought he was your primo guy."

"Couldn't pin anything on him," said Babcock. "Anything of substance, that is."

"Even though the guy's got a record?"

"As long as your arm," said Babcock. "Still . . . no concrete evidence. As far as *this* case goes, anyway."

"What about DNA?" Carmela asked. "Maybe some of Byrle's skin or hair was caught under his fingernails." Was she really having this conversation outside a church? Yes, she was. And at the scene of the crime, no less.

Babcock shrugged. "Doubtful."

"Still," Carmela persisted, "you ran all your little CSI tests, didn't you?"

"We did, yes, but . . ." Babcock shrugged. "It's going to take a while to process."

Carmela found that hard to believe. "Really? I thought you guys could do an analysis . . . like . . . overnight."

Babcock gave a rueful smile. "You shouldn't believe all that whiz-bang, rush-rush stuff you see on TV."

"Oh, but I do," said Carmela. Shows like *CSI, Law & Order,* and *Castle* fascinated her. So did reality shows that featured medical examiners and former FBI profilers. A little macabre, perhaps, but they also delivered an interesting jolt of reality.

"Unfortunately," said Babcock, "when citizens think we can work magic, that just puts more pressure on the police."

"So what now?" asked Carmela, wondering if she should share her suspicions with him. Her unrest about Norton Fried and Brother Paul. The innuendos Brother Paul had dropped about the Seekers. On the other hand, maybe not. Better to just keep snooping by herself.

"I had a meeting with the police commissioner this morning," said Babcock, "and it looks like we're going to ask the media for help. It's something I don't relish doing, but if they can get the word out . . . maybe we can begin to find a crack in this case."

Carmela wasn't enthusiastic about the media. "If you ask me," said Carmela, "TV people only want to get the word out to the public if they also get a big, juicy slice of the story."

"I understand that," said Babcock. "Still, it's what my boss decided. So we put the facts out there and ask the public for help. Did they see anything? Do they know anything? If so, please call the tip line. That type of thing."

"Won't you get tons of crank calls?" asked

Carmela.

Babcock rolled his eyes. "You have no idea."

"Just be careful," Carmela warned. "Any time you deal with the media, it can come back to bite you in the butt."

CHAPTER 16

Instead of heading for Memory Mine, Carmela dashed back to her apartment, jumped in her car, and sped off for the New Orleans Art Institute. Since she and Jekyl were official participants this coming Sunday, she'd put together some handouts that detailed the workings of the Children's Art Association, and she wanted to drop them off with Angela Boynton, one of the organizing curators.

So, a quick trip, Carmela thought to herself, as she nosed her car into the small parking lot that adjoined the museum. If only she could find . . . ah, a white Lexus was just backing out. Perfect.

Moments later Carmela was breezing down the marble hallway, feeling upbeat and thrilled to sip the heady and intoxicating aura of oil paintings, sculpture, and fine drawings. When she reached a door marked *Curatorial B,* she knocked twice, then popped her head into the small office.

"Is Angie around?" she asked the occupant, a curator who worked in the textile division and shared the small office with Angie. An office that was bursting with posters, brochures, Japanese obis, small Buddhist sculptures, a wall of books, and another wall where a red-and-purple brocade wedding kimono hung from a bamboo rod.

"Down the hall," said the woman. "She's supervising a hanging in the Price Gallery."

"Thanks." Carmela pulled the door shut and continued down the main corridor. She slowed as she passed a glass display case filled with French antiques. It was truly gorgeous stuff: a pair of ornate cobalt-blue vases, a Napoleon III rosewood-and-maple jardinière, and a Falence charger.

She walked slowly to the next case, admiring a silver dagger and then a silver chalice.

And that was where Carmela's progress suddenly ground to a halt. Because on the small white card in front of the chalice, way at the bottom, was a single line that caught her attention: *Donated by Norton Fried.*

What? Norton Fried donated this silver? What the . . . heck? Is he an actual collector or silver aficionado? And if so, isn't this an interesting piece of information?

226

Carmela kicked it into high gear as she continued down the hallway and spun into the Price Gallery.

Angie was there, all right, giving advice to two museum interns who were trying to hang a large, splashy contemporary painting in a vast gallery with a thirty-foot-high ceiling.

"A little bit lower on the left," Angie coached. The interns fussed, struggled, moved their ladder, then seemed to get it all figured out. When they'd made their final adjustment, Angie said, "Looks good to me."

"Is there no end to your job description?" Carmela asked. Her voice was a hollow echo in the cavernous gallery.

Angie turned to greet her, and a smile flashed across her lovely face. "With budgets getting slashed every six months, I'm going to be taking out the trash pretty soon," said Angie. She was a serious-looking woman in her midthirties, with shoulder-length light brown hair, green eyes, and a slight bump on her nose that made her look interesting and highly approachable. Today Angie was dressed in a beige tweed suit with a large, of-the-moment, gold squiggle pin pinned to her lapel.

"More money worries?" asked Carmela.

Angie nodded. "Every day seems to get more and more challenging."

"The large donors aren't kicking in like they used to?"

"No, they're not," replied Angie. "They're still running scared in this economy, just like everyone else. Sheltering assets and getting conservative."

"Which isn't always a *bad* thing," said Carmela.

"It's not," said Angie, as they strolled down the hallway together. "A tightening of belts can be a good thing. It makes you more mindful and appreciative of what you *do* have." She drew a deep breath. "Still, if the halcyon days of big private donations are over — and they just may be — then we're all going to have to get a whole lot more creative with our fund-raising."

"If there's anything I can do to help . . . ," said Carmela.

"Thanks," said Angie, "I may take you up on that."

Carmela paused in front of the silver chalice that Norton Fried had donated. "I didn't realize Norton Fried had donated a silver piece to the museum."

"Oh my, yes," said Angie, brightening. "Quite a few, in fact. Enough to quality Mr.

Fried for membership in our patrons' circle."

"Really," said Carmela. Thanks to the generosity of Shamus's family, Carmela also enjoyed membership in that very same patrons' circle. No big deal, really; it just meant you received invitations to gallery openings and private member events. Which entitled you to all the cheap white wine and cream cheese–stuffed cherry tomatoes you could gobble.

Angie gazed at the silver chalice and bobbed her head with enthusiasm. "This one's really marvelous, isn't it? It supposedly came from Chartres Cathedral."

"Interesting," said Carmela. For some reason, the notion that Fried was a silver collector was pinging unhappily inside her brain. After all, he'd been in the direct vicinity the morning Byrle had been killed. And, let's not forget, folks, an antique silver-and-gold crucifix *had* gone missing.

"But this isn't even the best of Mr. Fried's collection," Angie told her.

Carmela shook her head. "Excuse me?"

Angie glanced around and lowered her voice. "Apparently, Mr. Fried holds the very best pieces for his personal collection."

"Really," said Carmela. "Have you ever seen it? His personal collection, I mean."

Angie shook her head. "I don't know that anyone has. He's quite secretive about the whole thing." She smiled. "But that's the thing about collectors, isn't it? They're often a bit . . . quirky."

Carmela let this information sift through her brain. *A personal collection of antique silver that was secreted away.* Somehow that notion smacked of art collectors who locked stolen masterpieces inside a special vault, only to pull them out occasionally for their own personal enjoyment. Wasn't that what happened to the Rembrandts and Degas drawings that had been stolen from the Gardner Museum in Boston? They'd supposedly been on the so-called shopping list of a private collector? That had been the rumor anyway. The rumor according to Jekyl, who lived and breathed art history mysteries.

"Thanks," Carmela told Angie, as she handed her the stack of flyers. She was a little distracted, and new ideas were flying around inside her brain.

"Thank you," said Angie, balancing the flyers. "See you on Sunday!"

"Hey there!" Gabby called out, as Carmela breezed into the shop. "How was the funeral?"

"Tasteful and reflective," said Carmela, pausing at the front counter. "And very, very sad."

"I'll bet the church was packed with all sorts of people?" Gabby asked, as she focused bright, inquisitive eyes on Carmela.

"Yes, it was," said Carmela. She knew what Gabby was asking, in her subtle, roundabout way. "Unfortunately, no one stood out. Nobody, um, caught my attention."

"Too bad," Gabby murmured.

"Agreed," said Carmela. She glanced around and saw that Memory Mine was fairly busy this morning. Two women were perusing paper samples; three more were working away at the back table. And one customer, Louise Pattinson, a sort of regular, was examining specialty paper and sealing wax.

Carmela stowed her gear and headed for Louise. "Help you?" she asked.

Louise spun around, surprised, with a hand on her chest. "Oh, hi, Carmela, I didn't see you before. Probably because I've been so engrossed in all these wonderful papers and things."

"Lots of reds, bronzes, golds, and greens," said Carmela. "Perfect for card making, you know. Perfect for the holidays."

"That's what I was thinking," said Louise. "I'd love to create my own greeting cards, but . . ." Her voice trailed off.

"But you don't know where to start?"

Louise looked glum. "That's about the size of it."

"Card making is easier than you think," said Carmela.

"But all that measuring and cutting," said Louise, looking askance.

"No way," said Carmela, pulling down a package of blank white note cards and envelopes. "Just use these and add your own embellishments."

Louise still wasn't convinced. "Such as?"

Carmela grabbed a second pack of wine-red note cards. "Better yet, start with something really festive like these red note cards. Then maybe stencil on a gold fleur-de-lis." She reached over, grabbed a spool of wine-colored velvet ribbon, and spun it out. "Attach a bit of ribbon to the front of your card, use a dab of gold sealing wax in the center, and maybe stamp it with an angel seal."

"Ooh, I love that," cooed Louise. "And not so tricky."

"Or," said Carmela, "you can cut a few rough pieces of red brocade fabric, stick them inside your card, and then add a romantic photo or sentiment surrounded by bits of lace. And if you really want to kick things up a notch, just arrange *two* pieces of contrasting brocade fabric, one a bit smaller than the other, then add an even smaller piece of vellum, and then . . ."

"Add my photo and lace," finished Louise.

"That's right," said Carmela. "That will give you lots of interesting layers and textures."

"You're giving me some wonderful ideas," said Louise. "Got my brain percolating."

"That's why I'm here," said Carmela. She grinned, then moved off to help another customer, feeling more than a little fulfilled.

That was what this business was all about, of course. Helping people express their creativity, helping to open their eyes to all the various fun possibilities. And, if a customer needed a little nudge in the right direction, well, that was really the best part of owning a scrapbook shop, wasn't it?

Carmela smiled to herself as she helped select foil paper for another customer, rang up a couple of sales, and greeted the FedEx man, who was delivering what was probably a whole new batch of rubber stamps. The angels, wheat bundles, and slightly biblical-looking stamps that she'd ordered for

Christmas. And just in the nick of time, so to speak.

For the most part, Carmela didn't believe in premonitions, but standing at the front counter, pulling a package of silver and turquoise charms off a rack, she suddenly felt the tiny hairs on the back of her neck start to lift and prickle. And just when she was beginning to chide herself, just as she was telling her inner self to shrug it off, the front door flew open and Kimber Breeze from KBEZ-TV came storming in.

"What the . . . ?" said Gabby, glancing up.

"Oh no," Carmela muttered, under her breath. She'd had dealings with this crazy TV reporter before.

Lacquered blond hair swirling about her head, lips a bloodred pout, her forehead Botoxed until it was skating-rink smooth, Kimber Breeze quick-stepped toward Carmela. Her camera man, Harvey, video camera hoisted high on his shoulder, was but a half-pace behind.

Kimber raised a microphone to her burnished lips and, without preamble, began her report. "This is Kimber Breeze for KBEZ-TV reporting live from Memory Mine scrapbook shop in the heart of the French Quarter. We've just been told by a highly placed police official that the owner of this small shop was an actual *eyewitness* to the murder of Byrle Coopersmith, who was tragically bludgeoned in the hallowed sanctity of nearby St. Tristan's Church."

Kimber paused, took a deep breath, and then stuck the microphone in front of Carmela. Her look was sly and expectant.

"No," said Carmela.

"No what?" said Kimber. She tried to frown, but the stiffness from the Botox injections only allowed her an expression of mild concern.

"I wasn't an eyewitness and I have nothing to say to you," Carmela said, as she spun on her heels.

Kimber grimaced, then turned to Harvey and made a slashing-finger motion across her throat.

Nonplussed, Harvey lowered his camera and waited patiently. Harvey was no fool; he knew Kimber would poke and prod and eventually stir up her usual hornet's nest.

Kimber held her microphone at her side as she followed Carmela back to the craft table. "You'd be doing a public service," Kimber cajoled. "We've been asked by the chief of police, no less, to assist in drawing out any additional witnesses."

Carmela bristled. "I told you, I wasn't a

witness."

"But you were *there,*" Kimber pushed.

"Along with something like twenty other people," said Carmela, "so why don't you go pester one of them?"

"I probably will," said Kimber, managing a smarmy smile, "but you're at the top of my list."

"Then make a new list," said Carmela. She pulled a piece of mulberry paper from a flat file and slid the drawer shut with a bang.

"You're not helping," Kimber pouted.

"Neither are you," said Carmela. "And now, if you'll excuse me, I have customers to tend to." Carmela brushed past Kimber, heading back toward the front counter where Gabby waited nervously.

"Just one more question," said Kimber, gesturing for Harvey to shoulder his camera and resume shooting.

"No way," Carmela called over her shoulder.

"Please?" Kimber called, as she stumbled after her. That one word of politeness must have killed her.

"No," Carmela said again.

Gabby, who'd watched the entire exchange, waggled her fingers at the intruding but hapless Kimber. "Good-bye, Kimber.

Time to exit stage left."

"Thanks for nothing," Kimber muttered, as she threw them both a dirty look and stalked toward the door. Her perfectly made-up face now carried red blotches; her eyes were narrow slits. Then she turned to Harvey and muttered, "Change of plans, Harv. Let's head over to Big Haul Trucking and see if we can get something out of Johnny Otis."

"Sure thing," said Harvey. He'd kept the camera up on his shoulder, ready to shoot. "You want I should get an establishing shot, just in case you can pull something usable?"

"Do that," said Kimber, her hand wresting open the front door.

"No, don't do that!" said Gabby. She grabbed a broom that had been propped against the wall and gave a menacing shake in Harvey's direction. "Shoo! Get out of here!"

Harvey jumped back as if stung by a bee. "Jeez, lady, you almost clobbered me! And, if you don't mind, this equipment is expensive!"

Unfazed, Gabby shook her broom at him again. "I mean it, get out of this shop!"

Harvey backed out, but as he did, he continued to roll tape.

"Atta boy," Kimber chortled from out on

the street, "that's going to make great footage!"

"Gabby!" exclaimed Carmela, "that was very noble of you to come to my defense. Thank you."

"Kimber Breeze is a totally nasty person," Gabby grumbled. "I don't know how you tolerate her."

"I don't," said Carmela. "The trick is to not answer any questions, and just keep turning your back on her."

Gabby still looked angry. "You think the police *really* asked the media for help in finding witnesses?"

"I know they did," said Carmela. "Babcock told me they did."

"Then it's a sad day for the New Orleans Police," said Gabby, "to enlist the aid of TV people like that." She shook her head. "I really doubt they're going to shake anything loose or drum up new information."

"Actually," said Carmela, "Kimber just passed on a valuable piece of information."

"What?" Gabby looked puzzled. "Excuse me, did I just miss something?"

"She just revealed that Johnny Otis is employed by Big Haul Trucking."

Gabby blinked. "Okay."

Carmela's mouth pulled into a thin smile. "So that's where I'm going to look, too."

CHAPTER 17

First, however, Carmela had to dash over to the Belle Vie Hotel where she had a two o'clock meeting with Alex Goodman, the catering manager.

The Belle Vie was an elegant, four-star, antique-filled hotel nestled in the heart of the French Quarter. Its spendy rooms were lush and luxurious, its three sun-dappled courtyards filled with babbling fountains, baskets of bougainvilleas, and tropical banana trees. Here you could order a Sazerac cocktail, mint julep, or Ramos gin fizz and have it expertly prepared by a bartender who'd probably tended to celebrities, presidents, and even royalty.

Alex Goodman greeted her in the rather grand lobby with its painted murals, sparkling chandelier, and white marble floor.

"Alex," said Carmela, "sorry if I'm a little late."

With his ramrod posture, tweedy suit, and

bow tie knotted snugly about his neck, Goodman smiled a pat hotelier's smile. "Not at all," he told her. Goodman, though he'd grown up in Dubuque, Iowa, always affected a slight British accent. All it had taken was that one trip to London, the Cotswolds, and Windsor, and that distinctive British accent had stuck to him like glue.

Still, as Goodman guided her toward the Marquis Ballroom, he was most genial and accommodating.

"This," Goodman said, pushing open a pair of gold double doors, "should easily accommodate your event."

Carmela strode into the Marquis Ballroom and spun around. With its chandeliers, murals, and velvet-swagged windows, it was as grand and gaudy as she remembered it, and it was darn near perfect for Quigg's event.

"And you'll have it set up just the way we talked about?" said Carmela.

"String quartet at that end," Goodman told her, gesturing with one hand. "Then the four different wine stations, one in each corner, for St. Tammany Vineyard's best. The sparkling, the Sauvignon, the Syrah and Shiraz blend, and the Cabernet."

"With corresponding appetizers."

"Of course," said Goodman.

"And those will be . . . ?"

Goodman was already pulling out his cell phone. "Let's get Chef Rami down here to go over them with you personally."

"Tell him to meet us in the lobby," said Carmela, "then we can go over the red carpet setup, as well."

Chef Rami was a large African American man with twinkling eyes and a deep bass voice. The Michelin Guide had hailed him as the new Emeril, and Carmela figured it wouldn't be long before the good chef was honchoing a restaurant of his own.

"I'm surprised Quigg didn't want to do his own appetizers," Chef Rami said to Carmela, as he pulled a small piece of paper from the breast pocket of his extra-large white chef's jacket.

"He did," said Carmela. "I had to talk him out of it."

"We're glad you did," said Goodman. "This is a great opportunity for us, too."

"We don't usually get to do this kind of PR event," said Chef Rami. "With celebrities."

"I don't know how many celebrities will actually show up," said Carmela. "Mostly it will be fellow restaurateurs, wine sellers, and the media."

"The media loves anything that's free," said Goodman, who'd been around that block more than a few times.

"Don't they just," agreed Carmela. She smiled at Chef Rami. "So . . . the appetizer and wine pairings?"

Chef Rami turned serious. "For the Bayou Sparkler, the champagne, I want to do tuna carpaccio on toast crisps. And to accompany the Sauvignon, a tempura lobster roll."

"Perfect," said Carmela. Two down, two more to go.

"With the Syrah and Shiraz blend," said Chef Rami, "I'm recommending duck drummies. And with the Cabernet, I'm thinking blue cheese bites rolled in pecans."

"They all sound like perfect pairings," Carmela told him. "Couldn't be better."

"That went smoothly," said Goodman, obviously pleased.

"That's because you guys are pros," Carmela told him. She glanced down the set of low marble steps, her mind whirring. "Now, let's talk about the red carpet."

Chef Rami said his good-bye as Carmela and Goodman descended the half-dozen steps to the semicircular drive that snugged up to the front of the hotel.

"This should work really well," said Carmela, making a few quick calculations. "What you've got is a grand hotel entrance that allows limos to drive up and dispense guests."

"And when they're dispensed . . . ?" said Goodman.

"They'll stroll down a twenty-foot-long red carpet where we'll have them stop and pose in front of the step-and-repeat."

"And when's your step-and-repeat supposed to arrive?" asked Goodman.

"The printer promised to deliver it first thing Saturday morning," said Carmela. "They're also going to set it up . . ." Carmela glanced around, then made a quick gesture. "Probably against that wall of shrubbery. Is that okay with you?"

"I'll be here all day," said Goodman, "so I'll make sure it's positioned properly." He hesitated. "So . . . *are* you expecting celebrities?"

"Probably a few minor celebs just to make things interesting," said Carmela. "A couple of New Orleans Saints football players, a TV anchorman, the society photographer Nigel Prince, perhaps the mayor, and whatever ward politicians Quigg has invited."

"Very impressive," said Goodman.

"The celebs will draw media attention," Carmela told him, "and the presence of the media will make each and every guest feel important."

"Nicely done," said Goodman.

"In theory, anyway," said Carmela. She knew that no event ever went off without a glitch or two. Or three or four. But she wasn't a control freak, so . . . why worry? "Thank you," she added, shaking Goodman's hand, then giving a quick wave. "Call me with any question, big or small. Otherwise, I'll see you Saturday night."

Carmela skittered away, grabbed her cell phone out of her shoulder bag, and punched in the number for Edgar Babcock. He answered on the first ring.

"Your media ploy worked beautifully," she told him.

"Huh? Who is this?" A rustle of papers. "Carmela?"

"Kimber Breeze and her camera man stormed my shop this morning in a reenactment reminiscent of D-Day."

"What?" came his reply. "Somebody came to your shop?" He sounded a little foggy, like he'd been interrupted and lost his focus.

"Yes," said Carmela, "that idiot, Kimber Breeze. She came galumphing into Memory Mine on the pretext of doing an interview for the good of the public. But what Kimber *really* wanted to know was how it felt to

245

see my friend murdered right before my very eyes."

Babcock exhaled slowly, then said, with genuine sincerity in his voice, "I'm *so* sorry, Carmela. I had absolutely no idea the media would be that proactive."

"Proactive?" said Carmela. "Kimber was a rabid dog. If I'd had a gun handy, I would have shot her and passed it off as euthanasia."

"You want me to call the TV station?" asked Babcock. "Talk to her boss and have her reprimanded or something?"

"You really don't understand the media, do you?" asked Carmela. "Fact is, if Kimber *had* gotten her interview, her boss probably would have given her a raise!"

"Seriously?" said Babcock.

"I kid you not," said Carmela.

"Where are you right now?" asked Babcock. "At the shop?"

"Um . . . something like that."

"Can I call you back?"

"Anytime, sweetheart." Carmela punched the Off button on her phone and gazed down Esplanade. It was still cloudy and overcast, and yellow streetlamps glowed in front of Leboux Antiques, Chalmers Map Shop, and the Crooked Crayfish Restaurant. She wondered for a moment if she should just ankle back to her shop and drop this whole investigation. Let it go like so many autumn leaves floating down, then being carried away by a stream. She could retreat back to a calm, relatively peaceful, gratitude-filled life, and let Babcock and his fellow officers deal with the Byrle situation.

That was the ideal scenario, of course, except for one thing.

Carmela had made a solemn promise to Baby.

"Dispatch," said a gravelly voice on the other end of the line.

"Yes," said Carmela, clutching her cell phone, "is this Big Haul Trucking?"

"You got it," said the voice.

"I'm trying to get hold of Johnny Otis," said Carmela.

"You from the TV?" asked a man. He sounded weary and a little gun-shy, as if he'd already fielded a couple of similar calls.

"That's right," said Carmela. *Little white lie? Oh, for sure.*

"Johnny's busy right now," said the dispatcher. "He's out on a delivery."

"I figured that," said Carmela, "which is why I called you."

"Yeah?"

"Because I really need to speak with

247

Johnny," said Carmela. "And I give you my solemn promise that I won't hold Johnny up or anything. I just need a minute of his time."

"Yeah, well . . ." There was hesitation in the dispatcher's voice.

"Just a couple of quick questions." Carmela hesitated. "There's a rumor going around that the police may have cleared him." *And chalk up yet another white lie.*

"That so?" said the dispatcher, sounding a little less defensive.

"So you can see," said Carmela, "I'm only trying to set the record straight."

The dispatcher hesitated, then said, "According to my schedule, Johnny's over at Evangeline Furnishings right about now. So if you run into him, talk fast. Then we can get this whole episode over with and he can get his mind back on driving. Okay?"

"You got it," said Carmela.

Luckily for Carmela, Evangeline Furnishings was located in the French Quarter, about two blocks from where she was standing. She hotfooted down Esplanade and cut over on Chartres. Five minutes later she was standing directly in front of Evangeline Furnishings, staring at an obviously faux Louis XVI fainting couch that dominated the front window.

She spun around. There were parked cars, but no delivery truck.

"Back alley," Carmela said out loud, then dashed around the corner.

And found Johnny's truck, a rumbling white truck that belched purple gluts of oil. But no Johnny. Still the truck was running, so . . .

As if on cue, a man wearing blue coveralls, with lank, dark hair hanging down over the side of his face, emerged from the back door.

"Johnny Otis," she called out.

Otis steeled his shoulders and turned away from her. He was a narrow, wiry man with ropy muscles in his arms.

Carmela figured she didn't have anything to lose. "I heard you were at St. Tristan's on Monday when Byrle Coopersmith was killed."

Johnny Otis turned to stare at her with suspicious, hooded eyes. "So what," he said. "A lot of folks were at that church." He peered at her. "Maybe *you* were at that church."

Carmela pressed forward, even though his anger and hostility were so palpable he was positively frightening. "I understand you have a police record."

"That's all behind me." Johnny shrugged,

as he pulled open the driver's-side door and stuck the toe of a dirty work boot on the ledge. "Now I'm just a regular working stiff like everybody else." He offered her a barracuda smile. All teeth, no humor.

"An honest day's work for an honest day's pay?"

"That's right," said Johnny.

"No more shortcuts?" asked Carmela. "No more breaking and entering?"

Johnny stared at her with hatred suddenly flickering in his eyes. "Who are you again?"

"Carmela."

"Got a last name?" he snarled.

"Carmela . . . Meechum." At the last minute she decided it was safer to toss out her ex-husband's name. Let good old Shamus absorb any possible fallout.

Johnny hoisted himself up into the truck cab. "Anybody ever tell you to mind your own business, Carmela Meechum?"

"All the time, Johnny. All the time."

Carmela had every intention of returning to Memory Mine. She'd been walking purposely down Governor Nicholls Street, stopping just for an instant to admire a string of pistachio-colored baroque pearls in a jewelry shop window. That was when her cell phone rang.

"Get over here!" Ava shrilled into her ear.

The intensity of Ava's words jolted Carmela, the pearls suddenly forgotten. "Ava, what's wrong? Don't tell me Rain Monroe is making trouble for you again!"

With more urgency, Ava begged, "Please, just get over here!"

Ten minutes later, Carmela came crashing through Ava's front door for yet another emergency. "What?" she called out. "What's wrong?" She glanced around the dim little incense-filled shop, expecting to find Ava cowering and whimpering in a puddle of salty tears. Instead Ava was posturing and grinning like the proverbial Cheshire cat.

"I've got news," Ava chortled. "*Big* news."

Carmela's mind flashed immediately to Byrle's murder. And, for a split second, she figured there must have been a sudden break in the case. Maybe Babcock had called Ava's shop looking for her? Then dropped the welcome news on Ava?

"What?" asked Carmela, brushing at her flyaway hair, trying to pat it into submission.

"You know that exceedingly charming restaurant owner we met the other night?" Ava asked, dimpling prettily. "The one who owns Purgatoria?"

"Drew Gaspar," said Carmela, feeling

suddenly let down. Was this big emergency because Ava had been asked out on a date? But Ava went on dates all the time and didn't get nearly this revved up.

"Turns out," said Ava, "Gaspar is a partner in a brand-new fashion line."

"Fashion?" Carmela's words came out in a squeak. *The news was about fashion?*

Ava wrapped her arms around herself and let loose a high-pitched giggle. "Gaspar and his partners are calling their new line Voodoo Couture . . . and guess what!"

Carmela took a step backward. "What?"

"They want *me* to be their muse!" Ava delivered the news like she'd just struck gold by winning the lottery.

"A muse," said Carmela, a little stunned. This was clearly not the news she'd been hoping for. Not even close.

"Isn't that incredible!" Ava squealed. "Little old me . . . a fashion muse!"

"Um . . . what exactly does a muse do?" Carmela wondered out loud.

Ava spread her hands apart and wiggled her varnished red fingertips. "I have no earthly idea. But doesn't it *sound* utterly peachy? Like I'm some kind of wild, intuitive creative spirit?"

"Sure," said Carmela. "It's great."

Ava's smile slipped off her face as she

peered across a pile of black plastic shrunken heads. "I wish your tone carried a little more oomph and enthusiasm, Carmela." Her fingers reached out and toyed with the goat hair on the shrunken heads. "Are you not happy for me?"

Carmela leaned forward and put her hands on Ava's shoulders. "I'm thrilled for you, really. I can't think of a more . . . *appropriate* person to represent this Voodoo Couture clothing line."

"Thank you," said Ava.

Carmela released her hold on Ava. "What I'm not so thrilled about is Drew Gaspar."

Ava's lips crinkled into a semi-pout. "What are you talking about?"

"Frankly, Gaspar makes me a little nervous."

"Because he's handsome and urbane?" asked Ava. "Because he's a go-getter?"

"No," said Carmela. "Because his whole Purgatoria concept is slightly weird. Even Gabby thinks so. She met him when he dropped by my shop yesterday afternoon."

"Really?" Ava looked surprised. "Gabby didn't like him? But she likes *everybody.*"

"That's right," said Carmela. "Gabby's outlook is pretty much rainbows and dancing unicorns. But, quite honestly, she was put off by Gaspar. And, after hearing her reasoning, I have to confess that I am, too."

Ava cocked her head and said, "Explain, please. What are you talking about?"

Carmela swallowed hard. This wasn't going to be easy. "After I told Gabby about the . . . what would you call it? The *decorating* motif at Purgatoria, the gargoyles and church benches and crosses, Gabby thought maybe the police should take a hard look at Gaspar."

Ava gave a questioning glance. "For what?"

"For the murder of Byrle."

Ava's face crumpled. "Are you serious?"

"I'm afraid so."

CHAPTER 18

Ava had been so upset by Gabby's harsh accusation of Drew Gaspar that Carmela Bertrand, booster of frayed egos, rescuer of stray dogs, and picker-upper of trounced self-esteem, had invited Ava over for dinner tonight. She'd been chopping, stirring, and sautéing for the last forty-five minutes, planning to serve drunken pecan chicken along with corn pancakes. That is, if Boo and Poobah didn't storm the kitchen and snarf everything up first.

Tap-da-da-tap.

Ava's signature knock sounded at the front door.

"It's open," Carmela called out. "Just watch out for —"

"Boo! Poobah!" Ava sang out.

"— the dogs," finished Carmela.

Ava stuck her head around the corner. "Guess the little darlings didn't eat yet, huh? 'Cause their little pink tongues are lickin' me to death."

"They ate," said Carmela, as she tossed an extra tablespoon of butter into the frying pan. "Enough for four Great Danes and a Portuguese water dog thrown in for good measure." She watched the butter melt, then poured it over her mixture of sweet corn, red pepper, and onions.

"Boo, baby, stop it," Ava giggled, as the wiggly little Shar-Pei snuffled around Ava's bare ankles. "That tickles."

"Try to ignore her," said Carmela, as Ava held out a brown paper sack to her. "What's this?" she said, accepting the gift.

"Peace offering," said Ava.

"Did one of us break a treaty or something?" asked Carmela. She pulled a bottle of Beaujolais from the bag and nodded. "Because I sure don't remember . . ."

"It's an apology bottle," said Ava. "Because I was so grumpy earlier today."

"Oh, no problem," said Carmela. She carried the wine into the kitchen, opened a drawer, and pulled out her corkscrew.

"I was just, you know, disappointed," said Ava. "I thought I'd really scored a huge coup with the Voodoo Couture thing."

"You did," said Carmela. "So please don't pass up this opportunity to be a fashion muse on my account. Or because Gabby suddenly has a suspicious mind."

"Really?" said Ava. "You think I should do it?"

"I think you should," said Carmela. She popped the cork and poured two glasses of wine.

"You don't think my being a muse for Voodoo Couture would be a kind of . . . slap in the face? To you and Gabby?"

"Not at all," said Carmela. She handed Ava a glass of wine, then took her by the arm and led her to the dining table. They sat down, knees touching. "All I'm asking," said Carmela, "is for you to exercise caution."

"I will," said Ava, taking a sip of wine. "You know me, caution's always been my thing."

Carmela stared at her. "I mean really."

"Okay," said Ava. "Okay." She took another sip of wine. "Does this mean you're going to be investigating Drew Gaspar now?"

"I'm not sure," said Carmela. She moved her wineglass around in little circles on the table. "I don't have that part figured out yet."

"In that case, would you come with me Saturday afternoon to look at the Voodoo Couture clothes?"

"Will Drew Gaspar be there?"

Ava scratched her nose. "I don't think so. Not yet, anyway. There's this boutique on Magazine Street that's carrying the first dozen or so pieces. I was supposed to try them on and then . . . I don't know . . . think about the direction of the line, I guess."

"Of course, I'll go with you," said Carmela.

Ava grinned. "You're my BFF. Always got my back."

"I try to," said Carmela.

They were halfway through their drunken chicken when Carmela said, "I forgot to tell you. I talked to Johnny Otis today."

Ava's fork clattered to her dish. "You *what?*"

"I tracked Johnny Otis down."

"Isn't he Babcock's *numero uno* suspect?"

"He was until they had to kick him loose," said Carmela.

"And you talked to him," said Ava, dumbfounded. "A real-life career criminal. How did you manage that?"

"Not without some problems," said Carmela. "First Kimber Breeze came storming into my shop, trying to do an interview . . ."

"Hold everything," said Ava. "Please tell

258

me you shagged her scrawny butt right out of there?"

"Actually, Gabby did the honors on that. But not before Kimber let slip what trucking company Johnny Otis worked for. So I called up his dispatcher, found out where he was making a delivery, and went over there to *parlez-vous* with him."

"Girl, you've got some chutzpah!"

"Thank you," said Carmela.

"So what'd you say to him?"

"I told a few white lies about being a reporter and then asked a few questions."

"Weren't you scared?"

"A little," said Carmela. *Actually, a lot.*

"Because Johnny couldn't have been happy to see you."

"He was incredibly hostile," said Carmela. "Really angry."

"The kind of anger that could kill somebody?"

Carmela thought for a few moments. "It sure seemed that way when I was talking to him. Or *trying* to talk to him."

"There you go," said Ava, flipping a hand up. "Johnny's the guy you have to focus on."

"I don't know," said Carmela, thinking about Norton Fried and his silver collection. Suddenly, a whole lot of folks were looking more and more suspicious.

259

■ ■ ■ ■

"This is great coffee," said Ava. She was relaxing on the couch, a pillow behind her head and her legs stretched out. "Makes me want to just laze the night away." She raised her eyebrows and said, "What do you think? Should we order up a movie or something? A good, ten-tissue chick flick? Or maybe a comedy. Just not one of those goofy Pauly Shore or Harold and Kumar movies."

"I was thinking you and I should do something a little less passive," said Carmela.

Ava looked intrigued. "You want to hit some dance clubs? We haven't been to Dr. Boogie's since forever!"

"What about a drive out on Trempeleau Road?"

Ava's brows knit together. "Huh? What's out there?"

"Remember Brother Paul? He told us the Seekers had a church out that way?"

"Oh man," said Ava, holding the back of her hand to her head, "you want to *go* there and check them out? You *believed* Brother Paul?"

"Yes, I think I did."

"Well . . . turtle poop," said Ava. She blew

out air and sucked in her cheeks, giving a look of general discontent.

"Change of plans, then," said Carmela. "You stay here while I go snoop on my own." And she meant it, too. She could go solo. Might even be easier if she went alone.

"No way," said Ava, finally pushing herself up. "I'm not going to let you traipse around in the swamp all by your lonesome."

"It's not the swamp."

"If it's off the sidewalk, it's swamp."

"So you're coming?"

"Do chickens have lips?"

"We look like ninjas!" Ava chortled, as they sped down Highway 45. Both women had changed into black leggings and black oversized sweaters. Ava had even added a wide black headband to corral her mass of dark curly hair.

"I'm not sure ninjas wear cowl-neck Michael Kors sweaters," said Carmela, a smile twitching at her lips. For some reason, Ava had perked up considerably.

"They would if they were fashion-conscious ninjas," said Ava. "And watched *Project Runway*."

"You really are addicted to that show."

"Because that's my big dream," said Ava.

"You mean go to New York and take part

in a design competition? Try to create an honest-to-gosh collection?"

"No, silly. To look like Heidi Klum!"

They both fell silent then, watching the woods and fields disappear and the land turn more lush and verdant. Rain had lashed down earlier, but now it was barely sprinkling.

"We're out in the bayou," Ava observed as stands of tupelo trees flashed by, and blue-black stretches of brackish water.

"Not quite," said Carmela. "But we're getting awfully close."

"Gators around here?"

"Mmm, probably."

Ava glanced nervously out the passenger window, as if a twenty-foot albino alligator might be huffing alongside the car, wanting to take a chomp. "Who in their right mind would build a church way out here in the middle of nowhere?" she asked.

"Oh, just off the top of my head," said Carmela, as they breezed through the village of Mayport, "maybe . . . some sort of cult?"

"You think?" said Ava. "So maybe the Seekers *do* have something to hide?"

"Possibly," said Carmela. As they flashed past a dirt road with a leaning wooden signpost, she tapped her brakes and exclaimed, "Holy smokes, I think that was Trempeleau Road."

"That's where we're going? Where we're supposed to turn?"

"I think so." Carmela eased her foot off the brake and coasted over to the side of the road. "That's what we're here to find out." She K-turned her car, then headed down the narrow road.

"How far we gonna go?" asked Ava, after they'd bumped along for five minutes or so.

Carmela let the car roll to a stop. "This is probably as close as we should venture."

"But . . . you know where this church is located?" asked Ava.

Carmela frowned. "Not really."

"Then what makes you think it's around here?" asked Ava.

"For one thing," said Carmela, "the road pretty much ends here. She stared out the windshield at swaying trees. "For another . . . oh, just call it intuition? A hunch?"

That was good enough for Ava. "Okay."

As they climbed out of the car, Carmela said, "I left my keys in the ignition. Just in case."

Ava grabbed her arm. "Just in case what?"

"We have to make a fast getaway?"

"Let's hope it doesn't come down to that."

Carmela and Ava bushwhacked through a

263

stand of gum trees and emerged in a low, swampy area. Long grass squished and overhanging branches swatted their faces.

"Wet," said Ava, in a stage whisper.

Carmela backtracked a few steps, cut over to her left, then said, "Better here. There's a kind of trail. The grass is knocked down, so probably somebody drove this way not so long ago."

"Lucky us," said Ava.

"Where's your ninja sense of adventure?"

"Back home in my sock drawer?"

But a few minutes of pushing through the forest brought success.

"Does that look like a church to you?" Carmela asked. Some two hundred yards ahead of them, a white building seemed to shimmer through a tangle of trees.

"If it's a church," said Ava, "then it came complete with a silo." She hunkered down, hiding behind an overhanging tree branch. "See? It looks more like a barn. Where you'd keep cows and stuff."

"Wait a minute," said Carmela, crouching low, homing in on a small blaze that seemed to be growing brighter with every passing second. "I see people moving about now. See, over by that fire pit?"

"I think I see people," said Ava, squinting. "But they're wearing . . ."

"Robes," finished Carmela. "Brown robes." *Just like the killer at St. Tristan's had worn. Is this whack-a-doodle, or what?*

"Oh man," said Ava, looking spooked, "with the robes and flames and everything, this looks like something out of a John Carpenter movie. Like crazy devil worshippers. I mean, listen, do you hear that weird noise? They're, like, *chanting*."

"Yes, they are," said Carmela, locking her jaw tightly. Was this some sort of evil cult that Brother Paul had been up against? If so, why didn't he just launch a full-scale exposé? Take it to the media? Or make an appeal to local law enforcement?

"Holy shiitake mushrooms," said Ava, as more cult members appeared. "They look like a cross between the Klan and a bunch of Ozark Mountain snake handlers."

"Shh," cautioned Carmela. "Keep quiet and stay low."

"Don't worry," said Ava, "those guys look serious."

Carmela thought for a few moments. If she could ease herself a little closer, perhaps she could see what they were rallying around. Like maybe . . . a stolen crucifix?

"Stay here," she told Ava. "I want to inch closer and get a better look."

Ava's eyes went wide. "You're gonna leave

me here?"

"Just for a few minutes."

"No way," muttered Ava, "I'm tagging along. You're not gonna leave me stranded in buckthorn and poison oak, or whatever this stuff is."

"Okay," said Carmela, "but caution's the watchword."

"I'll try not to sneeze," said Ava.

They sneaked forward through the darkness, parting low branches as they went. The earth was cool, spongy, and wet underfoot, and Carmela could feel dampness seeping slowly through the soles of her shoes. Her shoes, great. Why had she worn Ferragamos tonight and not Keds? Or better yet, why hadn't she pulled on rubber wellies?

To make matters worse, the rain had started up again and now it pattered down, weighing down branches even more and making forward progress difficult and downright uncomfortable.

"Jeez," whispered Ava, "another storm's rolling in."

Rain poured down with greater intensity. Overhead, shards of lightning streaked across the blue-black sky.

"Not good," Carmela muttered as she crept forward. Thunder suddenly rumbled and roared, drowning out all night sounds.

Carmela used her sleeve to wipe rain from her eyes. If she could only get about ten feet closer . . . but first there was a clearing she had to wiggle across.

She tried to time her leap with the lightning. After the final crackle fizzled out, she dove from one sheltering clump of trees to the next.

Except it didn't quite work out that way. Right in the middle of her leap, a second flash of lighting exploded overhead, like a transformer gone haywire.

And Carmela and Ava were suddenly illuminated. Caught in nature's spotlight, like terrified actors on a stage!

Oh no!

Within moments, they were swarmed by robed figures. Two on either side of Ava, two more bookending Carmela. The robed figures didn't exactly force them to walk forward, but they weren't allowing a lot of other options, either.

"Hey, you goombahs," Ava screamed, "don't touch the merchandise!" She shrugged her shoulders and tried to pull away, but her guardians stuck tight as burs.

"Walk," ordered one of the hooded men.

"This is ridiculous!" Ava shrilled. "What's a bunch of guys like you doing in a dumb old swamp, anyway?" She tossed her head, trying to look coquettish. "I saw a cool roadhouse a couple miles back — Swamp Man Bobby's? Whaddya guys say we blow this pop stand and go grab ourselves a cold one, huh?"

Carmela glanced back over her shoulder. "They're not listening to you, Ava."

"I see that!" Ava fussed. "And, quite frankly, I'm shocked, since the two of us girls make a lovely combo platter."

"They're true believers," said Carmela.

"Yeah?" said Ava, still struggling. "That's just peachy-poo." Now her voice rose. "But will somebody please tell me exactly what it is they *believe* in!"

Carmela and Ava were marched inside the white barn and ordered to sit on a rough wooden bench. The place smelled of hay and goats, and, interestingly enough, freshly brewed coffee.

"Stay," ordered a gruff voice.

"Yeah, yeah," said Ava, giving a casual wave. But once the men had moved out of earshot, her fear exploded. "You don't think they're gonna drag us into the swamp and tie us to trees so crabs crawl all over us and pick us to death, are they?"

"No," said Carmela, "they're just being cautious. And a little paranoid."

"But paranoid people do crazy things."

"Don't worry," Carmela said, locking onto Ava's eyes, "nothing's going to happen. We're just . . . like . . . visitors."

But Ava's eyes had suddenly shifted elsewhere. "Who are you?" she demanded, gazing up at a tall man who'd pushed back his hood to reveal silvery-gray hair. A group of six more robed members stood behind him in a semicircle, like sentinels.

"I'm Frank Crowley," the man told her. He was craggy-faced, with heavy lids and lips. He also had a kind of crazy light dancing in his gray eyes. The kind of light Carmela pretty much characterized as belonging to a religious zealot. Not that there was anything *wrong* with being a zealot, it was just that they tended to be on the fringe versus the mainstream.

Carmela jumped to her feet. "I'm afraid your merry little band of men got a little overanxious tonight," she explained. "Forcibly hauling us down here."

"They were under orders," Crowley barked. "To capture any and all interlopers."

"That may be," said Carmela, "but they were wrong to do so." Carmela maintained a civil tone as she turned her palms upward, in a calm yet questioning gesture. Better, she decided, to remain peaceable and talk her way out.

Frank Crowley curled his lip and stuck his face a little too close to Carmela's face. "What were you two doing crawling around in the woods?" he crooned.

"They were spying on us!" shrilled a woman, who was standing nearby.

Now Ava was on her feet, looking shocked and a little indignant. "Don't get your undies in a twist! Because we . . . we came here in peace."

Carmela glanced sharply at Ava. *We what? Now what's she up to? Where's she going with this?*

"That's right," said Ava, winging it like crazy now, "we came out here to join your group!"

Carmela rolled her eyes. No way were they going to believe a story like *that!*

"I don't believe you," sneered Frank Crowley.

Carmela held up a hand. Ava had tossed out a wild fish story, now she had to serve it up and make it palatable. "Here's the thing. We heard about your group, all good things, of course. And we wanted to do a little investigating on our own."

Crowley glared at her. "You heard about the Seekers?"

"Yes, we did," said Carmela. She tried for

earnest, managed semi-sincere.

"From whom?" Crowley demanded.

"A friend," said Carmela, almost choking on her words. "A highly respectable man who's, in fact, a member of another religious order."

"You'll have to do better than that," Crowley said, "for me to believe you."

"Listen," said Carmela, "we're not here to start any sort of conflict or dispute. Truly. If anything, we're looking for concordance."

"You go, girl," said Ava, cheering her on. "Throw out some of those SAT words!"

Frank Crowley stared at Carmela for a few more moments, as if mulling over her words. Then he said, in a low voice, "Go. You're free to go." He cocked his head to one side and held up an index finger. "But don't come sneaking back here if you know what's good for you."

"Big threat," Ava snarled. "Maybe you wouldn't be so tough if you didn't have the seven dwarves there, backing you up."

But Carmela grabbed Ava's arm in a stranglehold and jerked hard, and slowly the two of them edged their way out of the barn.

When Carmela finally climbed into her car, she let loose a shaky breath. "What a whacked-out scene." She pulled her seat belt across and turned toward Ava. "And exactly what was that bit about 'we come in peace'?"

Ava grimaced. "It was all I could come up with at the moment. But I guess it didn't play too well."

"It sounded more like dialogue out of a fifties sci-fi movie."

"Thank you," said Ava, suddenly sounding pleased. "Because it was. I lifted it from *The Day the Earth Stood Still.* The original version, not the remake."

"Know what I think?" said Carmela, as her engine turned over and she slammed her stick shift into first. "I think they're all cuckaloo."

"You'll get no argument from me," said Ava.

"And you know what else?"

"What?" said Ava.

"I think Brother Paul tossed us a big fat red herring."

CHAPTER 19

They were rolling down Royal Street, windshield wipers beating out their syncopation, when Carmela said, "Let's run over to Storyville Outreach Center and have a little chat with Brother Paul." She was still smarting from their encounter with the irritable Frank Crowley.

Ava stretched languidly and yawned. "Waaaah?" She'd practically fallen asleep on the drive home. "You think? Really?"

"Yeah, I do," said Carmela. "I want to look directly into Brother Paul's beady little lying eyes and ask him why, exactly, he sent us on a snipe hunt."

"Snipe?" said Ava, tugging at her sweater and pulling herself upright. "What's this snipe? Some kind of animal?"

"It's a bad joke," Carmela explained. "A trick. Generally played at summer camp by someone with the mind-set of a fifth-grader."

"Yeah? How's it work?"

"It involves sending your bunk mates out into the dark woods with a flashlight and a pillowcase and telling them to hunt snipe," said Carmela. Her fingers clutched the steering wheel tighter.

"Which is basically . . . ," said Ava.

"A fool's errand."

"Hah," said Ava.

They crunched down Paris Street and pulled into the Storyville parking lot.

"Think they're still open?" asked Ava. The parking lot was sodden and dark, the building dimly lit.

"I know they are," said Carmela. "I can see people inside sitting on folding chairs."

"No place to go, I suppose," said Ava.

They slipped inside, where a low-key meeting seemed to be taking place. A dozen people were perched on wobbly folding chairs while a scruffy-looking man with a gray beard read to them from a small blue book. Once in a while, the group would nod en masse and mumble an answer.

"What is it?" Ava whispered. "A Bible reading?"

They stood for a few moments, listening, and then Carmela said, "I think they're making some sort of pledge."

"To pull their act together and get a job?"

asked Ava.

"More like never to drink again," said Carmela.

Ava grimaced. "Ooh, tough pledge."

A silver-haired woman, one they recognized from the kitchen last night, broke away from the group to greet them.

"You're back," she said, but in a cheerful, friendly manner. She wore a plain brown shirtwaist dress, the kind June Cleaver used to wear, once upon a time ago in TV land.

"We're looking for Brother Paul," Carmela told her.

The woman glanced at her wristwatch, a no-nonsense Timex. "He's saying devotions right now, so I hate to disturb him."

"We have some unfinished business to take care of," said Carmela.

The woman shifted from one foot to the other, looking indecisive.

"We wouldn't interrupt him if it weren't important," Carmela told her.

Something in Carmela's words must have resonated with the woman, because she said, "Brother Paul's quarters are at the back of the building." She waved at the door they'd just come through. "But you'll have to walk around outside to get there."

"Thanks much," said Carmela.

"Yet another challenge," commented Ava. "First we muck around in a swamp, now we stumble through a muddy parking lot."

"Just stick close to the building," Carmela advised, "where there's a little more terra firma."

"You think?" said Ava. Her toe struck a rock, her right ankle wobbled, and she almost went down. "Man, it's dark back here!"

Carmela had to agree. "You think there'd be a light over the door or something." They fumbled across the back of the building, then finally deciphered the murky outline of a back door.

Ava peered up. "There is a light. But the bulb's burned out, I guess."

"Or knocked out," said Carmela. "This isn't the greatest part of town."

"Pesky kids probably broke it," said Ava.

Carmela rapped her knuckles against the back door. It was a metal door that telegraphed hollow reverberations back to her.

"Nobody home?" asked Ava. She was more than ready to turn tail and get out of Dodge.

"He's supposed to be here," said Carmela.

"But he's saying devotions," said Ava. "Maybe Brother Paul gets into one of those religious ecstasy comas, where he's, like, totally focused."

"Or maybe he just doesn't want to talk to us," said Carmela. She rapped on the door again. "Brother Paul. You in there?" She had a bone to pick with him and wasn't about to give up.

"Try the door," Ava suggested. "Maybe there's a hallway or anteroom."

Carmela tugged at the door. It swung back easily on its hinges, revealing a ten-foot-long dark hallway with two old-fashioned wooden doors set on either side.

Carmela and Ava tiptoed in.

"Which door?" Carmela wondered.

Ava shrugged, then banged an open hand against the door that was closest to her, the door on the left. It rattled noisily, like the hinges might be loose. She waited a few moments, then said, "See? Nobody home."

Carmela crossed the hallway and knocked politely on the opposite door. She was still hoping to rouse Brother Paul. But here, too, there was no answer.

"Brother Paul's obviously not around," said Ava. "Maybe he skipped out for a bite to eat." She chuckled. "Or to enjoy a little liquid refreshment."

"Maybe," said Carmela. She was still reluctant to leave, so she thought, *What the heck.* Wrapping her hand firmly around the doorknob, she cranked it to the right and pushed.

The door swung silently inward.

"Oh hey!" said Ava.

They stood together and peered in. The room was a small study with cheap plywood paneling on the walls. A dim reading lamp stood next to a dilapidated purple velvet chair that looked like it had been salvaged from a thrift shop. A sagging bookshelf, laden with books, hunkered next to it.

"Maybe he *is* home," said Ava.

"Brother Paul?" Carmela called out. The confined space made her voice bounce and echo. "It's Carmela Bertrand."

Ava stepped across the threshold. "And Ava. Remember us? We worked in the kitchen last night? The two good-lookin' chicks?"

"That's helpful," Carmela whispered.

Ava shrugged.

"Brother Paul?" Carmela called again. As she stood there, feeling like an intruder, she gradually became aware that a slightly brighter light was shining through a doorway from an adjoining room.

"Maybe Brother Paul's on his knees

saying vespers or something," said Ava. "Maybe he really *is* in some kind of religious stupor."

"Maybe," said Carmela. She took a step forward and then another. For some reason — she had no idea why — she was drawn to that doorway. "Brother Paul?" she called again. "Are you okay? Because we're coming in. We *are* in."

Ava reached out and touched a hand to Carmela's shoulder. "Maybe we shouldn't be snooping, after all." Now she was the one getting cold feet.

But Carmela continued quietly across the room, heading for the adjoining room. When she was four steps from the doorway, she stopped abruptly and let out a surprised gasp. Then her hand flew to her mouth, and she barked out, "No!"

"Carmela?" Ava's voice was tremulous. "What's wrong?"

When Carmela didn't answer, Ava tiptoed across the room to see for herself. She gazed into the other room, doing a confused double take, not quite understanding what she was seeing at first.

Because Brother Paul was home, all right. Standing ramrod stiff in his monastic cell, staring directly at them. Except that his gaze was completely blank, his face was purple

279

and swollen, and his toes dangled six inches above the carpet!

There was no question whom Carmela would call, of course. She jerked her cell phone from her bag and, in spite of Ava's frightened mewling and gibbering, called Edgar Babcock.

The first unit arrived in about two minutes flat. A pair of fresh-faced uniformed officers came dashing in. When they saw what had happened, they escorted Carmela and Ava out of Brother Paul's room and stashed them in the back of their police cruiser. Then the officers dashed to the front of the building to secure the entire premises.

Babcock arrived amid a blat of sirens, riding in the passenger seat of another black-and-white. Before the car came to a complete stop, he leaped out, dressed casually in jeans and a brown suede jacket, but looking grim-faced and determined.

"What are you doing here?" was his first question to Carmela and Ava, as they scrambled out of the patrol car to greet him. "Did you touch anything?" was his rapid-fire second question.

"We wanted to talk to Brother Paul," said Carmela.

"No," said Ava.

Babcock looked from one to the other, confused. "Yes, you wanted to talk to him? Or no, you didn't?" he demanded.

Flustered, Carmela held up a hand, as much to stem his flow of questions as to steady her nerves. "Wait a minute. Yes, we stopped by to see Brother Paul. No, we didn't touch anything."

Babcock seemed angered as well as confused by their presence. "Imagine my surprise when this was called in, to learn that you two discovered the body!" He swallowed, angrily. "So why *exactly* are you here?"

"We were making an inquiry," said Carmela. Babcock was doing a slow simmer, but she knew he could explode like a runaway pressure cooker at any minute.

"It has to do with the circumstances surrounding, um, Byrle's death," said Ava, glancing sideways at Carmela.

"The Coopersmith homicide?" said Babcock, looking startled.

"That's right," said Carmela, fighting to remain calm.

"You're *investigating*," Babcock spat out. Before Carmela could open her mouth to protest or utter a peep, he said, "That wasn't a question."

"Okay," Carmela said, sounding properly meek.

"And you two just *happened* to discover the director of this place . . ." He glanced at the hastily scrawled notes he'd written on the way over. "You two found Brother Paul Lupori hanging from the rafters in his room?" Babcock was incredulous. "Which means the two of you actually went inside his . . . whatever it is . . . his living quarters, his apartment?"

"Yes," Carmela answered.

"Then you *did* touch something."

"Just the doorknob," said Ava. "Doorknobs."

"This is a bloody mess," Babcock fumed. He was stressing now, big-time. "Tell me *exactly* why you were here!"

"It's a long story," said Carmela.

"Try me," said Babcock.

"The thing is," said Carmela, "we ran into Brother Paul over at St. Tristan's."

"That's right," said Ava, jumping in. "The morning after Byrle was murdered."

"So, in your mind, that made Brother Paul a suspect?" Babcock asked. He seemed appalled by their faulty deductive reasoning.

"Well . . . something like that," said Ava.

"Not exactly," said Carmela.

Babcock was grim. "Please, one at a time.

Which is it?"

"We saw Brother Paul more as a person of interest," said Carmela. "And we thought . . . hoped, actually . . . that he might have some information for us."

"Which is the reason we stopped by last night," said Ava.

"You were here last night, too?" said Babcock. "Why?" A vein throbbed in his left temple, and Carmela hoped it wasn't a precursor to a heart attack.

"Helping in the kitchen," said Ava.

Babcock put his hands on his hips and hunched his shoulders. "Frankly, I don't care if you were weaving baskets," he said, in a tight-lipped growl. "Do you two know how *bad* this looks? Turning up at the scene of two different murders!"

"Was it murder?" Carmela asked, lifting her chin to indicate Brother Paul's living quarters. "Or suicide?" She glanced over Babcock's shoulder, where a team of crime-scene techs were pulling on blue latex rubber gloves and heading in with their equipment.

Babcock stuck both hands in the pockets of his suede jacket, turned his back on them, and strode forcefully away. He muttered to himself for a few moments, then came shuffling back.

"Here's what I want you to do," said Babcock. "I want you to leave. To go home. And not breathe a word about this to anyone!"

"You don't want to debrief us?" Ava asked.

"I don't want to even *look* at the two of you right now!" yelled Babcock.

It was almost ten o'clock by the time they stumbled into Carmela's apartment.

"Well, *that* was an exciting conclusion to a bizarre evening," Carmela said, as Boo and Poobah greeted her with exuberant snorts and wet kisses.

"I'm so upset I'm shaking," Ava confessed. "Even my toes are vibrating." Kicking off her muddy boots at the door, she added, "And when I get all wrought up like this, I burn energy like mad."

"Which means . . . ?" asked Carmela. She pulled off her sweater and smoothed the white T-shirt she'd worn under it.

"Well . . . it means I'm hungry," said Ava. She gave a guilty shrug. "Sorry. Sorry to always be imposing like this. Sorry to always be the needy girlfriend."

"You're not," said Carmela. "But I think I will put a tip jar on the counter." When she saw Ava's morose look, she said, "Don't worry about it. It'll do me good to fix us something to eat . . . help my brain refocus."

She added a shaky laugh. "Help me to . . . depressurize."

"You're a good mom," said Ava, gratefully sinking down on the sofa. She reached a hand out to stroke Boo's furry forehead. "Isn't she a good mom? Don't you lovey-wovey her?"

"Don't get too carried away in there," Carmela called, as she rattled dishes in the kitchen.

"Can I turn on the TV?" asked Ava.

"Be my guest. "You want your grilled cheese sandwich with Monterey Jack or cheddar?"

"Can I have both?" asked Ava. She hesitated. "Do you think Brother Paul was murdered? Or did he commit suicide?"

Carmela stuck her head around the corner. "Murdered. Definitely. The other is just too horrible to even contemplate."

"The sin for which there is no redemption," Ava muttered to herself, then made a hasty sign of the cross.

Carmela fixed two grilled cheese sandwiches, plated them, added dill pickle wedges and a handful of kettle chips, then carried everything into the living room.

"The news is just coming on," Ava told her, as she grabbed one of the plates.

They watched a montage of fast-paced

graphics that included snippets from Mardi Gras, scenes from Katrina, and a smiling news team standing in front of their mobile van. Then the camera moved in on Don Ankeny, KBEZ-TV's aging late-night newscaster.

"I don't think the TV guys will have picked up the Brother Paul thing yet," said Carmela, gazing at the newscaster with his eighties-looking hair. "It's too soon for . . ."

"Brother Paul Lupori is the latest victim in this city's rising tide of crime," announced Ankeny.

Both women stopped midbite and stared wide-eyed at the TV.

"Uh-oh," said Carmela, a bite of sandwich suddenly stuck in her gullet. "Looks like Brother Paul made the news, after all!"

CHAPTER 20

Ankeny, wearing his trust-me-I'm-serious news face, continued: "In an apparent murder at the Storyville Outreach Center, the director was found hanging in his small apartment at the rear of the building."

"Babcock's not gonna be happy about this," said Ava. She picked up her pickle wedge and crunched loudly, as if to add emphasis to her statement.

"You never know," said Carmela. "He could have tipped the TV station himself."

"You think?" said Ava. She popped a chip into her mouth and leaned back against the sofa.

Carmela thought for a minute. "Or maybe not. Babcock's your basic law enforcement control freak, and he didn't seem one bit in control an hour ago. So probably the TV guys sniffed this one out on their own."

"Uh-oh," said Ava, pointing at the screen. "Look who else is on. The Wicked Witch of the West. Kimber Breeze."

The camera switched from a two-shot of Ankeny and Kimber to a close-up of just Kimber.

"Does she look different to you?" asked Ava.

"Maybe . . . the Botox makes her look younger?"

"No," said Ava, "to look younger she'd need a time machine."

"Shhh," said Carmela, studying the screen now.

"In an interesting sidebar," said Kimber, smiling broadly, "Brother Paul Lupori was also affiliated with St. Tristan's Church, where the brutal murder of Byrle Cooper-smith took place just three short days ago. While it is not known at this time if the two murders are connected, informed sources tell me that Carmela Bertrand, who was an eyewitness in the Coopersmith murder, was also at the scene of tonight's crime." Kimber flashed her megawatt smile, then added, "Stay tuned to KBEZ for any and all break-ing news."

"Well, that's just fine and dandy!" said Carmela, throwing her hands up. "Now I'm publicly linked to *two* murders."

"Huh," said Ava. Then she turned to Carmela and said, in a thoughtful, questioning tone of voice, "Do you think maybe that's a good thing?"

Carmela exhaled with a loud whoosh. "Why on *earth* would you say that?"

"You've been poking around anyway," Ava reasoned.

"That's because Baby *asked* me to. As a favor."

"But now it's all out in the open. Your involvement, I mean."

Carmela touched an index finger to her lower lip, trying to decipher Ava's words. "So you're saying . . . what? That Kimber's announcement could shake something loose?"

Ava nodded. "It's possible."

"But who," said Carmela, looking pained, "killed these people? I mean, is it the same person or are there two different killers?"

"No clue," said Ava.

"Funny you should say that," said Carmela, "because that's exactly what we need. One good, solid clue."

"So let's put our heads together and try to figure out what happened tonight," said Ava. "Who would do this? Who would hang Brother Paul?"

"What I want to know is *how* they did it?" said Carmela. "How do you hang somebody against his will? Force him at gunpoint?

Knock him on the head and then string him up? I mean, how do you orchestrate this kind of grisly crime?"

"Scares the crap out of me just thinking about it," said Ava. She gathered her legs under her and sat cross-legged, her hand cupping her chin, looking contemplative. "My addled brain keeps circling back to *who.*"

"I hear you," said Carmela. She thought for a few minutes. "Tell me you're not thinking . . . Frank Crowley from the Seekers?"

"Dunno," said Ava.

"If Crowley engineered Brother Paul's murder, he had to drive a whole lot faster than we did to even get back to the city."

"Maybe Brother Paul's murder was already in the works," Ava theorized. "Maybe Crowley and Brother Paul didn't get along."

"I'm *positive* they didn't get along," said Carmela. "Brother Paul seemed to take a certain glee in siccing us on him."

"Good point."

"On the other hand," said Carmela, "it still could have been someone like Johnny Otis."

"That seems like a shaky theory," said Ava. "How would Otis figure in with Brother Paul?"

Carmela shrugged. "Maybe Johnny Otis was the one who killed Byrle and he pegged Brother Paul as a witness? Someone he had to get rid of, just to be sure."

Ava considered Carmela's words. "I can sort of see that."

"I can also think of a few other peripheral suspects."

"You mean like Drew Gaspar?" asked Ava. She shook her head and her lush hair tumbled down around her face. "Doubtful. I don't see how Gaspar could have possibly been involved."

"If Gaspar collects religious icons," said Carmela, "he might have stolen the crucifix, killed Byrle in the confusion, and . . ."

"And what?" said Ava.

"And Brother Paul could have *seen* something?"

"You keep coming back to that," said Ava. "Brother Paul as witness."

"I know that."

"That could be it right there," allowed Ava. "Though the reasoning feels a little forced and thin. Oh man, *everything* feels thin."

"But dead bodies keep piling up," said Carmela.

Ava gave a nervous shiver.

As if on cue, the phone shrilled loudly,

causing Ava to flinch. "Gotta be Babcock," she muttered.

"Bringing with him tons of fallout," said Carmela, wincing, as she snatched the receiver off its hook. "Hello?"

"Oh pussycat," trilled Jekyl, "I have *très* exciting news for you!"

Carmela put a hand over the receiver. "It's Jekyl. He says he has exciting news."

"Tell him about *our* news," said Ava.

"Is that Ava I hear in the background?" asked Jekyl.

"That's right," said Carmela. "And do we ever have news." Even though Babcock had warned her not to breathe a word about the murder to anyone, Brother Paul's murder had just been broadcast into every living room in the nearby eight parishes. So . . . it wasn't exactly a big hairy secret anymore, was it?

"Okay, lovey," said Jekyl, sounding intrigued. "You go first."

"Well," said Carmela, "if you turn your TV on right this instant, you might catch the tail end of a story about the murder of Brother Paul."

"Brother who?" said Jekyl.

"This guy who was affiliated with St. Tristan's," said Carmela.

"Wait a minute," said Jekyl. "The guy you

were going to question? You're saying he's been murdered?"

"Just happened," said Carmela. "And not only that, Ava and I were *there*. In fact . . . we found him hanging in his room at the outreach center where he works."

"All purple and blotchy-faced," said Ava.

"What?" screeched Jekyl.

Carmela filled him in quickly about Brother Paul, as well as how she'd been named by KBEZ-TV as the single eyewitness!

"That's awful!" Jekyl sympathized. "For you and for Brother Paul. But you make it sound as if Brother Paul might have been a little . . . intense. Of course, his heart was definitely in the right place." Jekyl sighed. "Now who's going to take care of those poor homeless guys?"

Carmela dropped the phone to her chest and gazed at Ava. "Jekyl wants to know who's going to take care of all those poor homeless guys now?"

Ava shook her head vigorously. "Not me, if that's what he's asking!"

"I don't know," said Carmela, back on the line again with Jekyl. "They'll probably fall through the cracks like everything else does in New Orleans."

"That's a rather sour indictment of our

city, wouldn't you say?" said Jekyl.

"Yes, well . . . there's a reason we're known as the Big Easy and not the Big We're Really on Top of It," said Carmela. "So . . . what was your news?"

"Well, certainly not as gruesome as yours," said Jekyl, "but major, nonetheless."

"Okay," said Carmela.

"I spoke with my friend Riley Simmonet," said Jekyl, "who's the art director at *Delta Living* magazine? And, guess what, sweetie, he wants to *photograph* your home!"

"Um . . . he what?" said Carmela.

"You know," said Jekyl, his excitement ratcheting in intensity, "he's hot to stage an actual photo shoot! With you as the subject! Do a real glamorous lady-of-the-manor-type thing."

Carmela's mouth drooped into a nervous frown. "You're not serious." Truth be told, she hated the idea. Posing, being a photographer's subject, just wasn't one of her favorite things.

"You're making a face, aren't you?" said Jekyl. "I can tell."

"No," Carmela lied, "I'm really not."

"I can absolutely envision the perfect photo layout," enthused Jekyl. "You wearing a romantic gown, posed in front of your marble fireplace. Or looking very Southern and fey as you lounge on that brocade fainting couch." He paused to catch his breath. "Exciting, no?"

"No," said Carmela.

"What?" Jekyl squawked. "Don't tell me you're not interested!"

"I'm not interested," said Carmela.

"What's he saying?" asked Ava, plucking at Carmela's sleeve.

"Jekyl wants me to do a photo spread for *Delta Living*," Carmela whispered.

"Yes!" said Ava, giving a vigorous fist pump. "You gotta do it!"

"I told him no," said Carmela.

"But it's a done deal," came Jekyl's pleading voice. "I made all the arrangements and scheduled the photo session for Saturday morning."

"*This* Saturday?" Carmela cried.

"Perfect!" Ava cheered.

"I really don't want to do this," Carmela pleaded. It just didn't feel right to her. Could she get out of it? She *had* to get out of it!

Jekyl let loose a colossal sigh. "Listen, Carmela, you want to sell that house of yours, don't you?" Now his voice carried an edge.

Carmela was taken aback. "How is selling my house connected to posing for a magazine?" It sounded stinky-fishy to her.

"It's all very intricately connected," Jekyl assured her. "A photo spread in *Delta Living* is the most powerful marketing tool you could ask for! Think how prospective buyers will eat it up!"

Carmela worried her lower lip with her front teeth. Jekyl made a good point. Homes that had been featured in fancy magazines *did* have a certain cachet attached to them. Fact was, buyers simply adored any publicity that was attached to their purchase.

"Okay," Carmela said, slowly. "I'll do it."

"Atta girl!" said Jekyl.

"On one condition," Carmela told him.

"What's that?"

"This photo shoot remains extremely low key."

"We have to call Baby and tell her about Brother Paul," said Ava. She'd ferried the dishes into the kitchen and was wiping her hands on a checked dish towel.

"Why?" said Carmela.

"Because you promised Baby you were going to investigate," Ava reasoned. "And tonight's murder goes hand in hand with your investigation." She paused, cocked her head, and gave a slightly apologetic smile. "You're Baby's secret agent."

"Lucky me."

"Better hurry up and do it fast," Ava prompted. "And hope Baby hasn't already heard about it on the ten o'clock news."

But when Carmela called Baby to tell her about stumbling around and finding the Seekers, then going to Storyville Outreach and finding Brother Paul dead, she was shocked beyond belief.

"No, I haven't seen the news," Baby fretted into the phone. "Oh, dear me, *another* murder." She paused for a few seconds. "And you think it's clearly related to St. Tristan's? That means you're on to something, Carmela!"

"If it does, then I'm not aware of what I'm on to," said Carmela. "There are dozens of loose threads hanging out there, but I don't seem to be able to pull anything together."

"Just that you seem to be getting close is exciting," said Baby.

"Not for me," said Carmela. "I just feel horribly guilty about the Brother Paul thing. Like I might have been somehow responsible!"

"How on earth do you figure that?" asked Baby.

"Because," said Carmela, "it feels like a nasty chain reaction. Brother Paul was the one who *told* us about the Seekers, and then Ava and I went there tonight and got discovered, and then . . ."

"Oh, honey, I don't think . . . ," said Baby.

Still, Carmela wasn't convinced. Her heart just felt sad and leaden.

"Did you tell Babcock you paid a visit to the Seekers?" asked Baby.

"No, I did not," said Carmela. "He was so crazed over Brother Paul's death and the fact that Ava and I were there that I figured I'd save that little surprise for later."

"But you are going to tell him?"

"I think I pretty much have to," said Carmela. "It could be related, and, well, I do have a guilty conscience."

"You'll do the right thing," Baby assured her.

Ava felt the same way.

"I agree with Baby," said Ava. "You have to tell Babcock where we were tonight and about running into the Seekers."

"You mean spill my guts about the whole sorry mess?"

"The whole rotten enchilada," said Ava. "Of course, I certainly don't envy you having that conversation with him." She tossed a furtive glance toward the door, obviously planning her escape route.

"What?" Carmela yelped. "You're not going to stick around and help me explain things? I have to go it alone?"

"He's *your* boyfriend!" Gingerly, Ava touched two fingers to her throat and added, "Besides, I think I might be coming down with something. All that traipsing around in the damp woods has left me feelin' under the weather."

Carmela was slightly suspicious of Ava's sudden ailment. "Maybe I should fix you a nice cup of tea with lemon?"

"No," said Ava, making a beeline for the door, "I'll just dump some Nyquil on the rocks and add a Kahlua chaser."

Edgar Babcock wasn't one bit happy when Carmela finally called him. In fact, when she gave him a kind of quick-fire synopsis, he was livid.

"You waited until *now* to tell me about the Seekers? Completely after the fact?"

"Um . . . it makes a difference?" said Carmela. She felt sheepish and stupid even asking the question.

"Of course, it does! Your foray to the Seekers church . . . er, place of worship . . . is a critical piece of information. Possibly even evidence."

"I don't see how it's actual evidence," said Carmela. "It's more just happenstance.

299

Kind of like our being at Storyville Outreach tonight. We happened to be there, Brother Paul happened to get killed."

"Don't try to double-talk me, Carmela," said Babcock. "You know very well I'm not a big believer in coincidences."

"I'll remember that," said Carmela, a chill in her voice now. "And did you by any chance happen to catch the ten o'clock news? Specifically KBEZ-TV?"

"Hardly," said Babcock, "since I've been mucking around at a murder scene. Why do you ask?"

"Then you missed Kimber Breeze naming me as the sole eyewitness — in Byrle's murder as well as Brother Paul's!"

"No way."

"Way," said Carmela. "Just off the top of my head, I'd say your department has a leak so big you could drive a truck through it."

"Excuse me?" said Babcock.

"With Kimber pegging me as a witness in Brother Paul's murder, the entire city is going to think I had a front-row seat — even though, once again, I really didn't see anything!" She blew out an angry glut of air. "Just had the bad luck to turn up there, too!"

"Aw jeez, Carmela." Now there was contriteness in Babcock's voice. "I didn't mean to drag you into this any more than you already are."

"I really want to believe you," said Carmela.

"Believe me," said Babcock. "These news people always go off half-cocked." He paused, thinking. "You think the other stations have it, too?"

"Probably."

"That's tough," said Babcock. "It means you're going to have to be doubly careful."

"Careful about what?" What was he talking about?

Babcock answered her in his serious, law enforcement voice. "You've been named publicly as a witness, Carmela. In two homicides. You're going to have to be careful about showing your face around town!"

"I don't like the sound of that at all."

Babcock mumbled something to himself, then said, "I'm going to put a car outside your apartment tonight."

An icicle of fear stabbed at Carmela's heart. "Seriously? You think that's necessary?"

"Yes, I do," said Babcock. "Considering your little shocker with Brother Paul and then your name being mentioned on the broadcast."

"Hmm," said Carmela. She wasn't sure if

she felt relieved or alarmed. Maybe a little of both?

"What are you up to tomorrow?" asked Babcock.

"I plan to be at Memory Mine most of the day, and then I'm going to Baby's house in the evening."

"Okay, we can cover you fairly easy. What about Saturday?"

"That's a little trickier," said Carmela.

"How so?"

"I've got a photo shoot at the Garden District house, and then I have the St. Tammany Vineyard press party at night."

"Can you skip it?"

"What?" Carmela's voice rose a couple of octaves. "Skip the press party? The one I've been working on nonstop for the past four weeks? No way. Not on your life."

"Because of that guy," said Babcock. Now he sounded just plain grumpy.

"You can say his name," said Carmela. "It's Quigg."

Babcock let loose an indelicate snort. "He'll always be *that guy* to me."

CHAPTER 21

"I can't believe it," Gabby said, in a voice that was both excited and filled with awe. "You landed smack-dab in the middle of trouble again! You're like some kind of rogue CIA agent or operative from *Mission Impossible*." She was hunched over a mug of steaming Darjeeling tea, sitting at the front counter. Carmela was perched across from her on a wooden stool and had just spent the last fifteen minutes recounting the bizarre events of last night.

"Maybe so," said Carmela, "but I can't say that I'm thrilled to be sitting at ground zero with Babcock telling me to mind my own business." Carmela was pretty much devastated at the way things had turned out with Brother Paul, but what could she do?

"What's your next move?" asked Gabby. "Or are you just going to lay low?"

"That's the general idea," said Carmela. "Oh!" She waved her fingers in front of

Gabby's face. "I forgot to tell you. Babcock put a guard on my apartment last night, and there's supposedly some sort of tail on me today."

"Seriously?" said Gabby. "Babcock's worried about your safety?"

"Uh-huh."

Spinning around, Gabby peered past a collection of altered books and a display of holiday scrapbook pages that she'd just arranged in the front window. "I don't see anyone waiting around out there."

"I don't think he'll be dressed in a trench coat and gray fedora and leaning against a lamppost," said Carmela. "He'll probably be more . . . incognito."

"I guess a tail is *supposed* to be invisible," said Gabby.

"I assume so," said Carmela. "If they're any good."

Gabby gazed at her. "You're not going to, like, dash down to Pirate's Alley Deli and try to draw this guy out into the open, are you?"

"If I do any deli dashing, it'll be to bring back a sack of cookies or cupcakes," Carmela assured her. "Not to willfully expose my police protection."

Tap tap tap. Someone was pecking gently at the front door.

Leaning forward, Gabby called out, "We're not open yet."

But Carmela had already slipped off her stool and was spinning the big brass latch. "It's Devon," she told Gabby, who was still tucked behind the counter.

A grin split Gabby's face. "Did he bring Mimi along?"

"Did I bring Mimi?" came a friendly, high-pitched voice. "Do I go anywhere without my sweet little princess?" Devon Dowling, the antiques dealer who owned Dulcimer's Antiques just around the corner, came strolling in with Mimi the pug tucked securely in his pudgy arms. "I never leave my baby girl at home." He tilted his head forward and planted a kiss on Mimi's furry, wrinkled forehead.

Gabby scurried around the counter, the better to greet Mimi. "Hello, sweetheart," she cooed, as Devon transferred the imperious, flat-faced, wide-eyed Mimi into Gabby's outstretched arms.

"What brings you out so early?" asked Carmela. As if she couldn't guess. Devon Dowling was the neighborhood gossip. Correction, make that neighborhood snoop. Nothing got by Devon that didn't warrant an acerbic comment or probing question. And, probably, Devon's probing questions were about to commence right now.

Devon stuck a hand on one hip, posturing grandly, as he said to Carmela, "You were on television last night, you naughty girl."

"Not my doing," said Carmela. She knew she was going to get fallout, she just didn't realize it would come spattering down on her head so quickly.

"Realize," continued Devon, "it's not such a big deal to witness one murder in New Orleans." He shrugged, rolled his eyes heavenward, and threw up a hand in a casual gesture to clearly indicate that times were, indeed, trying. "The crime rate being what it is in our fair city. But *two* murders in one week! That sort of accomplishment should be listed in the *Guinness Book of World Records.*"

"I didn't actually witness two murders," Carmela told him. "Ava and I were in the vicinity when Byrle was killed at St. Tristan's, and then we kind of stumbled upon the aftermath of last night's murder."

"*Aftermath* being a dead body," said Devon.

"Well, yes," said Carmela.

"And you were at that awful place just off Paris Street," said Devon, visibly flinching.

"Not so awful," Carmela told him, "if you're homeless and hungry. Then the

306

Storyville Outreach Center might be a welcoming sight."

"But will it remain welcoming?" Devon asked.

Carmela shrugged. "Good question. My guess is Brother Paul was probably the driving force behind it, but we can only hope there are other committed volunteers. People who recognize the good that's being done there and who'll work to keep it open."

"Ooh," said Devon, touching a roll of silk ribbon with his fingertips. "This is lovely."

"Charmeuse silk," said Carmela, eager to change the subject.

"Very classy," said Devon, cocking his head sideways in thought. "You think I could use something like this to attach my price tags?"

"I think it would be perfect," said Carmela. "You want me to order a couple of rolls for you?"

"Do that," said Devon, looking pleased. Then he focused intently on Carmela again. "If you ask me, this trouble all harks back to that stolen crucifix."

This time, Carmela all but pounced on Devon's words. "Yes! That's exactly what I think, too! But why do *you* say that?"

"Because of all the enormous publicity when that silver crucifix was unearthed," said Devon. "Especially among the arts and antiques community. Père Etienne and all that early French Quarter history. And now, *quelle horreur,* some aficionado has actually gone ahead and *collected* the crucifix. And I use that term loosely."

"You think the crucifix was stolen by a collector?" asked Carmela.

Devon cupped a hand to one ear. "Is there an echo in here?"

"Why a collector?" asked Gabby, sidling over to join them as she continued to cradle a snuggled-up Mimi.

"Because, dear ladies, collectors tend to be crazier than bedbugs," Devon proclaimed. "I've met collectors who would walk barefoot across a bed of hot coals just to acquire a rare postage stamp, a carved Japanese netsuke, or even a sixteenth-century doubloon. Do you know, there was even a natural history museum in England that had its rare bird collection stolen? And we're talking *taxidermy* birds — skins or pelts or whatever the sad little things were — all because a collector coveted them!"

"Thou shall not covet thy neighbor's goods," murmured Gabby. Mimi was nestled against her shoulder and appeared to be half-asleep, lulled by the conversation and Gabby's swaying movements.

Devon turned toward Gabby. "But people do covet, don't they? And they always will. It's simply human nature."

"Devon," said Carmela, "do you know any collectors who are crazy over religious icons?"

Devon looked a little insulted. "Realize, please, that I deal predominantly in high-end French and English antiquities." He pursed his lips, then added, "Of course, there is the odd Early American andiron or crock that creeps into my shop, but that's another story entirely."

"Religious icons?" said Carmela, trying to bring the conversation back to the subject at hand.

"Oh, I run across the occasional collector," said Devon. "Someone who pops in, looking for old statuary or religious oil paintings."

"Could you share any names?"

Devon looked annoyed. "No one person comes to mind at the moment, but if you want to wander over sometime, we can prowl through my customer list. Who knows? Maybe something will ring a bell."

"Couldn't hurt," said Gabby, gazing at Carmela.

Just as Gabby finally relinquished the adorable Mimi, Shamus called.

"What?" said Carmela, impatience evident in her voice. A call from her ex was the last thing she needed today. But Shamus never missed a chance to criticize or snoop.

"What's this happy crap I saw on TV last night?" Shamus demanded. "You're involved in some murder investigation?"

"Not really," said Carmela.

"Babe," said Shamus, "that's what they said on TV."

"You know how the media confuses things," Carmela told him.

"They didn't sound confused," Shamus countered. "They made it sound like you were Johnny-on-the-spot for both murders."

"Shamus," said Carmela, "was there something you specifically wanted? Because I'm awfully busy right now."

"That's what you always say," Shamus whined. "You're always too busy."

And you were too busy to pay attention to our marriage, thought Carmela.

"Sorry," said Carmela, "what did you want?"

"You're still hosting that wine thing tomorrow night?"

"Something like that," said Carmela.

"Think I could wangle an invitation?" Now he was using his aw-shucks, I'm-a-good-old-boy voice.

"Invitation singular?" asked Carmela. "Or *invitations?"* Of course, he wanted to bring a date. Wanted to show off.

"Okay," said Shamus. "Invitations. You win. You always win."

"It isn't about winning, Shamus."

"Oh yeah?"

"Come if you want," said Carmela. "Bring a guest if you want. Just don't . . ."

"Don't what?" asked Shamus.

"Don't get in my hair."

Business turned brisk that Friday morning. Three regulars came in, laden with scrapbook tote bags, and promptly took up residence at the craft table in back. A couple of tourists wandered in, glanced about expectantly, then proceeded to go absolutely crazy when they discovered Carmela's cache of unusual fibers and ephemera.

Andrea Banning, a customer who was planning a large holiday dinner, came rushing in to ask Carmela for help in designing name cards. After determining that Andrea's tablescape colors were cream, gold, and white, Carmela helped her select a paper made with fibers of Irish moss, then showed her how to stencil a gold border design around the edge of the cards.

"I wish there were something else I could

do," Andrea said to Carmela. "Something that relates to the whole notion of thankfulness and Thanksgiving."

"What if you wrote quotations or interesting sayings on slips of paper and put them in a small glass vase? Then everyone could draw out a slip and read it?"

"I love the idea," said Andrea. "You have paper for something like that?"

"What about linen paper?" said Carmela.

Around ten thirty, Baby came rushing in, a tiny blond dynamo in a stylish coral tweed suit with a matching Chanel bag swinging against her hip.

"How's it going?" Baby asked Carmela in a stage whisper. "Any fallout from last night?"

"Not so much," Carmela told her. "At least I haven't had any TV reporters parachute in yet."

Baby glanced around the shop, taking stock of the dozen or so customers who were shopping and crafting. "And your shop is busy. Nice."

"Remember a couple of days ago," said Carmela, "when we talked about mini clipboards?" Baby had asked about designing special clipboards to give to all the homeowners she'd roped into participating in Holidazzle.

Baby waved a hand. "You don't have time for that now."

"Actually," said Carmela, "I gave it a little thought. And came up with kind of a neat idea."

"Really?" said Baby, suddenly intrigued.

Carmela led Baby back to her office and grabbed a small Lucite clipboard. "Mini clipboards," she said, handing one to Baby. "But we jazz it up by covering it with some interesting paper."

"Maybe that neat snowflake-and-swirl pattern you just got in?" asked Baby.

"Perfect," said Carmela. "Then we loop white velvet ribbon around the clip, make a poufy bow, and attach a white silk flower. At the bottom of the clipboard, we'll stencil on some letters that spell out *Holidazzle.*"

"I like it," enthused Baby. "We could even attach a mini pen." She nodded to herself. "Very crafty."

"The clipboards pretty much work for anything," said Carmela. "You can personalize clipboards for your grandkids, garden club, tea club . . . well, you get the idea."

But Baby had other things on her mind, too.

"You're still coming to the meeting tonight, right?" asked Baby.

"Are you sure you need my help?" said

Carmela. Considering the two murders and Babcock being upset with her, it seemed like a fine night to snuggle in at home. Put on a comfy T-shirt and jammie bottoms and just flake out in front of the TV.

"No, no," Baby proclaimed. "You're my ace in the hole. I'm the new kid on the block as far as the mayor's Cultural Advisory Board is concerned, but you're the one with credibility."

"Not really," said Carmela. The lure of jammies and a movie still loomed large.

"Sure, you do," said Baby. "You've done freelance projects for the Art Institute, served on the board of the Children's Art Association, and done fund-raising for a couple of local theaters. Plus, you're a bona fide designer."

"Scrapbook shop owner now," smiled Carmela.

"Don't try to wiggle out of it," said Baby. "Fact is, you're a wildly creative woman who's vitally connected to the arts."

"Such as they are," said Carmela, remembering how the budget for the Oliphant Theater had been obliterated.

It was three in the afternoon when Ava called. Carmela had been busy all through lunch and well into the early afternoon. In fact, she'd managed to wolf down only half a roast beef po'boy. But Ava was seriously jazzed and asking her to hurry over.

"You mind if I take off?" Carmela asked Gabby.

"It's Friday," said Gabby, "and you're the boss."

"Not really," said Carmela. "It feels like we're in this together."

"The shop, yes. Your murder investigation . . . investigations . . . no."

"Ava's got her undies in a bunch over something and wants me to swing by. Yet again."

"Then you'd better swing by," said Gabby.

After checking on a couple of scrapbookers, Carmela slipped out the back door and hurried down the back alley. And when she pulled open the door and entered Juju Voodoo, she found Marilyn Casey standing at the counter, deep in conversation with Ava.

"Ava, hi," said Carmela. Her eyes skittered over to Marilyn, who seemed to be shuffling a deck of tarot cards. "And Marilyn. How's the writing going? Making progress on your book?"

That was when the cards slipped from Marilyn's hand and her face crumpled.

Ava looked serious. "We need to talk."

Warning bells clanged in Carmela's head. "Now what's wrong?"

Marilyn shot Ava a worried glance and said, "I'm afraid my book's taken a crazy turn." She lifted her hands in a helpless, wounded-bird gesture, and added, "It seems like *everything's* taken a crazy turn."

"What makes you say that?" asked Carmela. "What happened?"

Marilyn hesitated, looking miserable.

"Tell her," said Ava.

Marilyn cleared her throat. "I'm feeling extremely queasy over Brother Paul's death."

"Excuse me?" said Carmela.

Marilyn's eyes welled with tears. "I know you two were there last night. At Brother Paul's soup kitchen. I saw it all on the news."

"We weren't really there when the murder took place," said Carmela, wondering how often she was going to have to repeat herself. "We just sort of *found* him afterward."

"The weird thing is," said Marilyn, touching her thumb to her chest, "the reason I'm so upset is because I stopped by his mission yesterday to interview him."

The earth seemed to tilt crazily on its axis for Carmela. "Seriously?" she said. "Why?

What for?"

"Mostly because Brother Paul was present at St. Tristan's the day of Byrle Coopersmith's murder," said Marilyn. "I kept thinking that his being there had to be somehow relevant. Or that, since a few days had passed, his memory might have dredged up some extra little detail. Something that mattered." Her brows pulled together. "Something I could include in my book."

"So you talked to him . . . when?" asked Carmela. "Wait, you already said . . . yesterday afternoon?"

"That's right," said Marilyn. "I had a two o'clock meeting with him, though he kept me waiting until two thirty."

"But she still *parlez-voused* with him," said Ava.

"What kind of questions did you ask?" said Carmela. Could Marilyn's visit have somehow prompted Brother Paul's murder? If so, why? And by whom? The thing was, Marilyn was just a fledgling author, one of thousands who was trying her hand at mystery writing. And probably, Carmela figured, she was just bumbling her way along. Her interview with Brother Paul couldn't have yielded anything significant, could it?

A single tear trickled down Marilyn's

cheek. It left a faint trail in her otherwise flawless makeup. "I just asked Brother Paul what he was doing at St. Tristan's the morning of the murder."

"What did he tell you?" asked Ava, jumping in.

"He said he was puttering around," said Marilyn. "He'd apparently attended some sort of board meeting where he'd put in a request for funds."

"Funds for what?" asked Carmela. This came as new information to her.

"I assumed for his soup kitchen," said Marilyn.

"Outreach center," said Ava.

"What else did he say?" Carmela asked.

"That's the funny thing," said Marilyn. "Brother Paul kind of hemmed and hawed. He didn't exactly give me straight answers."

"Did he mention anything about the Seekers?" asked Ava.

Marilyn's brows furrowed again. "I don't think so. Nothing that I recall."

"So what time did you leave?" asked Carmela.

"Around three," said Marilyn. "I went home, typed my notes, and didn't give him another thought until I turned on the ten o'clock news." She swallowed hard. "That's when I found out that Brother Paul was . . ."

She choked on her final word. "Dead."

Carmela swirled this new information around in her brain for a few seconds. "Did you tell the police that you'd met with Brother Paul?"

"Yes, of course," said Marilyn, looking alarmed. "In fact, I called them first thing this morning. I figured it was the least I could do, since they've been so cooperative."

"Hmm," said Carmela. The police, Babcock specifically, hadn't given her one ounce of cooperation. Then again, she wasn't writing a book. Maybe that was what it took. You had to be a would-be Joseph Wambaugh to grab their attention.

"Anyway," said Marilyn, "I thought you two would want to know." She turned mournful eyes on Carmela. "Since you've been digging into things yourself."

"Thanks," said Carmela. "I appreciate the information." She hesitated. "And I'm sorry that all this has thrown you for such a loop." Maybe writing about true crime was a little too gritty for Marilyn's sensibilities?

"I can't imagine what you two went through last night," said Marilyn, her eyes going large.

"It was pretty awful," admitted Ava. "He was all purple and his eyes were kind of poked out."

Marilyn opened her wallet and pulled out two business cards. She handed one to Ava and the second to Carmela. "Should you need to get in touch . . ." Her words trailed off.

Carmela stared at Marilyn's card. It had a swirly little pen-and-ink logo and listed her name and cell phone number, and a street address over near Tulane. "Okay," she said. "Thanks."

Marilyn nodded numbly.

"It's not your fault, you know," Carmela told her. "Just because you talked to Brother Paul doesn't mean you're in any way responsible for his death. Try not to . . ." She was going to say *obsess,* then amended her words to, "Try not to worry about it."

Marilyn's voice was filled with genuine misery. "I'll try."

"Dang," said Ava, once Marilyn had left her shop. "What do you make of all that?"

"I'd say it pretty much confirms our suspicions," said Carmela. "That somebody, probably our killer, believes Brother Paul witnessed something."

"But who dat?" asked Ava, puzzling.

Who indeed, thought Carmela, as the back door to Ava's shop opened and the sudden suck of air caused overhead felt bats to flut-

320

ter and white wooden skeletons to click and clack.

"Eldora?" called Ava. She leaned forward over the counter, knocking over a saint candle and almost sending a display of silk voodoo charms crashing to the floor. "Is that you?"

"It's me," called Eldora, poking her head around a display of blue, purple, and red evil eye necklaces strung on black leather cords. "I've got two readings this afternoon, but I'm a little early. Hope you don't mind, hope I'm not interrupting."

"No problem," said Ava, as Eldora slipped quietly toward the back reading room.

"Eldora's still working out?" Carmela asked.

"She's a hoot," said Ava. Reaching out, she touched a finger to a small white plaster skull that sat on her counter. "My customers couldn't be happier. And she really is a whiz when it comes to interpreting a crystal ball."

"In that case," said Carmela, "maybe we should ask Eldora what's going on."

Ava made a face. "I said she was good, I didn't say she was the oracle at Delphi."

Carmela thought for a minute. "Do you think Eldora would be willing to appear at my wine-tasting event tomorrow night?"

Ava shrugged. "Maybe. If she doesn't have a gig someplace else."

"Bringing in a psychic would help make it more of a fun social event and less hard sell on the wine."

"I can see that," said Ava. "If folks have a good time, they'll come away with nice warm feelings about St. Tammany Vineyard."

"That would be the general idea."

"So ask her," said Ava.

Chapter 22

Opulent and, at the same time, slightly frayed at the seams, the Garden District remained one of the most photographed, beloved, and coveted neighborhoods in all of New Orleans. Elegant Italianate, Greek Revival, and Moorish-style mansions lined the streets, all looking like giant, delicious cookies that had been painstakingly frosted with squiggles of wrought iron, finials, filigrees, and every other exotic adornment.

"Here we are," said Carmela, as she nosed her car down Third Street. Wrought-iron streetlamps flickered in the darkness, spilling welcome little puddles of yellow light. She coasted to the curb in front of a stunningly large Italianate home and cut the engine. "Baby's place." In honor of the occasion, she'd worn a cobalt-blue cowl-neck dress with black suede boots. Ava wore her de rigueur leather pants and a bright red sweater cinched with a studded leather belt.

"Yowza," said Ava, as they hustled up the front walk. "I can never quite get used to the fact that Baby and her husband have so much money."

"Does it bother you?" asked Carmela, as she pressed the bell.

"No," said Ava, "I rather like it."

And, lucky for Baby Fontaine, she had just as much taste as she had money. And her beautifully furnished home reflected it. In the entry hall, Prussian blue silk covered the walls while shining brass sconces flanked a wall mirror set in a Rococo brass frame with an inlay of tortoiseshell. Carved cypress moldings crowned the entry room, and an enormous crystal chandelier dangled enticingly above a huge circular staircase that curled its way up to the second floor. The overall effect was *Real Housewives of Beverly Hills* meets *Gone with the Wind*.

Baby's husband, Del, greeted them at the door. "Welcome, ladies," he drawled. "Come in and make yourselves at home." He was tall, handsome, and effusive, a prominent lawyer from an old New Orleans family and a member of the high-society Comus krewe.

Carmela gave Del a chaste air kiss, while Ava simply said, "I'm just here with Carmela."

"And we're so glad you are!" enthused

324

Del. He lowered his voice and said, "I don't know what the deal is with this mayor's Cultural Advisory Board. To be perfectly honest, my idea of culture is a fine mahogany-stock rifle, a good bluetick hound, and a smooth twenty-year-old brandy. Not necessarily in that order, of course. Or enjoyed at the same time."

Ava dimpled prettily. "My idea of culture is Lady Gaga."

"Nothing wrong with that, my dear," said Del. "Say, how would you like a glass of champagne?"

"Good stuff?" inquired Ava.

Del winked at her. "I think, perhaps, we could rustle up a flute of Cristal."

Ava beamed, as if she'd been offered the Hope Diamond. "Oh yeah!"

Rain Monroe confronted Carmela head-on in the front parlor. "I still don't see why *you're* here!" she said in an icy drawl. She wore a tight red knit dress that showed off her hip bones to perfection. Her feet, tucked into black stiletto-heeled booties, were planted firmly and wide apart on the wine-red Aubusson carpet. Rain's mouth twitched and she seemed to be itching for a good scrap.

In one smooth move, Baby swept up behind Carmela and entwined a protective arm around her waist. "Carmela's my guest," said Baby. Her tone was friendly but insistent. "I wanted her here tonight as my personal arts consultant."

Rain's eyes blazed, then narrowed into unhappy slits. "I can't believe you need an *advocate*," she spat out. "After all, Baby, a person of your stature in the community has served on countless committees. You're well aware of the protocol for these meetings."

"But nothing quite this artsy," purred Baby. She tilted her head, as if she were considering something quite wonderful, then said, "Now, if you ladies are interested, and I do hope you are, I've set out some lovely tea and pastries in my dining room." She made a genteel shooing motion. "So y'all just run ahead and please help yourself."

Carmela, who made it a point never to pass on dessert of any kind, met up with Ava in the dining room.

"Champagne," said Ava, tipping her crystal glass from side to side.

"I see you've been served the finest of the manor." Carmela grinned. "While I, on the other hand, just had what was practically an eye-gouging conversation with the indomitable Rain Monroe."

"Oh man," said Ava, contorting her face, "I'm, like, one hundred percent sure she's the one who got me kicked off the Angel Auxiliary."

"Which is why I'm going to talk to her," said Carmela. "See if I can reason with her."

"Impossible to reason with crazy people," Ava said in a matter-of-fact tone, then reached out to snare a small square of pecan pie.

"But I'm still going to try," said Carmela. "Because I know how much that Angel Auxiliary means to you."

"You're such a good BFF," said Ava, grabbing a miniature chocolate napoleon.

Carmela placed a mini wedge of cheesecake on her plate, then searched the tabletop for a second goody. She saw bread pudding, pralines, cake with lemon cream, and a pear torte. It would be nice to dig into a slice of each, but not if she wanted to fit into her clothes. Not if she wanted to someday fit into jeans as skinny as Ava's. As she debated caloric merits, Carmela slowly became aware of a woman standing at her left elbow. A large, lumpy woman who was breathing with an exaggerated wheeze. She turned her head slightly, then practically jumped out of her skin when she saw who it was. "Glory!" she exclaimed.

Glory Meechum was Shamus's mean-spirited big sister who, by dint of her senior status in the Meechum family pecking order, now ruled the Crescent City Banks with an iron fist. Never a fashion plate to begin with, Glory wore a severe-looking gray dress that seemed to eerily complement her gray helmet hair. Her feet were encased in a pair of black shoes with squatty little heels. Carmela figured Glory's color wheel had to be gray and black. Or, if you wanted to be kind, anthracite and zinc.

"Why is *she* here?" Ava suddenly whispered, at Carmela's other elbow. Ava loathed Glory and considered her the scourge of the planet. Of course, Glory thought Ava was the devil's harlot.

Carmela," Glory began, in her flat, even bray. "What brings you here?" Glory stuck out her hand to shake with Carmela. It was a stiff gesture, cool and businesslike and devoid of any former-sister-in-law warmth. It was as if Glory had just walked into a deposition and been grudgingly introduced to opposing counsel.

"Baby invited me to sit in on tonight's meeting," Carmela hastily explained to Glory. "Just as a sort of . . . consultant." For some reason, her answer sounded lame to her. But Glory seemed to approve of her presence.

"That's fine," said Glory, nodding her oversized head. "It's good you're back in your old neighborhood." Her eyes wonked sideways for a moment, taking in Ava, and then she focused on Carmela again. "It's been rather unseemly, you living in that nasty apartment across from that ridiculous little magic store."

"Oh, you misunderstand," said Ava, her voice dripping with a lethal combination of honey and venom. "Carmela's not moving back here. She's putting the Garden District house up for sale."

Glory clutched a hand at her bosom, as if she'd felt the first painful stirrings of a cardiac infarction. "What? What?" she shrilled, in a pained, hysterical tone of voice. "You're *selling* the house?"

"She sure is," Ava chortled. It wasn't often she had a chance to drive a stake through Glory's heart, and Ava was relishing every single minute of it.

"This can't be happening," Glory spat out. Her face had turned ashen and her left eye twitched uncontrollably. "This is . . . catastrophic!"

Glory's theatrics were so over the top, Carmela had to fight hard to keep a straight face. "Glory, surely this news isn't coming

329

at you like a bolt from the blue. I'm positive Shamus mentioned the possibility of my selling the house." In fact, Carmela was pretty sure she'd had this same conversation with Glory a couple of months ago. With pretty much the same hysterical reaction.

Glory shook her head with unbound fury. Amazingly, her helmet of hair barely moved. Carmela figured Glory must be gelled and shellacked in perpetuity.

"No, no!" cried Glory. "This home sale comes as a complete shock to me!" Her voice trembled with anger fueled by outrage. "If I'd known you were going to *sell* it, I never would have agreed to the terms of your divorce."

"Sure you would," said Ava. "Because it was *her* divorce, not yours."

"Does Shamus know about this . . . um . . . impending sale?" asked Glory.

Carmela was getting tired of playing this little game. Selling the Garden District house, which was legally hers, had been discussed ad nauseam. By any and all parties concerned. "Of course Shamus knows," said Carmela. "And, truth be told, he really doesn't care that much." The Meechum family owned three other homes nearby, and Shamus hadn't shown much interest in any of them. Since he'd reverted to his bachelor ways, he'd moved into a bachelor apartment. Doorman, cleaning lady once a week, neighbors who included lots of single ladies.

"That home is his birthright!" hissed Glory.

Carmela glanced up, certain Glory's ferocity was going to cause the overhead chandelier to come tinkling down upon them. Luckily, it was only swaying slightly.

"The divorce is signed, sealed, and duly recorded with the State of Louisiana," said Carmela. "The Garden District house is mine, free and clear, to do with what I want."

"Have you no heart?" Glory muttered. She snatched up her dessert plate; hastily piled on cookies, cakes, and bread pudding; then grabbed a double slice of rhubarb torte and toddled away.

"Apparently not," said Carmela. "But at least I'm not testing the boundaries of coronary disease."

Still, the evening remained rife with conflict. Because, upon seeing Glory's grumpy departure, Rain Monroe circled back to the dining room to have another go at Carmela.

"It's bad enough you're here," snarled Rain. "But to bring your trampy friend

331

along — shame on you."

"I'm guessing," said Carmela, "that your rather uncharitable reference is to Ava here?"

Rain gave an acknowledging shrug.

"Aw," said Ava, "and here I was afraid you hadn't even noticed me. Boo-hoo."

"Ava's a guest in Baby's home," said Carmela, trying to remain calm. "As such, she should be accorded the utmost courtesy."

This time Rain let loose an audible snort.

"And since we have a moment before the meeting begins," said Carmela, "I'd like to talk to you about a couple of things."

"What do you mean?" Rain demanded. She'd gone from looking outraged to being fidgety.

"You're on the board at St. Tristan's," said Carmela. It was a statement, not a question.

Rain's nod was almost imperceptible.

Carmela dove in. "Monday morning, the morning Byrle was killed, did Brother Paul appear at your board meeting?"

Rain plucked an imaginary piece of lint from her dress. "What's it to you?"

Carmela tried to ignore Rain's rudeness. "Was he requesting funding for the Storyville Outreach Center?"

Now Rain just looked bored. "He might have."

"Excuse me," said Carmela, "this information isn't exactly a closely guarded state secret. Either he did or he didn't. Now which is it?"

"He did," said Rain, "but the board turned him down flat. Brother Paul's work just didn't align with our interests."

"Charity isn't one of your interests?" Carmela asked, her tone bitingly crisp. Then she directed her gaze toward Ava and inclined her head sideways. A signal for Ava to leave her alone with Rain. Ava's brows shot up in surprise, but after a few seconds she slipped away.

"You know what I mean," said Rain, backpedaling a little, trying not to look like a complete philistine. "We're a poor parish, still fighting the bouts of a bad recession. We can't be expected to fund every little thing."

"Whatever," said Carmela. "Next question. Since you're an influential board member at St. Tristan's, I was wondering if you could find it in your heart to have Ava reinstated?"

Rain clenched her jaw so hard, Carmela could hear her mandibles click.

"Are you serious?" was Rain's terse reply.

"Dead serious," said Carmela. She'd made up her mind to be polite to a fault, but no way was she going to wheedle or beg. This was just a simple request.

"Not a chance," Rain spat out. She paused to gather a small amount of outrage, then said, "Do you know what she *does?*"

"Of course," said Carmela. "Ava helps dust benches and altars at St. Tristan's. Sometimes she brings in fresh flower arrangements and passes out palm branches on Palm Sunday."

"She runs a voodoo shop!" Rain shrilled. "How do you think that looks?"

"Are you serious?" said Carmela, trying hard to contain her rapidly building fury. "Half the people in New Orleans have been through Ava's shop. Buying crazy things for their Mardi Gras or Halloween parties. It's basically a gift shop with saint candles and harmless little red silk bags filled with aromatic herbs and spices. The kind you probably stuff inside your turkey every Thanksgiving."

"And now she's got a psychic working there!" spat out Rain. "A woman who purports to tell fortunes! Who claims she can see into the great beyond!"

"What do you want me to do?" asked Carmela. "Report Ava to the paranormal police?"

Rain glared as she fingered the silver cross that was strung around her neck on a black silk cord. "You have to understand, Carmela, I'm a very devout person."

"Then as a charitable act, could you please . . . ?"

"No!" screamed Rain, and this time a few people turned to look at them. "No," Rain said, dialing back the volume. "That's never going to happen."

After all the contentious rankling, the meeting itself was practically an afterthought. Baby sat primly and took copious notes, ducking her head from time to time to whisper questions to Carmela. Ava drifted in and out, almost always with a full glass of champagne in hand. A gaggle of old money and nouveau riche haggled over allocations of money to theater groups, dance companies, and artist consortiums. Once they'd drawn up a sort of short list, they began arguing about amounts. Finally, at ten o'clock, with amounts still not decided and not much accomplished in the way of fostering the arts, the committee chairman thanked everyone for their hard work and declared the meeting over.

"Thank goodness," said Carmela, as they

headed for her car. The cool air felt welcome and refreshing, even though little splotches of rain had started to plop down again.

"Thanks for talking to Rain," said Ava, as they both walked along, stiff-legged and a little hunched over from sitting so long. "At least you scored an *A* for effort."

"Little good it did us," said Carmela, pulling open the driver's-side door and hopping in.

Ava folded her long legs into the passenger seat. "Still, you gave it a shot."

"Rain says she's upset over the voodoo thing," said Carmela. "Claims she's very religious."

"Maybe Rain is religious like Mel Gibson's religious," said Ava. She twirled a finger next to her ear. "A little . . . over the edge."

Carmela drove slowly down Third Street, then turned onto Annunciation. "We'll be back here tomorrow," she murmured. She wasn't looking forward to the photo shoot one bit. Even though scrapbooking was all about displaying photos in exciting, creative ways, she pretty much dreaded being the subject of a photo. Probably, Carmela decided, that discomfort harked back to third grade and a disastrous school picture that had made her look like a scrawny kid with spiky, artichoke-inspired hair. Then again, maybe everyone had a bad class picture experience buried deep down inside their flawed childhood psyche.

They hit Jackson, then hung a right on Rousseau and bumped along near the river. Carmela's father had made his living working on river barges. And even though he'd been killed many years ago, she still felt a certain kinship with this industrial, riverfront part of New Orleans. Maybe, out there in the spirit realm, her father's ghost still hovered, keeping a watchful eye on Mississippi barge traffic.

"Spooky over here," said Ava. "All these dark, lurking warehouses."

"It's just the industrial side of New Orleans," said Carmela, as her little car skirted a pothole. "After all, we're a major port city that moves five hundred tons of cargo every year."

"The stuff tourists never see," said Ava. "Oh man!" she squeaked, as they rattled over another stretch of bumps and potholes. "You could bust an axle on this road." New Orleans's streets were notorious for being pebbled, pocked, and pitted, and this route seemed to sport more potholes than autos.

Carmela glanced up sharply and squinted into her rearview mirror. "I just wish that jerk would stop tailgating us."

"Maybe it's the protective tail Babcock put on you," Ava suggested.

Carmela had practically forgotten about the police tail. She'd been far more concerned with business at her shop, Brother Paul's murder, and Baby's arts meeting.

"Maybe it's somebody cute," said Ava. She shook her hair back and let loose a girlish giggle. "Nothing like a tall, dark, handsome man in uniform."

"Unless he's in plainclothes," said Carmela.

"I can take care of his clothes," grinned Ava.

"Probably," said Carmela, "it's some poor schlump who's simply driving home after a hard day at work."

Ava swiveled in her seat. "He is following close."

"He sure is." Carmela touched her toe to her brake pedal. She knew if her brake lights flared, the average person's response would be to hit their brakes and drop back.

This guy stuck like a burr.

"Who is that?" she wondered aloud.

"Somebody *really* following you?" asked Ava. She digested this for a millisecond, then said, "Following us?"

"I hope not," said Carmela, just as the

heavens seemed to open and spill down a torrent of rain.

"Yipes!" Ava cried, as rain pinged furiously on the roof of the car and sloshed across the windshield in undulating waves. Carmela's windshield wipers were suddenly working overtime, barely keeping up. "This downpour oughta make him back off," she added.

But the car following closely behind them didn't back off one iota.

"Doggone," said Carmela, fighting to make out the boundaries of the road while still managing a quick glance in the mirror. "I think that idiot is going to . . ."

Crunch! Metal scraped against metal.

"Hit us!" Carmela cried. "Doggone, he *did* hit us!"

"Tapped your bumper, anyway," said Ava. "He probably lost sight of us in this downpour." She leaned forward and peered out the front window. "Hard to see anything out there!" Ava gathered part of her sleeve in her hand and wiped at the window.

Carmela reached down and flipped her defroster to high.

"Better," said Ava.

But it wasn't. Not really.

Once again the car approached them from behind and nudged against Carmela's back

339

bumper. Harder this time.

A little shot of adrenaline squirted through Carmela's body, pushing her into fight-or-flight alert. She reacted instantly by tromping down hard on the accelerator. Everything inside her told her to shake this guy, to try to lose him.

"Holy moly!" Ava cried, "that was intentional! He wants to run us off the road!"

Carmela accelerated into a turn. "Try to read his license plate, okay?"

Ava turned and squinted as the car spun through the turn with them. "I can't quite make it out; he's just far enough back and it's raining too hard."

"Okay, then peek out the back window and see if you can figure out what kind of car it is." If she could get the model and make, she could call in a report to the police. *Yes, the police. Where are they? Where's the security tail Babcock supposedly arranged? Taking a break? Just when I need them most?*

Ava pulled her knees up and swiveled around in her seat again. Scrunched up and hanging over the back of the seat, she peered out the back window. "It's, like, really big and black."

"Like an SUV?" Carmela edged her speed up to forty-five. Off to her right, dingy

340

warehouses flew by.

Ava shook her head. "No, I think it's a regular car."

"What's the make? Can you tell?"

"Uh, maybe a Ford?"

"You sure about that?" *Who do I know drives a big black Ford? Basically . . . nobody.*

"Or," said Ava, "it could be a . . . BMW?"

"Ava, there's a world of difference between a Ford and a BMW!"

Ava swung back around, frustrated. "Not to me there isn't! Last I looked, I wasn't a contributing editor to *Car and Driver.* All I care about is if a car gets me from point A to point B."

"Well, whoever's trying to cream my bumper," said Carmela, "means business!" The car was about thirty feet behind them now, but was steadily keeping pace.

"Can't you lose them?" asked Ava, pulling her seat belt across and snapping it closed. "Or, better yet, lay down a spray of tacks or an oil slick?"

"Only if I were James Bond or Batman," said Carmela. "But I'm gonna try to outrun him." Carmela cranked her wheel hard, sending them into a tight turn down Tchoupitoulas. "Maybe we can lose them along here," she cried, the Mississippi hard on their right.

"Lordy, Lordy," mewled Ava. "Tell me we're not gonna do a Thelma and Louise and jump this car into the river!"

"Not a chance," said Carmela. She cranked her steering wheel hard again and flew down Felicity. Somewhere ahead, she knew there was a little café with a narrow cobblestone alley running directly behind it. Her Mercedes was small and nimble and cornered like a race car. If she could hit that turn and slip down the alley, she could outmaneuver this joker once and for all!

"You gained a pretty good lead on that last turn," said Ava, whipping her head around, "but he's still following." She gulped. "Oops, coming on stronger now."

"Not for long," Carmela muttered, through clenched teeth. She blinked and poked her head forward, searching frantically for that café. But all she saw was darkness, plunging trees, and rain slashing down. "Gotta be here," she muttered, unless she was completely turned around in her directions.

"He's pulling closer," said Ava, fear tingeing her voice.

Carmela ground her teeth together in frustration. If only she could . . .

Suddenly, she spotted the colorful purple-and-orange painted sign of the Xanadu

Café. Here was her chance to outmaneuver and outsmart this creep! Wrenching the steering wheel, she bumped the right side of her car up and over the curb, jolting them hard, like the starting jerk of a roller coaster. Then Carmela was pretty much driving straight down the cracked sidewalk, her car pointed directly at a dejected banana tree and five small wrought-iron tables that made up Xanadu's outdoor café. The closer she came, the harder she gunned her engine.

"You're gonna hit . . . !" Ava cried.

Carmela's front bumper missed the tables by inches and, instead, dinged the tall, metal outdoor heater. The six-foot-high heater teetered back and forth on its base like a giant sippy cup, and then Carmela slipped by and was bumping hard down the alley. Directly behind her, the outdoor heater toppled over and clattered against the cobblestones, forming a nifty, temporary barricade.

A metallic crunch rang out as the black car smacked nose first against the fallen heater, then came to an abrupt, jouncing stop.

"Holy Coupe de Ville!" came Ava's excited shriek. "You did it!"

CHAPTER 23

A web of photographer's lights and alumi-
num stands formed a cluttered, shiny barricade in the living room of Carmela's
Garden District house. Accompanying
hoods, snoods, scrims, and battery packs
were scattered everywhere. Off in the dining room, a professional makeup artist had
set up a temporary studio on Carmela's
heirloom dining room table. Palettes of eye
shadow, blush, and highlighter glistened in
sparkly, almost Crayola-like colors.

"You call this low key?" Carmela gasped.
She sat ramrod stiff in a chair, bare face
tilted upward as if in supplication, a towel
draped across her front and shoulders.
Besides Jilly, the hair and makeup artist
who'd just begun working on her, Jekyl and
Ava hovered nearby. The photographer, his
assistant, and a lighting guy popped strobe
lights and conferred over test shots.

Gazing at Carmela's unhappy, naked face,

Jekyl muttered, "Thank goodness I hired Jilly."

"She doesn't look half bad," observed Ava. "Dab a little concealer under her eyes and they'll brighten right up."

"She's got great bone structure," Jilly told them, "so I intend to play that up." Jilly looked exactly like you'd imagine a movie makeup artist would look. Slat thin, spiked blond hair, eyeliner (guyliner?), tight white T-shirt, designer jeans, and an upper arm covered with elaborate tribal tattoos.

"That's right," said Carmela, hating all the fuss, knowing it would only get worse once the photographer started shooting. "Go ahead and talk about me like I'm not even here."

"Sorry, love," said Jilly, as he twiddled a brush.

"So let's just spackle my face and get it over with." Carmela sounded just this side of cranky.

Jilly leaned forward, a sympathetic look on his face. "What do you usually use?" he asked. He had a slightly high, crackly voice.

"Just a little foundation and mascara," Carmela told him.

Jilly poured a puddle of light beige liquid into his hand. "But we're making you up for the camera lens, which reads differently than the human eye. So we'll have to go a little more dramatic, a little more extreme."

"Which means what?" asked Carmela, finally favoring him with a half-smile. For some reason, she felt she could trust this young man with his endearing, crackly voice.

Jilly took a wedge-shaped sponge and began daubing makeup onto Carmela's face. "First I'll do a light base coat to even out the skin tone, then I'll apply foundation and a few dabs of highlighter."

"Sounds like an artist gessoing a canvas," Carmela observed.

"That's a fun analogy," said Jilly, working swiftly.

"And don't forget eyeliner," said Ava, hovering close by. "Give her lots and lots of eyeliner and mascara."

"But no tarantula eyes," said Carmela, glancing at Ava as Jilly continued to daub away. Ava could sometimes overdo it on mascara.

"No tarantula," Ava agreed. "For you, just — kaboom — big, dramatic eyes!"

Minutes later, Jekyl bustled in, holding up two long dresses that swished and rustled in his arms. "I took the liberty of bringing along a couple of gowns for you to choose from." One gown looked like liquid pewter; the other was a midnight-blue velvet.

This was news to Carmela. "I can't wear what I have on?"

Jekyl rolled his eyes. "Sweetie, c'mon. You're wearing beige slacks and a sweater. How let's-drive-to-the-mall-in-the-minivan is that?"

"Camel," Carmela said, in an insistent tone. "Not beige. Camel is very in this season."

Jekyl let loose a deep sigh and said, deadpan, "Yawn."

"Not *yawn*," said Carmela. "Classic."

"Honey," said Jekyl, "the name of the magazine is *Delta Living*, not *Night of the Living Dead*."

Ava knelt at Carmela's side. "Just try the gowns, *cher*. I know one of them is going to look super fantastic on you!"

"And pin a little extra hair on her, too," Jekyl advised.

Carmela's hands flew to her head. "What!" she squawked. "Now I need hair?"

"Couldn't hurt," said Jilly.

Ava nodded sagely. "There isn't a woman alive who couldn't use a little extra hair."

Carmela narrowed her eyes and peered at Ava's flowing locks. "You've got extra hair pinned in?"

Ava held an index finger to her lips, as if it were a secret worthy of the Knights Templar. "Just three or four little ol' extensions. But when it's a major occasion, like Halloween or Mardi Gras, watch out! Then I go for the full lioness look!"

"Perfection!" Jekyl declared, when Carmela's hair and makeup was finally finished.

"You think?" Carmela gazed into the smoked mirror on the breakfront, not recognizing the exotic-looking woman who stared back at her. She'd been transformed into a creature with big doe eyes, a pouty mouth, and a wild mane of hair.

"Oh yeah," said Jekyl, impressed, "a terrific makeover."

"I think I'd rather just go home now," said Carmela.

"Not gonna happen," said Ava, happily. "Now it's time to play dress-up."

Jekyl tugged on Carmela's arm. "Come on, lovey, slip into one of these gowns, then come and meet Twig. He's in the parlor, doing a final lighting check."

"What's a Twig?" asked Carmela.

"The photographer," said Jekyl. "Twig Dillon. Surely you've heard of him?"

Carmela shook her head. "Sorry. No."

"Goodness," said Jekyl, taking a deep breath, "Twig's just about the most creative and wildly popular photographer in New Orleans today. Seriously, the man's an absolute genius!"

Turns out, Twig wasn't just a genius photographer, he was a nice guy, too.

"Photography isn't just about me and the camera," Twig explained to Carmela. "Ninety percent of my energy is expended in front of the lens, while maybe ten percent is spent behind the lens."

Curious, Carmela said, "What do you mean? Explain, please."

"The most important job for a photographer is to put his subject completely at ease," said Twig. "Because any discomfort or nervousness will be reflected in their face and body language."

"I can understand that," said Ava. "Of course, I'm always comfortable in my body."

"Say I shoot the CEO of a company," Twig continued. "I chat him up a bit, get him talking about the big deals he's working on, and then ask him to point his belly button toward the Mississippi."

"You disarm him," said Carmela.

"Sort of," said Twig. "But mostly, I try to establish a sense of trust." He took Carmela's arm, guided her over to where he'd closed a set of blue velvet curtains, and posed her accordingly. "I like that pewter dress, by the way. Makes the color of your eyes more vivid."

"Is this part of making me feel comfortable?" asked Carmela.

"Yes and no," said Twig. "From my perspective, you already look comfortable."

"You're good," said Carmela.

They tried a few shots in front of the curtains, then reclining on the fainting couch. Then Twig moved Carmela in front of the fireplace.

"The fireplace," said Jekyl, knowingly, "that's the best pose yet."

"Maybe rest one hand on your hip and the other on the mantel," Ava suggested. "Try to look casually elegant."

Carmela lifted her hand and felt the tickle of dust on the mantel. She grimaced.

"And lift your chin slightly," Jekyl coached. "Ah, perfection!" he declared, as the shutter snapped and blinding light exploded in Carmela's eyes.

"Can we try that again?" asked Carmela. "I think I . . . blinked."

"Just look this way, sweetheart," said Twig. "And relax your face — no, now you're scrunching. Just think serene thoughts, but don't be afraid to give me a little attitude, too."

"Let the fierceness emanate from your eyes," said Ava. "Think starving super-model. Pretend you've been living on Red Bull and cigarettes for the last three weeks."

"And that you're jet-lagged from too many trips to Paris and Milan," added Jekyl. "Think . . . Kate Moss!"

And then Twig was at her side, talking to her, coaching her to tilt her head a certain way, showing her how to relax her shoulders and just go with the flow.

"Just remember," said Twig, "when you want to dissipate tension, put your lips together and make a long, drawn-out hum."

"What does that do?" asked Carmela.

"Any kind of humming resonates in your nose, mouth, and upper jaw," Twig told her. "And causes instant relaxation."

Carmela tilted her head, gently put her lips together, and smiled. "Yummmm. Hummmm."

"Perfect!" declared Twig.

"Fantastic!" said Jekyl. "To the manor born."

But Carmela didn't feel like she'd been born with a silver spoon in her mouth. "I'm not totally confident with this pose," she told Twig. "It feels more like the posture of a madam."

"Nothing wrong with that," Ava chuckled.

"There's *everything* wrong with that," Carmela shot back.

Twenty minutes later it was all over. Carmela was back in her own clothes, though her hair and makeup were still amazingly exotic.

"Will this last until tonight?" Ava asked Jilly. "I mean, Carmela's hair and makeup?"

Jilly gave a vigorous nod. "Between the multiple layers of makeup and hair spray, her look should actually last several days. That's if she sleeps upright in a chair," he added.

"See, hon?" cooed Ava. "You're already perfectly coiffed and made up for the wine-tasting event tonight."

"So there really is an upside to all of this," said Carmela. She strolled back into the parlor, where Twig, his assistant, and the lighting guy were busy packing up. "Thanks so much," Carmela said to Twig. She gave a little wave. "To all of you."

"Here," said Twig, handing her a large black leather portfolio. "If you or your clients ever need a bit of photography, perhaps you'll . . . consider hiring me."

"This is your book?" Carmela asked. From her days as a designer, Carmela was familiar with what was termed in the industry as a *book*. It was generally a large loose-leaf portfolio with plastic sleeves that held samples of an artist's work. Books were commonly used to showcase photographers', designers', and illustrators' samples in hopes of generating future work.

"Besides photographing home interiors," Twig told her, "my bread and butter is pretty much portrait shots. You'd be surprised at how many wealthy women want their portraits done."

No, I wouldn't, thought Carmela. She'd visited countless Garden District and lakeside area homes where the common denominator was often an elaborately done portrait of the lady of the house, usually hung directly above the fireplace for guests to see and admire.

"A lot of women hit forty," said Twig, "and they think . . . Ooh, I need to memorialize this, because from here on it's all downhill."

"Which it really is," said Ava.

Carrying the book over to a wing chair, Carmela sat down and started flipping through it. Ten pages in, she came upon a dramatic black-and-white photo of Rain Monroe, posed next to a marble sculpture of an angel. "This is interesting," said Carmela, trying to keep her voice even, "you shot a portrait of Rain Monroe."

"Now she was an unusual subject," said Twig, coming over to join her. "Her dark hair was a tad difficult to light. But her face has lots of angles and planes."

"That's 'cause Rain's always in skinny-bitch mode," sniped Ava, from across the room. "Always starving herself to stay a size two."

"But, honey," said Twig, giving Ava a quick smile, "*you're* a size six, aren't you?"

Ava's face lit up. "You're right. I am."

"You did a great job," said Carmela, as she flipped to the next page. "Oh, here she is again and . . ."

Time suddenly stood still for Carmela as she focused on Rain, who was posed in a long, black, severe-looking dress. But it was the background that stunned Carmela. Directly behind Rain was a stark white wall hung with dozens of crucifixes.

Carmela tried to gather her thoughts. "This is . . . an unusual setting," she finally stammered out. "I take it this backdrop is of some significance to her?"

Twig gave the page a cursory glance. "For sure," he said. "Ms. Monroe has a huge collection of crosses." He let loose a discreet sniff. "In fact, she even fancies herself as some kind of amateur archaeologist."

"Really," said Carmela. "Isn't that interesting."

"Ready to go?" Ava called to Carmela. Carmela had been paging slowly through the rest of Twig's book, looking at photos but not really absorbing them. Her mind was whirring over Rain. Rain, who had been at St. Tristan's when Byrle was murdered. Rain, who, interestingly enough, collected crucifixes.

What did all this mean? Carmela wondered. That Rain was a highly religious person? That Rain had an odd sense of decorating? Or that Rain was a vicious, scheming, possibly murderous woman who would stop at nothing to add to her collection?

Carmela snapped the book closed, slipped out of her chair, and sprinted for the stairway.

"Where are you going?" Ava called after her. She was anxious to get moving. Their next stop was Lacy Lady, where she was supposed to get her first peek at Drew Gaspar's Voodoo Couture line.

Carmela spun around when she hit the landing and held up two fingers. "Two minutes," she called down to Ava. "I'll be back in two minutes."

Taking the rest of the stairs two at a time, Carmela hit the landing, then dashed into her old bedroom.

It hadn't changed one bit since Shamus had slipped into his boogie shoes and ducked out of their marriage. The big old sleigh bed still looked cushy and comfortable, the draperies plush and velvety, and the wavering baroque mirror on the opposite wall still gave the whole room a certain edgy elegance.

Carmela put her head down and tried to steel herself from thinking about the moments she and Shamus had shared together in that old sleigh bed — the languid mornings and lush evenings. Instead, she stepped into her walk-in closet, flipped on the light, and looked around. A half-dozen dresses still hung there. Old evening gowns, left over from happier, more carefree times when she'd attended formal parties with Shamus, as well as the Pluvius and Rex Mardi Gras balls. Now the gowns just looked sad and forlorn in a spooky, Miss Haversham sort of way. Probably, they were completely out of style, too.

Carmela dropped to her knees and bent forward. Running her hands across the cushy, cream-colored carpet, she felt around for a few moments. Finally, the tips of her fingers located the seam she knew was there. She gently peeled back the carpet and gazed at the floor. Set into the narrow wooden floorboards was a small metal safe, something Shamus had installed for her in their first rapturous weeks of marriage. His rationale had been that it would be a safe place to keep her good jewelry. Interestingly, not a lot of precious gems, diamonds, or gold had been forthcoming in those early years. So, instead, it evolved into a place to stick her passport, a couple of emergency fifties, and a few mementos.

Spinning the combination — her birth year — Carmela heard a soft click as the tumbler fell into place. Open sesame. She raised the metal lid and gazed inside. She'd long since removed her money, passport, and small cache of jewelry, but had left her gun. A small revolver that, once upon a time, back in their married years, Shamus had given to her for protection and that she'd never had to use.

The gun was small, dull gray, and ugly. Probably Shamus had forgotten all about it. But Carmela hadn't. She hesitated for a moment, then reached down and picked it up between her thumb and forefinger. Gingerly, as if she were handling a dead mouse, she dropped the gun into her purse. A small

box of bullets tumbled in after it.
   Just in case.

CHAPTER 24

"That was fairly weird," said Carmela. They were speeding down Magazine Street, her foot pressed hard against the accelerator, as if she were trying to outrun the memories of this morning's photo shoot.

"Oh yeah," said Ava. "But really great." She tapped her bright red nails against the dashboard. "Wish I could do a photo shoot like that."

"I meant the photos of Rain Monroe," said Carmela.

Ava ducked her head and squinted at Carmela. "You think Rain had something to do with Byrle's death?"

"I'm not sure what to think anymore."

"I can see her clobbering poor Byrle," said Ava. "Maybe she didn't intend to actually *kill* Byrle, but things just got out of hand." She gave a self-satisfied nod. "So it's still technically murder."

"Do you think Rain killed Brother Paul,

too?" asked Carmela.

"She would if she thought we were following a trail and were getting too close," said Ava. "Plus she collects crucifixes. And she's crazy."

"Just because Rain collects crucifixes doesn't mean she's crazy," said Carmela, backpedaling a little. "I mean, lots of people have religious icons in their home." She knew that Jekyl had a large statue of St. Stephen in his parlor and an enormous black wrought-iron candelabra in his dining room. Both had been deacquisitioned from churches.

"I think Rain's crazy," said Ava, "because she really *is* crazy. If that makes any sense."

"Some," said Carmela.

"So," said Ava, "if Rain moves to the head of the line as far as suspects go, would that mean you're less down on Drew Gaspar?"

Carmela lifted her shoulders in an imperceptible shrug. "I guess I'm just taking a wait-and-see attitude."

"And you're waiting for . . . what?" asked Ava.

"I don't know," said Carmela. "All I hope is we don't . . ."

"There it is!" Ava squealed, cutting off Carmela's sentence. "Lacy Lady!" Lacy Lady was one of the newer boutiques that had sprung up along Magazine Street, a colorful, cosmopolitan part of the city where art galleries, trendy restaurants, and clothing boutiques were clustered.

Carmela nosed her car into an empty parking spot on the street. "Okay," she said, as the engine ticked down. "Let's hope this all works out for you."

Ava gave a lopsided grin. "I just hope everything fits!"

"We're the first shop to carry the Voodoo Couture line," cooed Sally Barnes, the manager of the small, well-edited boutique. Sally had long blond hair and dressed bohemian chic, which meant she wore a skintight tank top and a filmy, flowing designer skirt with her sky-high Manolos.

"And how many pieces in the collection so far?" asked Ava. She was fairly quivering with anticipation.

"Twenty," said Sally, as she led them past tables piled with cashmere sweaters and silk scarves. "But I expect Voodoo Couture will take off like crazy once the company has its official launch."

"What does an official launch entail?" asked Carmela.

"Dozens of different components," said Sally. "But, most importantly, the line needs to have a national network of sales reps, garner some favorable press in the trade papers, and stage an industry-centric fashion show. It doesn't have to be at New York's Fashion Week, but it certainly should be at some of the regional venues."

"And I'd be the muse," chortled Ava.

"You'll have to excuse my friend," said Carmela. "As you can see, she's head over heels."

"Can't say I blame her," said Sally.

As Carmela scanned the racks and shelves at Lacy Lady, she was reminded of a sparkling little jewel box. There were racks of Cosabella lingerie, trays of enormous statement rings, fluttering silk scarves, stacks of True Religion jeans, James Perse T-shirts, racks of elegant evening gowns, a rack of colorful faux furs, and a table filled with long leather gloves and Miu Miu purses.

"You have a very tasty selection," Carmela told Sally.

"Tantalizing," said Ava. A scarlet peignoir with matching froufrou mules had caught her eye.

"Thank you," said Sally. "We like to think of ourselves as a carefully edited shop for women with refined taste."

"And you carry all my favorites," trilled Ava. "Gucci, Pucci, and Fiorucci."

"And she can rap, too," laughed Carmela.

"A lady who knows her labels," said Sally, smiling.

"Usually," said Ava, "we shop down the block at The Latest Wrinkle." She leaned in closer to Sally and said in a stage whisper, "The resale shop."

"Hey," said Sally, brightening, "that's a terrific place. I picked up a vintage Ungaro jacket there not so long ago."

"Well . . . yeah!" cheered Ava.

"You ready to try things on?" asked Sally.

"Just show me the dressing room!" said Ava.

Sally fingered the Voodoo Couture rack. "What size?"

"A California extra-large," said Ava.

Sally paused. "Pardon?"

"That would be a size six," said Carmela. "Ava's idea of a little joke."

"Yes," agreed Sally, "some of those ladies who live in Bel Air and Beverly Hills are quite tiny."

While Ava sequestered herself in a dressing room, Carmela pulled out her cell phone and dialed Babcock's number.

"Hey," she said, when she got him on the line. "Just wondering what's going on." She was referring, of course, to the two murder investigations.

But Babcock pretty much brushed off her question.

"What are you up to?" he asked.

"I just finished that photo shoot I told you about," said Carmela.

"Now you're a big star," said Babcock. "You won't want to hang around a poor civil servant like me."

"Not to worry," said Carmela. "But what I really called about was — do you still have a tail on me?"

"Of course," said Babcock. "Why?" He was instantly on alert. "Is there a problem? Did something happen?"

Carmela weighed his words for about a millisecond, then decided not to tell him about the car that followed her last night. She didn't want to get his officer in trouble, and she didn't want him to clamp down on her activities for the rest of the day. After all, the wine-tasting event was tonight.

"No problem really," said Carmela. "I'm just sort of . . . checking in."

"Why don't you blow off this thing tonight?" he said to her. "And we'll go out. I'll call in a marker or two and line up a table at Galatoire's. We can enjoy some oysters en brochette or the crabmeat Yvonne. What do you say?"

Carmela wanted to say yes, she really did.

But when she promised someone she'd do something, she always kept her word. "Not tonight," she told Babcock. "I've got to see this event through."

"And then you're done with it?" asked Babcock. What he really meant was, *And then you're done with Quigg Brevard?*

"Yes," said Carmela, wishing she'd never taken on Quigg's project. Wishing she hadn't phoned Babcock. "And then I'm done. It's all done." *Except, of course, for solving Byrle's murder.*

"Excellent."

"I feel like . . . you're not sharing any information about the two murders," said Carmela.

Babcock's voice went quiet. "Probably because there isn't a lot of information to share."

"You're keeping me out intentionally," she said. Not in an accusing tone, just stating the fact.

Babcock countered with, "Don't you think you're in enough trouble already?"

"Well, no. Not really," said Carmela.

"Good-bye, Carmela," said Babcock.

"Carmela!" came Ava's excited voice. "Come take a look at this!"

Carmela hit the Off button on her phone and spun around to face Ava.

"You like?" asked Ava, striking a pose in front of the three-way mirror.

"Wow," said Carmela. Ava was swanning around in a long black velvet gown with a strip of jet beads accenting the semi-plunging neckline. "Are all the pieces so Goth?"

"No, absolutely they're not," said Sally. "In fact, most of them are quite appropriate for day."

"Sure, if you happen to be taking tea at Carfax Abbey," Carmela murmured in a voice so low neither Ava nor Sally could hear. Then again, the line was called Voodoo Couture and not Suits for Ladies Who Lunch. So . . . whatever.

As Ava emerged from the dressing room wearing a short red dress, Carmela's cell phone beeped. Babcock calling back? With an apology? She gave the phone a querulous look and pushed On.

"Carmela," came a high-pitched voice.

"Yes?" said Carmela. She crossed a thread-worn Oriental rug and slid behind a rack of fur and brocade-trimmed jean jackets, the better for privacy.

"It's Devon. Devon Dowling. I called your shop, but your assistant said you were out and about."

"What's up?" she asked. A tingle suddenly

slid down her spine.

"All this nasty rain has substantially cut into my walk-in traffic," complained Devon. "So I took some time this morning to look through my customer cards. You know, like we talked about?"

"Yes, Devon?" Had he actually found something?

"Because you wanted to know about people who were interested in . . ."

"Religious icons," finished Carmela. "That's right."

"Does the name Frank Crowley mean anything to you?" asked Devon.

"The Seekers," Carmela muttered to herself. "Yes, Devon," she said. "That name does mean something to me." *And,* she thought to herself, *it just might be connected to two murder investigations.*

So, of course Carmela immediately got Babcock back on the phone.

"Here's the thing," she told him. "I just spoke with Devon Dowling, the antiques dealer down the street from me. And he came up with Frank Crowley's name in his customer cards." Silence spun out for a few moments, then she said, "Frank Crowley, from the Seekers?"

"We've already spoken with him," said

Babcock. "He gave us the names of twenty people who swear he was with them that entire night. At their meeting hall or whatever it is out on Trempeleau Road."

"Did you actually talk to any of these people?"

"Obviously, we did," said Babcock.

"But they're *followers*," Carmela sputtered. "They're like, 'Let's drink the Kool-Aid and say whatever Crowley tells us to say.' "

"I think you're way off the mark on this one," said Babcock.

"You don't see Crowley as a suspect?" said Carmela. "Seriously?"

"If he is, he's a long shot," said Babcock. "And I rarely put my money on long shots."

"Okay," said Carmela, "what about Rain Monroe?"

"What about her?"

"Did you know she has a collection of crucifixes?"

"No, I did not," said Babcock.

"Well, she does," said Carmela. "Don't you find that highly unusual?"

"In this town," said Babcock, "pretty much everyone and his brother-in-law is unusual. If I ran around arresting all the eccentrics and oddballs, our jails would be filled." He gave a low chuckle. "And I'd be out of a job."

"I'm going to figure this out, you know," Carmela told him. "I'm going to get to the bottom of Byrle's murder."

"Please," said Babcock. And now his voice sounded pained. "Please don't get any more involved than you already are."

"Excuse me," said Carmela, with some force. "The only way I could be any more involved is if I stumbled upon a *third* dead body!"

When Carmela finally swung by Memory Mine, her wine carriers were stacked neatly on the front counter, all wrapped, glued, and elegantly finished.

"Oh my gosh!" Carmela exclaimed. "They're all done?"

Two heads suddenly popped up from behind the row of wine carriers.

"You like 'em?" asked Gabby. She hooked a thumb and pointed at Marilyn Casey. "You can thank my cohort here. I wrapped and did the finishing work, but Marilyn did most of the gluing."

"I felt like I was back in kindergarten," Marilyn laughed, "licking white paste off my fingers."

"Oh, you darlings!" said Carmela. "You saved me so much work!"

369

"The shop wasn't all that busy," said Gabby, pleased that Carmela was pleased, "so why not?"

"And my writing hit a major roadblock," said Marilyn, "so I dropped by to see if there was anything new in your investigation and . . . poof . . . I got roped in."

"You volunteered!" said Gabby.

"Absolutely, I did," said Marilyn. "And had a fun time to boot. I'm going to have to stop by more often."

"Do that," said Carmela.

"Marilyn even helped write an invitation for one of our customers," said Gabby.

"It wasn't much," said Marilyn. "She just needed the right words to invite her friends to a holiday party."

"But it turned out really neat," said Gabby. "Almost poetic."

"Nothing like a real writer's touch," Carmela said to Marilyn. She sometimes wished she had the ability to pile up words on paper, too. Pen a mystery or even a romance.

"Don't I wish," said Marilyn. "I've got a whiz-bang outline for my mystery. But now I have no idea how to end it."

"Maybe," said Carmela, picking up one of the wine carriers and admiring the yellow tassel that Gabby had attached, "you just need to stick around and see what happens with the investigation."

Marilyn looked skeptical. "Just let it all unfold?"

"If it ever does," said Gabby.

"We can only hope," said Carmela.

CHAPTER 25

Black shiny limos slid up to the front door of the Belle Vie Hotel and cameras flashed as Carmela mumbled hasty thank-yous to the rain gods, whose benevolence had seemingly held off yet another downpour.

"This is going, great, huh?" asked Quigg. With his hair slicked back, dressed in a slim-cut tuxedo with a gold brocade cummerbund, he stood next to Carmela on the red carpet, looking dapper and elegant with a touch of Las Vegas showbiz tossed in for good measure.

"We lucked out," said Carmela, as one black limo pulled away and a white stretch limo swung in to take its place.

"Luck had nothing to do with it, sweetheart," said Quigg. "You made this happen."

"But it was a slam dunk from the get-go," Carmela told him, with an impish grin. "When you send out fancy invitations and invite people for free food and drinks and a chance at publicity, not many people are going to say no." She smoothed the skirt on her long dark blue taffeta skirt. Paired with a pale blue silk blouse, her outfit looked fancy and slightly formal but didn't restrict movement. And as she would be schmoozing close to one hundred fifty guests tonight, along with honchoing chefs, servers, and musicians, movement was of the essence.

"It's a party town," Quigg acknowledged, as they watched the preening guests. "Plus, you persuaded the media to turn out, too."

"Saturday night's a dead night newswise," Carmela told him. "So whatever print or broadcast crew is working, they're happy to come out to an event like this and then be invited to join the party."

"Is that what you're going to do? Invite them to join the party?"

"Sure," said Carmela. "Once our guests have all walked the red carpet and posed in front of the step-and-repeat." Besides hiring two professional photographers, Carmela was thrilled that crews from three TV stations and two newspapers had turned up. It was tantamount to a public relations coup!

Five minutes later, Ava arrived, squired by Jekyl and three of his friends. Copious air kisses were exchanged, Carmela was fawned over greatly, and then Jekyl and company headed inside to hit the food and drink.

"You look fabulous!" Carmela told Ava, who lingered in front of the step-and-repeat. Ava looked both high fashion and lethal in her black strapless gown with marabou trim at the bottom.

"Thank you," said Ava, pushing back massive waves of dark hair as she smiled demurely for the cameras.

"And why are you suddenly looking even more skinny?" Carmela whispered. "It's as if you dropped ten pounds in the last two hours. What's your secret? Some kind of magical mystery cleanse?"

"I owe it all to modern engineering," said Ava, running a palm slowly across her flat tummy. "I'm wearing three sets of Spanx."

"You're not!" said Carmela. She could barely squiggle into one pair, let alone three.

"Honey," said Ava, "if you bounced a quarter off my derriere right now, it would ricochet back and punch out your eye."

"Whatever you're wearing," laughed Carmela, "it works."

"Now," said Ava, lifting her chin and glancing about, "where are those TV cameras?"

The scene inside the Marquis Ballroom was one of excitement coupled with mad hilarity. The string quartet played a jazzed-up version of "Days of Wine and Roses." Madame Blavatsky, seated at a round table covered with a fringed paisley shawl, had already collected a discreet line of guests waiting to have their fortunes told. Bartenders at each of the four wine stations busily poured glasses of wine. And tiny hors d'oeuvres were being eagerly snapped up by everyone.

"Look at this party," squealed Ava, as they wandered through the ballroom. "Fantastic. You really pulled it off."

"Want to get a drink?" Carmela asked. "Along with the wine we're pouring here tonight, Quigg created a couple of wine cocktails, too."

Ava cocked her head to one side. "Cocktails are an art form and I consider myself a patron of the arts."

"Plus, you've got to try the food," Carmela urged. "Especially the lobster rolls and duck drummies. The Belle Vie went all out."

"Actually," said Quigg, suddenly appearing at their elbow, "Chef Rami went all out." He was accompanied by Chef Rami, wearing a pristine white jacket but without his trademark chef's hat. The chef beamed at Carmela and Ava.

"And this is Chef Rami?" asked Ava, sticking out a hand to greet him as she popped a drummy into her mouth.

"Nice to meet you," said Chef Rami, accepting her hand.

"Great food," Ava enthused, as she chewed.

"I've been secretly trying to woo Chef Rami away from here and get him to come work for me," said Quigg. "You know, he's a graduate of CIA."

Ava swallowed with a gulp and let loose an amused shiver. "Oooh, you used to be a spy?"

"Culinary Institute of America," Chef Rami told her. "The *other* CIA."

"Ah," said Ava. "The other one."

"By the way," Quigg said to Carmela, "I love that you brought in a psychic. It gives the whole event a very offbeat touch."

"Nothing like a string quartet and a psychic to get the party rolling," Ava chortled.

"Along with a boatload of wine," added Carmela. She slipped away from the group and surveyed the room. The media had finally swept in like a horde of marauding Mongols and were attacking two of the wine stations. But that was okay. They had dozens of cases of Bayou Sparkler and Sauvignon Silver. No way would this crowd drink their way through everything.

Looking around, Carmela also spotted plenty of restaurateurs and wine shop proprietors. Perfect. Couldn't be better. She knew they were pretty much the decision makers who'd make or break St. Tammany Vineyards. If they decided to stock Quigg's wines or add them to their wine lists, then he was pretty much guaranteed success. And if they didn't . . . well, maybe Quigg could let his wine age for a few years in a nice hot shed and go into the vinegar business.

"Carmela!" exclaimed a pretty African American woman. "Remember me?"

"Ardice!" said Carmela, giving her a quick hug. Ardice was midthirties, cute, and dressed in a tailored black cocktail dress. She was the business manager at St. Tammany Vineyards and also did the buying for the gift shop.

"Aren't you the PR whiz," said Ardice. "You even got some of our local media to show up."

"That was always the hopeful part of the plan," said Carmela, pleased that Ardice had noticed.

"That reporter for KBEZ," said Ardice, "the one with all the blond hair and Botox?"

"Kimber Breeze?" said Carmela.

"She kind of waylaid me outside," said Ardice. "She asked a couple questions about Quigg's wine, but I think she really wanted to know about you."

"Oh no," said Carmela, looking around. "Is she here?" All she needed was to have Kimber Breeze hijack this event. To shift attention from Quigg's wines to the murder investigations.

"She's here somewhere," said Ardice, her long gold earrings dangling, "so be careful!"

Carmela wandered past the Cabernet station, making sure things were running smoothly, then circled back to Madame Blavatsky's table. That was where she ran smack-dab into Ava, clinging to the arm of Drew Gaspar.

"Look who I found!" crowed Ava. "None other than handsome Mr. Gaspar, a partner in the very amazing Voodoo Couture line."

"Nice to see you again," said Carmela. She was friendly, but reserved.

"I was just telling Mr. Gaspar how much I enjoyed modeling his clothes this afternoon," said Ava.

"I wish I could have been there," said Gaspar, giving her a wink and a wide grin.

"I wish you could have been there, too," giggled Ava.

"Have you had a chance to taste any of

the St. Tammany wines yet?" Carmela asked.

Gaspar continued to grin at Ava. "Indeed, I have. Very fine quality. I wouldn't mind adding them to my wine list, such as it is."

"That's what we like to hear," said Carmela. She gave a business-friendly smile and said, "I take it you're still tinkering with food and wine for Purgatoria?"

"It's never ending," said Gaspar.

"And the décor?" she asked, thinking about the stolen crucifix.

"We can always find a niche or nook for another gargoyle or candlestick," said Gaspar, happily. "It's that kind of place."

"I'm sure it is," said Carmela. "By the way, our host tonight, Quigg Brevard, is spearheading a restaurateurs' food donation drive."

"He is?" said Ava.

Carmela was completely winging it now as her words poured out. "He's going to be asking restaurants to donate extra staples to the Storyville Outreach Center." She paused for a beat. "Does that interest you?" She watched for any flicker of familiarity and saw none. Either Gaspar was an exceedingly good liar or he'd never heard of the place.

"Count me in," said Gaspar. "I'm always willing to help out."

"Kind of you," said Carmela. "I'll be sure to pass that along to Quigg."

"Do that," said Gaspar. He whispered something in Ava's ear, then slipped away from her.

"You're getting close to him," said Carmela, in a slightly accusing tone. "You know that worries the heck out of me."

"He didn't *do* anything," said Ava. "Really. He's just a good guy. You wait and see. Any suspicions you have are completely unfounded."

"I hope so," said Carmela, as they threaded their way through the press of guests. Pretty much everyone had tasted each of the different wines by now, which added up to a whole lot of merriment.

Unfortunately, all of Carmela's feelings of accomplishment burst like a soap bubble when she ran smack-dab into Rain Monroe.

"Rain!" Carmela exclaimed. "What are you doing here?" Carmela was dismayed to see her, Rain being the killjoy that she was. And Ava, with a few drinks under her belt, might just decide to haul off and smack her.

Rain put a hand on her hip and postured grandly in her sleek ivory cocktail dress. "I came with Peter Johns, owner of Griffin Bistro."

"Wonderful," said Carmela, though her

words lacked enthusiasm. Ava just stood at Carmela's elbow, giving Rain a cold, calculating stare.

"Although," Rain continued in a bored tone, "I doubt we'll stay long." Now her true colors began to emerge as she shook her head and asked, "Have you actually *tasted* this wine?" Rain's upper lip curled in sublime distaste. "From St. Tammany Vineyards?"

"Yes, Rain, I have," said Carmela. "In fact, I organized this event."

"Too bad for you," Rain continued. "The Sauvignon is reminiscent of paint thinner, and please don't get me started on that presumptuous Cabernet."

"I'm sorry it's not to your liking," said Carmela, as Ava gave her a subtle nudge. "But, truth be told, we've been getting raves."

"I suppose there's no accounting for taste," Rain sniffed.

"You know, Rain," said Ava, her eyes glimmering wickedly, "that's a very interesting dress."

"Why . . . thank you," Rain said, startled by Ava's comment.

Ava took a step back, as if to study Rain's cocktail dress and matching clutch purse. "But I'm thinking that dress would look better with a black bag — over your head."

The look of pure shock on Rain's face was the delicious swirl of frosting on Carmela's evening.

Rain, on the other hand, let loose a howl. "Well, I never!" she cried, then flounced away, her heels clicking like angry castanets.

"Good one," said Carmela, giving Ava a discreet high five. "But why does she have this hunger inside that drives her to be so mean and snarky?"

"She's a lily-livered snake," Ava explained. "She slithers around, making observations that pretend to sound learned, but beneath it all she's just a tired old cottonmouth."

By ten o'clock the crowd had thinned considerably. By ten thirty, the event was virtually over. Only about a half-dozen hangers-on remained, chatting with Quigg as they continued to quaff glasses of wine. Even though Carmela hoped they were talking business, they probably weren't.

"My feet are killing me," Ava lamented, as they waited for the valet to bring Carmela's car around. "I've probably got at least a dozen hammertoes."

"You suddenly grew extra digits?"

Ava gave a lopsided grin. "Okay, smarty, ten hammertoes."

"That's what you get for wearing sky-high stilettos."

"Which, I might add, earned me invitations to three dinners and one concert."

Carmela peered down at Ava's shoes. "What do you know, they're even more magical than ruby slippers."

Just as they pulled away from the Belle Vie, the rain started up again.

"Right on cue," said Carmela.

"At least it didn't rain on your step-and-repeat."

"Why does that sound like a country-western song?" asked Carmela.

"Don't let it rain on my step-and-repeat," Ava sang with off-key gusto. "Don't want the party to go downbeat. Walkin' and talkin' and struttin' my stuff . . . am I really askin' that much?"

"Nice try, Dolly Parton."

"Doesn't work?"

"Um, let's say songwriting's not exactly your forte."

"Singing?"

"Let's say it's right up there with the one-hit wonders some of those Real Housewives recorded."

"Okay," said Ava, sinking back in her seat. " 'Nuff said." She was relaxed and sated from an evening of food, wine, and compliments. All in all, not a bad combination.

"Where did Jekyl and company run off to?" asked Carmela, as they spun down Bourbon Street. The blue, red, and yellow neon lights from the bars and clubs reflected brightly in the wet street, giving the illusion of a parallel universe. A universe that was probably just as rowdy and bawdy.

"He and his buddies went to this big party over in —" began Ava.

Her words were suddenly cut short by the earsplitting clang of a bell. A clang that spun out into a metallic hammering that sounded as if a gigantic alien spacecraft had just crash-landed.

"Holy angels!" cried Ava. "What was that?" The noise continued to reverberate like some kind of dour warning.

"I bet one of the church towers got hit by lightning," said Carmela. She was relieved they were in her car, grounded by four fat rubber tires.

"Do you think it was St. Tristan's?" asked Ava, her happy mood suddenly evaporating.

"I don't know," said Carmela, squinting at the road ahead. "Maybe."

"What if it's, like, some kind of ghostly warning from the netherworld?" said Ava. "Protesting Byrle's murder." She hesitated. "Or maybe the world's coming to an end?"

"Naw," said Carmela, as she turned and crept down her back alley. "That's not going to happen for a long, long time."

Rain continued to pound down as they scurried across the courtyard, heading for Carmela's front door.

Ten feet away, they heard the dogs barking frantically. Deep, angry, if-I-could-just-sink-my-teeth-into-you barks.

"Sounds like something got them riled," said Ava. "Maybe that bell scared the livin' —"

"Oh crap," said Carmela, as they ducked beneath the overhang that stuck out above her front door. "Somebody left a note."

"Maybe Babcock?" Ava asked, as they huddled together. "What's it say?"

Carmela reached up and grabbed the note that had been tucked in the metal grating. As she touched heavy, crisp paper, she was also aware of something wet and sticky.

"What's that dripping from the note?" asked Ava. "Ink that smeared?"

Carmela held the note under the faint light of the outside brass lamp. Something red had stained her fingers and smeared the note. She gaped at the mess, not quite believing what she saw. "I . . . I think it's blood."

"What!" yelped Ava. "Jeez . . . that's crazy

creepy!" Her eyes were huge and darting from side to side. "What's the note say?" She made a nervous hand gesture.

Carmela flipped open the bloodied note and read it. Color drained from her face. "It says — *You've been warned.*"

"Holy chimichanga!" said Ava. "Who would write . . . ?" Her words ended as a strangled choke. "Who would smear their own *blood* on something like this?"

Carmela stared into the darkness of the courtyard, wondering if someone might be lurking in the swirl of shadows, just on the other side of the archway. "I don't know," she said, slowly. "Probably . . . a crazy person?"

CHAPTER 26

So, of course, they were once again forced to call Babcock.

"Well, this is fairly bizarre," he told them, as he stood dripping on Carmela's carpet, studying the strange note. "Obviously, you've stepped down hard on someone's toes."

"Carmela wouldn't do that," said Ava.

"Of course, she would," said Babcock. He edged closer to Carmela and asked, "Where have you been snooping this time?"

"We weren't," said Carmela. "We just returned from that wine-tasting event I honchoed."

"Huh," said Babcock. His handsome face looked tired and drawn. With genuine worry thrown in for good measure.

"I *told* you about that," said Carmela. "Umpteen times."

"Still," said Babcock, "you've been snooping around, obviously ruffling more feathers. You know it and I know it."

"Looks to me," said Ava, "as if Carmela got to someone."

"You think so?" asked Babcock. His words sounded just this side of sarcastic.

Ava gave a vigorous bob of her head. "Somebody's worried. Probably the somebody who wrote that note."

"Who have you been bothering?" Babcock asked Carmela again.

Carmela's brows shot up. "I don't know!" she cried.

"Think," said Babcock. "Think really hard. And, this time, I would really like an answer from you."

Carmela gazed at Ava. A what-do-you-think? gaze.

"Rain?" said Ava, in a small voice.

"Rain Monroe?" said Babcock. "The lady with all the crucifixes?"

"Yeah," said Carmela. "That would be my first guess."

"You're not hurling accusations at Crowley anymore?" asked Babcock.

"Could be him," said Carmela.

"Not likely," said Babcock. He let loose a deep and mournful sigh.

"The question is," said Carmela, "what do we do now? I mean . . . does this note imply that . . . um . . . someone might . . . ?"

"Come back and harm you?" finished Babcock.

"I wasn't going to make it sound quite so dire," said Carmela.

"Maybe we are in danger," said Ava. "So we should sit tight and lock our doors."

Babcock looked undecided for a few moments. He stood with his fists thrust into his pockets, jingling change, rocking back on his heels. Finally he said, "Is there someplace you two can go where you'll be safe?"

"How about your place?" asked Carmela. Babcock lived in a renovated brownstone town house just south of the CBD, or Central Business District.

"Ha ha," said Babcock, "very funny."

"Why not?" asked Ava.

"Here's why not," said Babcock. "When somebody spills their Type A blood all over a note, it generally indicates they mean business. And if this sick, twisted someone knows precisely where you live, they've probably figured out that we're involved."

"Is that what we are?" asked Carmela. "Involved?"

Babcock put both hands on Carmela's shoulders. "Sometimes a little too involved," he murmured.

"You can tell from just looking at that note that it's Type A blood?" asked Ava.

"No," said Babcock, "but I'm afraid the next blood spilled could be yours." He turned to gaze solemnly at Carmela. "Or yours."

Ava hovered nervously on the balls of her feet. Then she grimaced and said, "Um . . . maybe we should tell him about the car last night?"

The question ripped from Babcock's mouth. "What car?"

Ava ducked her head, looking flustered. "The one that tried to run us off the road?"

"Carmela!" said Babcock. "This isn't the first time someone's come after you?"

"I didn't view it quite that way," Carmela said, contriteness in her voice.

"So you think somebody is seriously after us?" asked Ava.

Babcock exhaled slowly. "It would seem that way. So it's probably best if you stay at a hotel or something for the night. I need to get my team together and see what we can figure out."

"How about going back to the hotel we were just at?" asked Ava. "We could probably wangle a good deal. Heck, maybe they'd even comp us a room."

"Not with the dogs," said Carmela, her

mind clicking along at a dizzying speed. "But that's okay, I know a better place to hide out."

"And it can't be your Garden District house," said Babcock. "With multiple entrance points, it wouldn't be secure enough."

"Now you're really scaring me," said Ava.

"I meant to," said Babcock. "So I want you two to pack a few things and go, okay?" He glanced at Ava. "You run across the courtyard while I stand guard right here in the doorway. I'll keep an eye on the both of you."

"Okay," said Ava. She ducked her head and scurried out across the courtyard into the rain.

Carmela just stood there, staring at Babcock, looking nervous, scared, and more than a little baffled.

"Go ahead," he told her, in a kinder, gentle tone of voice. "Get your things."

"What are we going to do about the dogs?" Ava asked as they drove down Rampart Street. Carmela's little Mercedes was packed to the gills. The two of them sat in the front seat with overnight bags jammed between their knees; the dogs were scrunched into the back of the car, where there wasn't really a seat but a shelf. Boo and Poobah were panting and snorting with excitement at being out so late, steaming up the windows like crazy. Smelling up the car a little, too.

"I'm gonna drop Boo and Poobah with Shamus," said Carmela.

"Think he'll take them?" asked Ava.

"Oh yeah," said Carmela. "He's crazy over them; they're his little darlings."

One quick phone call and five minutes later they were parked in front of Shamus's condo. He'd been waiting for them on the sidewalk and dashed eagerly up to the car to greet them.

"Oh, Boo doo doo," Shamus cooed to Boo, tapping the back window. "Woof you, woof you, fur babies."

"Is that an actual language?" Ava asked, as she pushed open her door and climbed out.

"Dog language," said Shamus. "Can't you see how much they love it? Really eat it up?"

Shamus helped Carmela out, then reached back and snapped a leash on a somewhat bored Boo, then a second leash on Poobah. When the dogs had jumped out and were happily sniffing about the boulevard, he said, "Come on, kids, let's go watch TV and snarf some pizza."

"No pizza," said Carmela.

"Aw, gee," said Shamus, frowning at her. "You're no fun." He bent down and kissed Boo on the top of her furry head. "Mommy's no fun, is she? Mommy's never any fun."

"No pizza," Carmela said again.

"Yeah, yeah," Shamus muttered. Then a grin stole across his handsome face. "Where are you girls off to? Some late-night wild party out in the bayou? Gonna have yourselves a little . . . heh-heh . . . overnight?" Shamus suddenly looked a little wistful. As if he wanted to grab a bottle of Wild Turkey and head out with them.

"That's the other thing I wanted to talk to you about," said Carmela. "We're in a . . . I guess you could call it a spot of trouble."

"Sounds familiar," Shamus snorted. "Does it have something to do with that church murder?"

"And the one at Storyville Outreach Center," said Carmela. "Yes, I'm afraid so. The thing is, Ava and I need to stay out of sight for a while. So I was wondering if we could use your camp house?" The Meechum family owned a small camp house in the Baritaria Bayou that they used for hunting and fishing. Sometimes it even served as home base for Shamus's occasional photog-

393

raphy projects.

"It's okay with me," said Shamus, "but, jeez, nobody's been out there in a coon's age. There's probably an inch of dust covering everything." He suddenly looked agitated, like he had a bad taste in his mouth. "And spiderwebs. Those doggone wolf spiders are all over the darn place."

Carmela stifled a grin. Shamus had a real phobia about spiders. She was pleased to see it still bothered him.

"And you're gonna have to fire up the generator and prime the pump," he reminded her. "You remember how to work the pump?"

"Of course, I do," said Carmela. "It's not exactly the same degree of difficulty as disarming a nuclear warhead."

"I'm just sayin'," said Shamus. He dug into his pocket and came up with a Gucci key chain. He worked a small brass key off it, then pressed the key into Carmela's open palm.

"Okay," said Carmela, deciding it was better to remain peaceable. Especially since he'd agreed to dog-sit. "Okay, thanks."

Shamus fixed her with a crooked smile and a wistful gaze. "Those were the good old days, huh, babe? You and me hanging out at the camp house?" He nodded to himself as a look of fond regret crept across his face. "Sleeping late, catching a bucket of mudbugs, drinking beer, and crawling into . . ."

"Shamus," Carmela snapped, "I'm afraid you have a very selective memory."

Shamus gave a knowing grin. "I'm like a computer, sweetheart." He tapped an index finger against the side of his head. "It's all up here in my hard drive."

"Maybe," said Carmela, "it's time to hit the Delete button."

They barreled down Highway 23 toward the Baritaria Bayou, passing through the small, sleeping towns of Port Nickel, Jesuit Bent, and Naomi.

"Whoa," Ava remarked, as Carmela edged the needle up to seventy, "you've got yourself a lead foot tonight."

"Just blowing out the carbon," said Carmela, finally slowing as she came upon Myrtle Grove. It wouldn't do to have the local constable issue a speeding ticket. When she reached a well-lit stretch of road, Carmela pulled in at an all-night Save Mart.

"I hope some peckerwood doesn't decide to rob this joint while we're shopping," said Ava, as they picked up milk, eggs, bread, butter, coffee, and a few other essentials. As an afterthought, Ava tossed in a couple of MoonPies and a Zagnut bar.

Just before they started up again, Carmela checked her phone for messages. One missed call. And she recognized the number. Babcock. She scrolled down to his name and hit the button to return his call. Maybe he'd found something out?

"Who you calling?" asked Ava. She was already unwrapping one of the MoonPies.

"Babcock. But he's not answering."

"Have a MoonPie," said Ava.

"Ah," said Carmela, disappointed at not reaching him, "maybe later."

"Zagnut bar?" Ava offered. When Carmela shook her head, Ava plopped the candy bar into her handbag. "I wonder if you can make candy bar pie out of Zagnut bars? You think?"

"I think," said Carmela, "you can make candy bar pie using *any* kind of candy bar and it will probably turn out just grand."

From Myrtle Grove it was a twisting fifteen miles of seashell roads through dark swampland and the occasional dark, piney forest until they arrived at the tiny village of Baptiste Creek.

"This looks more like a fish camp," said Ava, peering out the window as they slid down the main drag.

"Some of it is," said Carmela. Many of the inhabitants were fishermen or trappers by trade, and the buildings, which had withstood floods, hurricanes, salt air, high humidity, and the march of time, looked a little ramshackle. Add in a stilt building or two that had your basic fishnet, alligator hide, or tin sign nailed to the outside, and you had yourself a picturesque little place with wide appeal to sportsmen.

"This is where you usually pick up a boat," said Ava, as they bumped along.

"At Toler Boat and Bait," said Carmela. Ned Toler, the proprietor, was a crackerjack fishing guide who owned a passel of brown-spotted hounds.

"But tonight we're going to *drive* in," said Ava. She sounded edgy and nervous. "I always thought the only way in was by boat."

"That's the fun way in," said Carmela, "but there's a back way, too. The road's kind of muddy and rutty, but I think we can make it."

"You *think* we can?"

"I know we can," said Carmela. "I've done it a couple of times."

"But it's been raining. Don't you think we need a four-wheel-drive vehicle?"

"It helps," said Carmela. Then she saw the look of concern on Ava's face and said,

"Really, we'll be fine."

They clattered across a narrow, one-lane wooden bridge. Underneath, the water looked sluggish, dark, and ominous. Like maybe an alligator or two might be lurking. Then, two hundred yards beyond, the road dwindled to a muddy rut and the bayou closed in on them.

Carmela crept along steadily as swamp privet and buttonbush whispered against her windshield and caressed the sides of her car. She knew if she kept a steady pace, didn't accelerate and spin her wheels, didn't slow down and get bogged, she'd be fine. After all, she'd done this before. Just never at night.

"Doggone, this is creepy," said Ava. She was clutching the dashboard, her knuckles gone white, gazing out at brackish water populated by stands of black gum and bald cypress.

"It's primordial," said Carmela. "An exotic tangle of swamp, jungle, saltwater intrusion from the Gulf of Mexico, and waterlogged trees."

"And critters," added Ava.

"Opossum, nutria, heron, bald eagles, loggerhead turtles, and alligators," said Carmela. "As well as redfish, black drum, speckled trout, and black bass, if you happen to be into fishing."

"Fishing, no. Fashion, yes," said Ava. "Um . . . how close are we?"

"It's not too far now, we just have to . . . oh, man." Carmela took her foot off the accelerator and let her car coast to a stop.

"Why are we stopping!" Ava shrilled.

Carmela lifted a hand from the steering wheel and pointed. Ten feet ahead, the road turned into a quagmire.

"Can we make it through that?" asked Ava.

"Hope so," said Carmela. She put her car into reverse, spun it back a good fifty feet or so, then double-clutched into second. "Hang on!" She sped forward at a good clip. Ten, twenty, now thirty miles an hour. Hitting the mud, Carmela felt her tires sink in and her engine rev higher as it fought its way through. Chunks of mud flew past them as they ground away. And then, just when Carmela could see dry land again, just like that she was stuck.

"What happened?" cried Ava. She'd been rocking backward and forward, as if being synced with the car could help propel it forward.

"We're stuck," said Carmela.

Ava let the news sink in. "Can we get a tow truck?"

"Nope."

"What are we going to do?"

Carmela let go of the steering wheel and flexed her fingers. "Push?"

"You're not serious," said Ava. "I . . . I can't push. I'm a one-hundred-thirty-pound weakling!"

Carmela chuckled. "You always told me you weighed a hundred and twenty."

"I lied," said Ava, who was way past hitting the panic button. She was venturing into hysteria territory. "But that's beside the point. The thing is, what are we going to *do?*"

"Not many choices," said Carmela. She slipped off her shoes, then pushed open the driver's-side door and dangled a bare foot above the mud. "You scoot over here and drive. I'll jump out and push."

"Drive?" said Ava. "But your car's a *stick* shift!"

"Just put it in first gear, and once we get going, pop it into second."

"Wait a minute, wait a minute!" said Ava, waving her hands wildly. "Your instructions . . . you're making it very complicated."

Carmela was incredulous. "Excuse me. A gal from Alabama who can't drive a stick shift?"

Ava gave a vigorous head shake. "Not for years. Not since I stole my cousin Jethro's pickup when I was fifteen and desperate to get to a dance over in Rock City."

"Well . . . tell me about that. Did you make it?"

"Yes, of course. I danced every dance and made out with Huey Everet behind the outhouse."

"Then just pretend you're in the same situation, only with modern plumbing."

Ava blinked rapidly as she tried to process this information. Then a sly grin stole across her face. "I guess when you put it that way . . . move over, honey!"

CHAPTER 27

Built on stilts and hunkered into a grove of saw palmetto and tupelo trees, the Meechums' camp house was built of cypress and cedar boards that had been painstakingly split, sawed, planed, and nailed into place by hand. Windows were hinged on top and opened outward to allow breezes to sift through. Of course, the house could also be battened down in a heartbeat in case of bad weather. An open-air porch wrapped around the front and two sides; the steeply pitched roof was covered with corrugated tin.

Inside, the first level was a combination living room/kitchen area with a small partitioned-off storage room. Up a narrow flight of stairs and stuck up in the rafters was the bedroom loft. Carmela had turned on the generator, so now the place was moody and lit with soft lighting.

"Oh my gosh," Ava trilled, as they clomped into the camp house with all their gear and groceries, "this is so cozy."

"It's homey but dusty," said Carmela, stifling a sneeze. Shamus had been right. The place was thick with dust and the corners of the room festooned with spiderwebs.

But thirty minutes later, they'd pulled sheets off the leather sofa and chairs, wiped down the counters as well as the kitchen table and chairs, mopped up the cobwebs, primed the pump, and even started a fire in the small stone fireplace. Suddenly the camp house felt very warm and cheery and lived in. The rain had started up again and pattered down on the tin roof, lending a homey if not slightly melancholy sound effect.

Ava had changed into an oversized T-shirt and high-heeled fuzzy slippers and was curled up on the couch. "It's like staying in a lodge."

"Without the amenity of room service," said Carmela.

Ava gave a slow wink. "But I've got you."

"If you don't mind scrambled eggs and toast, you'll be fine."

"Works for me," said Ava. She leaned back against the sofa, looking sleepy and content. "Hey, there's a cassette player." She pointed to a bookshelf tucked under one of the windows. "We could play some music."

"If you're a fan of Alabama and the Carpenters."

"Pass," said Ava. "Too old-school." But she was still contemplating the cassette player. "Isn't it weird how music has progressed, over the years, from albums to cassettes to CDs to iPods? I mean, what's next?"

"I don't know," said Carmela, "Maybe implant a chip in your brain?"

"Hope not," said Ava. She stretched out a long, bare leg and rested it on a leather hassock. "You think I should get a tattoo?"

"Why not?" said Carmela. "They're doing such great things with lasers these days."

Ava stifled a giggle. "If I got a tattoo, there'd be no turning back. I'd keep it forever."

Carmela lifted a single eyebrow. "What kind of design did you have in mind? And what part of your body would showcase this magnificent design?"

"I don't know. Maybe a yellow rose just above my sweet little dimpled knee?"

"Why not a magnolia blossom?" asked Carmela, playing along.

"Too complicated," said Ava. An imp-like smile stole across her face. "You get one, too," she urged. "We'll both pay a visit to

404

Crazy Ink and make it a girls' bonding experience. Maybe meet some cool biker guys, too."

"I'm really not a tramp-stamp kind of girl."

"Think of it as scrapbooking your bod," Ava teased. "You could do a fun design or some cool calligraphy or . . ."

A heavy thunk sounded on the roof. Like a weight being dropped from the heavens above. There was a moment of hesitation, then a loud, metallic tumbling as something rolled and bounced its way down the corrugated roof, picking up speed as it went.

Ava hit the deck like she was sliding into first base. Carmela ducked behind the sofa.

"Holy frizolli!" Ava yelped. "What was that?"

"Rock," said Carmela. She said it calmly and without emotion. The same as if she'd uttered the words *dog poop*. "I think somebody tossed a rock onto the roof."

"Who would do that?" hissed Ava. "I mean, out *here*?"

Carmela shook her head. "Don't know. Trapper, poacher, swamp rat, meth lab lowlife? Take your pick." She was just thankful the windows were shut and latched. On the other hand, the camp house was solid, but no way was it an impenetrable fortress.

"Oh crap!" Ava clapped a hand over her mouth. "Do you think somebody followed us?"

Carmela was already running various permutations through her brain. None of them were good. "Maybe," she allowed.

"Like the same person who left the note?"

"I don't know." Carmela scanned the interior, looking for soft points. Places someone could force or batter their way in. Besides the front door, she didn't think there were any. At least she *hoped* there weren't.

"So you think it's just some good-ol'-boy hunter stumbling around out there?" said Ava.

"Trying to scare us? Could be."

"But you're not sure."

Carmela shook her head. She was concentrating, listening hard with every fiber of her being, waiting to see if there might be a repeat performance. So far, there wasn't. So . . .

Footsteps sounded on the front porch. Slow and deliberate. Someone was walking the length of the porch. They stopped, paused, then turned back.

"Is the door locked?" Ava whimpered.

"Yes," said Carmela, as she focused on the front door. Seven feet high and con-

406

structed of solid oak, it was a considerable barrier. There was no window or peephole in the door, only a small arched window high above it.

"What if it's that guy from the Seekers?" asked Ava.

But Carmela wondered if it might not be Johnny Otis. After all, she'd given him Shamus's last name. Could Otis have tracked her that way? Maybe looked up property records? Had he left the note on her door and then tailed them here tonight? Or was someone else prowling around out there?

Staying low, Carmela scrabbled across the room and grabbed her bag off the kitchen table. Five seconds later she was back behind the sofa, digging through it.

"Phone?" asked Ava.

Carmela pulled out her cell phone as well as her handgun.

"You've got a gun?" Ava hissed.

Carmela nodded.

"With real bullets?"

"Yes."

"Have you ever fired it?"

Carmela grimaced. "Once. At a firing range." Then she added, "I don't want to use it, but if we're pushed . . ." She dropped the gun into the right-hand pocket of her sweater, keenly aware of its lumpiness and heft.

Ava looked genuinely frightened. "Better we try to get help. Is there cell phone service out here?"

"Sometimes. But it's spotty, at best."

"Still," said Ava, "you gotta try!"

Carmela tried. First she punched 911. No dice. Nothing happened at all. Just dead air. Then she punched in Babcock's cell phone number. She managed to coax out one strangled ring before it went dead. "Nothing's working," Carmela whispered.

"Try again," urged Ava.

"Try who?" asked Carmela.

"Anybody!"

Carmela thought for a minute, then punched in Shamus's phone number.

He answered on the fourth ring, with a sleepy, discombobulated "Hello?" that told her he'd been fast asleep.

"Shamus! Did somebody call you? Was somebody looking for me tonight?"

"Huh?" said Shamus. Then, sounding perturbed, he said, "I was asleep. You woke me up." His voice was peevish and scratchy, like that of an unhappy five-year-old.

"Shamus, pay attention!" Carmela hissed.

But Shamus only coughed and mumbled, "What time is it?"

"Did someone call your house, Shamus?" Carmela asked. "After we stopped by? Was someone looking for us?"

"Um . . ."

"Think, Shamus!" Carmela ordered. She could sense his wheels turning, but very slowwwly.

"I guess so," said Shamus. "Yeah, yeah they did."

"Who was it?" asked Carmela.

"Um . . . it was Baby," said Shamus. "Baby called."

"Are you sure it was Baby?" asked Carmela. "Because we're at the camp house and somebody's outside harassing us. And, just off the top of my head, I don't think it's our old friend Baby."

"Whoever called *said* it was Baby," Shamus whined.

"And it was a woman?"

"Ah . . . yes."

"And you took her at her word?" Carmela screeched. "And told her exactly where we were?"

"Well, yeah," said Shamus, yawning. "Um . . . *what* time did you say it was?"

"Shamus," said Carmela, "this is important. This is critically important. You must call Edgar Babcock right now and tell him exactly where we are. Tell him we might be

409

in danger and have him send somebody out here immediately. And by somebody I mean police, sheriff, Coast Guard, or Fish and Wildlife Services. Now, will you do that? Can you do that?"

"I guess."

"Then do it *now*, Shamus, and please don't let me down!"

"Jeez, Carmela," Shamus croaked, "I'm not a moron!"

"Just make the call, Shamus." Carmela clicked the Off button.

"What?" asked Ava. She was curled into a ball, halfway under a low wooden table.

"Some woman phoned Shamus, looking for us. He thought it was probably Baby, so he kind of revealed our location." She chewed at her lower lip nervously. "But it wasn't Baby. Couldn't have been."

"Then who?"

"Rain?" said Carmela. "Rain Monroe?"

"Oh, great," said Ava. "Now we've got a crazy lady stalking us."

"Don't make this worse than it is," said Carmela. "Don't let your mind run wild."

"But Rain could have a gun, too!"

"We don't know that," said Carmela.

"Think about it!" said Ava. "If Rain's the one who killed Byrle and Brother Paul, then maybe she's come here to kill us!"

"We're going to be okay," Carmela said. She tried to keep her voice calm. "We haven't heard anything from outside for a couple of minutes, so that's a good thing. We'll just stay right here with the doors and windows locked."

"Okay." Ava gave a stuttering nod. "Whatever you say."

"And then, in about fifteen or twenty minutes, someone from the sheriff's department or Fish and Wildlife Services is going to knock on our door. And then we really will be perfectly fine."

Ava glanced toward the door. "If somebody's still out there, can they see through that window up there?"

"Not unless they stand on something," said Carmela. "And that's probably not . . ."

The window above the door suddenly exploded inward, sending shards of glass ripping through the camp house. Carmela threw up her arms and turned her head away. "Gun blast!" she cried.

"Ayyy!" Ava's high-pitched scream rent the air.

Oh no! Ava hit?

"Are you hit?" Carmela screamed as she got her knees under her and made a frantic, stumbling dive toward Ava. "Are you hit?"

"I don't know!" Um . . ." Ava pressed the

411

back of her shaking hand to her forehead. When she took it away, bright red blood was smeared across her brows and forehead. Ava's eyes went wide and her face turned deathly pale. "Oh jeez, Carmela. I'm hit, I am hit!"

CHAPTER 28

Carmela pulled the scarf from around her neck, prepared to make a tourniquet. "Let me see!"

But Ava was terror-stricken. "How bad?" she gibbered. "Do you think the bullet's lodged in my brain? Am I going to end up a vegetable?"

Carmela put her arms around Ava and gently pushed back a hank of dark curly hair. A quick, cursory inspection revealed the problem. "You weren't hit by the bullet. But you've got a small shard of glass stuck in your forehead."

"Pull it out!" Ava screeched.

Carmela hesitated. "It could hurt." She could also mess up big-time, leaving her friend with an ugly scar.

"Please!" Ava pleaded. "I don't want a hunk of glass sticking in me!"

"Okay, okay," said Carmela. "Then just . . . try to hold still."

"I will, I will." Shaking like a leaf and practically stupefied, Ava hunched forward.

Carmela pinched at the glass with her thumb and forefinger but wasn't able to get a good grip. "Doggone." Between the ooze of blood and Ava's trembling . . .

"Just do it!" Ava begged. "Yank it out!"

Carmela gulped a quick breath and steeled herself. She got what she hoped was a firm pincerlike grip and gave a sudden yank. And she got it! The glass, thankfully, came out clean.

"Am I gonna have a scar?" asked Ava. "Will I need a plastic surgeon?"

"Shh," said Carmela, wiping at Ava's forehead with her scarf. "Maybe a single stitch at best. Or just a Steri-Strip. It's not bad at all."

Ava touched a finger to her wound. "But I'm still bleeding!"

"Head wounds always bleed like crazy," Carmela murmured. "But that's not our problem right now." She shot another quick, worried look toward the front door.

"Can they get in here?"

"We're not going to stick around to find out," said Carmela. She grabbed Ava's wrist and pulled her to her feet. "Come on," she said, as she hauled her friend toward the narrow stairway.

Which was exactly when the lights winked out and the entire camp house was plunged into total darkness.

"What happened?" cried Ava. They'd only made it up the first step. Now Ava clung to Carmela as if she were a lifeline.

"Somebody cut the generator."

"So we clamber around in the dark?"

"Wait here," Carmela told her. Putting her hands in front of her, she shuttled her way to the bookcase, where she knew a flashlight was always stashed. Batting her hands around crazily, she knocked a row of books to the floor.

"What's happening?" asked Ava.

Carmela's fingers finally touched the reassuring rubber grip of the flashlight. "Nothing. I got it." She snapped the light on. "Let's get upstairs." She waved the thin beam in an upward motion.

"Won't we be trapped?" Ava quavered, as they climbed the stairs.

"No," said Carmela. They scrambled up and she flashed her light around the small loft, revealing a bed, small table, and dresser. "We'll be safe." Depositing Ava on the bed and the flashlight on the small table, Carmela scurried back and dropped the trapdoor into place. It slammed shut with a satisfying bang.

"What if whoever's outside gets *inside?*" worried Ava. "What if they climb the steps after us?"

Carmela grasped the four-drawer wooden dresser and muscled it across the floor until it sat squarely atop the trapdoor. "They won't. And if they do, that's gonna hold them."

"Now what?" asked Ava. She was still dabbing at her forehead, still coming away with touches of blood.

"What I'm going to do is take a look out there," said Carmela.

"Out there?" said Ava, not quite comprehending. "You mean *out* out there!"

"That's right." Carmela crept over to a small cantilevered window and unscrewed the latch. She had to see what she was up against!

"Please don't!" Ava cried. "Stay here!"

Carmela hesitated at the window. Should she go? Or wait here and hope help showed up? No, she didn't want to articulate her base fear to Ava, but maybe a rescue brigade *wouldn't* arrive. Maybe Shamus would mess up, or Babcock wouldn't be home, or the local sheriff would be too busy with some other sort of emergency.

Slowly, quietly, Carmela raised the hinged window. Cold rain lashed in, instantly chill-

416

ing her to the bone. Holding a finger to her mouth, Carmela said, in a low whisper, "One quick peek."

Ava shook her head vehemently. No, she didn't want Carmela to go.

"You just hunker down," Carmela whispered. "You'll be okay." She propped open the window, took a deep breath, and put one foot on the roof.

Instantly, she was hit with a swirl of wind and rain. It flattened her hair, soaked her clothes, obscured her vision, and scared her to death.

Still, Carmela kept moving. She ducked through the window frame, scrunched around, then pulled her other leg through. With barely a glance backward, she stepped out onto the tin roof.

Rain sliced down in torrents now as Carmela crept along the roof. The footing was slippery at best, and Carmela prayed to the Lord above that she wouldn't fall. *Oh please, don't let me slide down, hit the ground, and break a hip. Oh yeah, and get shot in the head while I'm lying in the mud, writhing in pain.*

Thunder rumbled like a bowling alley in the heavens, and streaks of lightning slashed the sky. Still Carmela walked the ridgeline of the roof like a tightrope walker, placing one foot carefully before the other, arms extended for balance.

She reached the edge and hesitated. Brushed rain from her eyes, took a deep breath. This was the tricky part. She had to keep her balance and still look down without succumbing to vertigo.

Suddenly, a brilliant flash of lightning illuminated the sky. And in one quick, starkly revealed instant, like a camera flash exploding, Carmela caught sight of a woman sneaking along the side of the camp house. The woman's head was down, her shoulders hunched forward as she stealthily picked her way.

Carmela's gun lay heavy in her pocket. If push came to shove, did she dare use it? If she shot someone, would it be classified as self-defense or would she be convicted of manslaughter?

Another flash of lightning gave her a flash of insight. Yes, she'd use her gun. Because in that quick moment, she'd seen a gun clutched in the woman's hand, a gun that was pointed even and straight, ready to fire.

Was this Rain Monroe? Carmela ground her teeth together and made a shallow growl. Had to be! And how dare she come after them! How dare she stalk them and terrorize them! Carmela's fury rose up inside her like molten lava and she screamed, as loud as she could, "Rain!"

The woman below jerked as if she'd been hit with a muscle spasm. She flung herself to the left, then the right. Not seeing anyone, the woman hesitated for one startled moment, then cranked her head back and looked up.

Another bolt of lightning tore across the sky, and the woman — not Rain — stared directly at Carmela! As their eyes met, a knowing, feral look crossed the woman's face.

Fumbling for her own gun now, realizing she had to defend herself, Carmela struggled to drag it from her pocket.

That was when Marilyn Casey, wannabe mystery writer and certified crazy lady, slowly raised her gun at what appeared to be an easy target.

Time slowed to a crawl for Carmela as she juggled her weapon and tried to maintain balance on the slippery roof.

But Marilyn had the upper hand by a couple of seconds. Enough to let her take careful aim at Carmela's fluttering heart!

At that precise moment, Carmela's feet shot out from under her and she fell flat on her back.

Marilyn's shot ripped across Carmela's

left shoulder as Carmela slid wildly down the angled roof of the camp house, as if she were careening full tilt down a giant waterslide.

For a few sickening, heart-stopping moments, Carmela was airborne, catapulted almost horizontally through the air. Then she was falling, falling, falling, letting loose a shrill scream that reverberated in her head and seemed to go on forever. Still clutching her gun, she landed on her back with a bone-rattling, teeth-jangling thump.

Wind knocked from her lungs, head befuddled, Carmela found herself sprawled awkwardly in six inches of sticky mud and decaying vegetation. Blinking away rain, Carmela stared up at the woman who had a gun in her hand and murder in her eyes.

But this time Carmela had the advantage of a precise and perfect angle. Without an eyelash of hesitation, Carmela pulled back on the trigger and felt the gun buck hotly in her hand. She gasped as her shot hit its mark!

Marilyn cried in pain and fired one useless shot into the air. Then her gun flew from her hand and Marilyn, howling like a banshee in the forest, dropped in the dirt like a sack of spilled canned goods.

CHAPTER 29

Throwing back her head, neck straining with pain, Marilyn Casey let loose a strangled, enraged howl. "Owwww!" She twisted and contorted herself back and forth, clutching her wounded knee as blood spurted everywhere. "You shot me!" Marilyn's voice was a high-pitched, agonized gurgle. "I'm going to get you for that! I'll *kill* you!"

Carmela knew she wasn't out of the woods yet. Marilyn's gun had flown out of her hand, but it lay somewhere nearby. Struggling to sit up, every muscle and fiber in her back screaming in protest, Carmela glanced wildly about. Where was Marilyn's gun?

Marilyn continued to groan and thrash, jabbing her good leg at Carmela and kicking at her head. Then Marilyn seemed to lose interest in that and began frantically patting the ground around her, trying to locate her gun.

"I will kill you!" Marilyn growled as she gnashed her teeth and bits of foam and spittle flew from her mouth.

"Stop it!" Carmela cried, aiming her gun at her. "Stop or I'll shoot again!" If she could just pull herself up . . . if only her back didn't feel like it was alive with hot coals.

Marilyn's eyes rolled wildly in her head as she pawed around. Then, a sudden, demonic glint shone in her eyes.

Carmela saw instantly what Marilyn was after. Marilyn's gun lay maybe six feet away.

"Don't!" Carmela warned, still struggling to get her feet under her and failing miserably.

Marilyn flopped over onto her stomach, flailing and trying to pull herself along on her elbows.

"Stop it!" Carmela warned again.

Now Marilyn was three feet from her gun, her arm straining to reach it, her fingers working reflexively.

Wrenching herself around, Carmela kicked frantically at Marilyn's outstretched arm.

"Arwahhh!" wailed Marilyn.

With no tricks up her sleeve, other than shooting Marilyn, Carmela spun herself about in the sucking muck. With one final effort, she flopped both legs across Marilyn's outstretched arms and pinned her down tightly.

They were still struggling weakly when Carmela heard the first hint of a motorboat putt-putting up to the dock. Hurried footsteps splashed toward them. Then, through the curtain of rain, a pair of mud-splattered boots slowly appeared. A kindly-looking man in his early fifties, wearing a khaki brown uniform with a yellow Fish and Wildlife Services patch on his arm, shone a bright light on them. "Holy horse pucky," he muttered.

"Help me," Carmela cried out weakly, as she stared up at her rescuer. "She's got a gun!"

The Fish and Wildlife guy took a step closer and planted his size-twelve boot on top of Marilyn's gun. "Not now she doesn't."

Five minutes later, it was pretty much over. At least the exciting, shooting part, anyway.

Marilyn sat handcuffed and dripping on a straight-backed wooden chair just inside the door, a tourniquet applied to her injured leg. She muttered and mumbled to herself like a person possessed, shaking her head as if the entire episode had been one huge misunderstanding.

Ava was splayed out on the sofa, casting angry looks at Marilyn. If she'd been imbued with supernatural powers, she'd have cast a spell and turned Marilyn into a garden-variety toad.

The Fish and Wildlife Services officer, whose name Carmela came to learn was Bobby Stump, chattered madly via radio to the local law enforcement center.

And, wonder of wonders, Carmela had finally been able to reach Edgar Babcock by phone.

"She shot at me!" Carmela cried, hot tears trickling down her cheeks. "She tried to kill me!" Standing on the front porch, she gazed into the purple darkness of the bayou. Raindrops still pattered down, and the occasional streak of lightning lanced the sky.

"You're safe now," Babcock crooned. "You're okay, you did good, sweetheart. Time to stand down."

"But I . . . but I . . . I'm all the way out here in the bayou." A small sob escaped Carmela's lips. "Kind of in the middle of nowhere. And Ava's hurt! She got hit by a chunk of flying glass."

"I understand all that," Babcock soothed. "We'll take care of it, we'll get her to a hospital."

"It was Marilyn Casey all along!" Carmela cried. She wanted to kick herself for not seeing it earlier.

"We just figured it out," said Babcock, sounding excited. "We took the note back to the lab and one of my guys — he wasn't even supposed to be there — thought the handwriting looked familiar."

Carmela sniffled. "Seriously?"

"Yes. It seems Marilyn had been interviewing him and she left a list of questions."

"Bold," said Carmela.

"Brazen," agreed Babcock. "But that's how criminals often operate. They think they're smart, so they do stupid, arrogant things."

"She was writing that wretched book," said Carmela.

"That's right. And, apparently, she didn't think a historical thriller was exciting enough. She wanted to write about true crime. And probably gain an instant local readership."

"Crimes that *she* committed," Carmela mourned. She clutched her phone tighter. "Awful," she said. "Poor Byrle. And then Brother Paul."

"Just because you were getting close," said Babcock.

"And she needed an exciting ending," said Carmela. "Really . . . abominable."

"But she didn't get away with it," said Babcock. "Thanks to you."

"Me?" Carmela said, with a strangled gasp. "I didn't do anything. All I did was . . ."

"Shoot her," said Babcock. There was grudging approval in his voice.

But Babcock's voice seemed to be fading in and out for Carmela. Or else she was descending into some kind of posttraumatic shock. Carmela wasn't exactly sure what was happening. All she knew was she seemed to be losing her tenuous connection to Babcock, who, right now, was proving to be not only her boyfriend, but her rock and champion.

"I wish you were here!" she told him, in a gush of emotion. "I wish you could just hold me!" Standing on the front porch, she collapsed back against the outside wall and slid down until she landed in a cross-legged, hunched sprawl. "I just feel so . . . alone." *And miserable,* she thought to herself.

"A mistake!" Marilyn shrilled from inside. "A huge mistake!"

"Shut up!" came Ava's angry voice. "Shut up or I'll whack you upside the head!"

Carmela squeezed her eyes closed, trying

to shut out the noise from inside. She just wanted to make it all go away.

"Are you there?" came Babcock's voice.

Carmela ducked and blinked as a flash of light strobed before her eyes. This time she knew she was slipping into shock. Or . . . maybe the sun was just beginning to rise on the bayou? Could that be happening? Had she and Ava spent the entire agonizing night out here? Yes, probably they had.

"I'm coming," Babcock told her. "I'll be there."

Carmela clutched the phone, as if his voice alone could sustain her.

A low thumping pounded in her temples and then seemed to telegraph through her entire being. *Heart attack? I'm having a heart attack? Or, worse yet, a stroke?*

And then a light shone even brighter and the rotor blades of a helicopter sounded distinctly, beating their whap-whap-whap out across the sparkling water, whipping out concentric circles of ripples.

"That's you?" Carmela cried out, when she suddenly realized what was happening. "That's you?" Now a top note of joy colored her voice as she pulled herself to her feet.

"Landing in two minutes," Babcock told her.

"The cavalry coming to the rescue,"

427

Carmela murmured. Her head throbbed, her back ached, her nerves felt like they'd been shot through with electrical current. On top of that, she was ready to collapse.

"From the way Officer Stump tells it," said Babcock, as the helicopter swooped down onto a jetty of soft land, "you're the one who did the rescuing."

"You think?" said Carmela. She could see a set of impossibly long legs dangling out the side of the helicopter. Then a man in a flapping leather jacket with a phone pressed tightly to his ear hurried toward her.

"Job well done," Babcock told her, as Carmela's own phone slipped from her hand and she flew into his outstretched arms. "You saved the day."

"I think," said Carmela, hugging him tightly, "we saved each other."

SCRAPBOOK, STAMPING, AND CRAFT TIPS FROM LAURA CHILDS

Candle Magic

Metal embellishments and charms are lovely when applied to large pillar candles. Think silver dragonflies on white candles, perhaps a bronze Celtic cross on a maroon candle, or gold keys on a yellow candle. For a more ornate candle, glue on some beads and tie a piece of sheer ribbon around it.

Gatefold Cards

This triptych style of card is showy but easy to create. Simply start with a piece of card stock that measures six by twelve inches. Then find the middle of your length of card stock and mark it with a pencil. Then find the quarter points and mark those with a pencil. Now score only the quarter lines and fold carefully so the two sides meet in the middle. From here, simply decorate your card, front and inside, just as you would your traditional cards.

Wooden Birdhouses

Transform a simple wooden birdhouse into a table centerpiece using decoupage. For winter months, decoupage using tortoiseshell or velvet paper and enhance with bits of brocade or velvet ribbon and Paperclay birds that have been painted gold. For warmer months, select floral papers and then embellish with pressed paper dragonflies and silk butterflies.

Paper Flowers

If you have a one- to two-inch heart punch, you can easily create a beautiful flower! Choose yellow or gold paper and punch out seven hearts to use as petals. Now add a bit of gold paint to give your petals some depth. Then assemble your flower by overlapping each petal and using a dab of glue to hold them all together. These flat flowers work perfectly in a scrapbook, or you can bend the petals slightly before assembly to create dimension.

Instant Papier-Mâché

Don't toss out those mounds of shredded packing paper! Instead, mix them with a simple flour-and-water paste to create instant papier-mâché. Mardi Gras masks, anyone? Or cover an old wine bottle with papier-mâché to create a bumpy artifact look. When it dries, simply rub on colored paint to simulate an antique bronzed effect.

Seed Packets

Small envelopes filled with seeds make wonderful gifts or favors. Just select your favorite envelopes from the craft store, then embellish by rubber-stamping them with floral and leaf motifs. Gild the edges and hand-letter a greeting or floral sentiment (such as *Where flowers bloom, so does hope*). Then fill with your favorite seeds (think wildflower or zinnia seeds), tie on a bit of sheer ribbon, and your gift is ready to share with all your green-thumb friends.

FAVORITE NEW ORLEANS RECIPES

CARMELA'S
CHICKEN JAMBALAYA

2 Tbsp. butter
1/4 cup onion, chopped
1/4 cup celery, chopped
1/4 cup green bell pepper, chopped
1 can (14.5 oz.) diced tomatoes
1 1/2 cups chicken broth
2/3 cup white rice
1/4 tsp. garlic salt
1/4 tsp. black pepper
1/4 tsp. hot pepper sauce
2 cups cooked, diced chicken

Melt the butter in a skillet over medium heat. Add the onion, celery, and bell pepper and sauté until tender. Stir in the tomatoes, broth, rice, garlic salt, black pepper, and hot pepper sauce. Bring to a boil, then reduce the heat. Cover and simmer for about 20 minutes, or until the rice is cooked. Stir in the chicken and heat thoroughly. Serves 4.

Brown Sugar Quick Bread

2 1/4 cups flour, sifted
2 tsp. baking powder
1/2 tsp. baking soda
1/4 tsp. salt
1/2 tsp. cinnamon
1/4 tsp. nutmeg
1 cup brown sugar, packed
1 egg, beaten
1 cup buttermilk
2 Tbsp. butter, melted
1 cup pecans, chopped

Preheat the oven to 350 degrees F. Stir together the flour, baking powder, baking soda, salt, cinnamon, and nutmeg. Blend in the brown sugar. In a separate bowl, combine the beaten egg, buttermilk, and melted butter. Add to the flour mixture and combine well. Stir in the chopped pecans. Pour the batter into a greased and floured 5-by-9-inch loaf pan. Bake for 45 to 50 minutes, or until a toothpick inserted in the center comes out clean.

BABY'S CHOCOLATE STREUSEL BARS

1 3/4 cups flour
1 1/2 cups powdered sugar
1/2 cup cocoa powder
1 cup butter
1 pkg. (8 oz.) cream cheese, softened
1 can (14 fl. oz.) sweetened condensed milk
1 egg
2 tsp. vanilla extract
1/2 cup pecans or walnuts, chopped

Preheat the oven to 350 degrees F. In a large bowl, combine the flour, powdered sugar, and cocoa powder. Cut in the butter until the mixture is crumbly. Set aside 2 cups of the crumb mixture and press the remaining mixture on the bottom of a 9-by-12-inch baking pan. Bake for 15 minutes. In a large bowl, beat the cream cheese until fluffy. Gradually beat in the condensed milk until smooth. Add the egg and vanilla and mix well. Pour the mixture over the baked crust and smooth out. Combine the nuts with the reserved crumb mixture and spread on top. Bake for 25 minutes. Let cool, then cut into bars.

BAYOU BACON-WRAPPED SHRIMP

Zest of 1 lime
Juice of 1 lime (2 Tbsp.)

2 Tbsp. olive oil
12 large raw shrimp, peeled and deveined
6 strips bacon, cut in half lengthwise to
  make 12 strips

Preheat the oven to 400 degrees F. Mix the
lime zest, lime juice, and olive oil in a small
bowl. Add the shrimp to the lime mixture
and let marinate for 10 minutes, making
sure all of the shrimp are coated.

Wrap a half-slice of bacon around each
shrimp and secure with a toothpick. Place
the finished shrimp on a slotted baking pan
and brush any remaining lime mixture on
top. Bake for 10 to 14 minutes, until the
shrimp are pink and the bacon is crispy.

BIG EASY BROWN SUGAR BEANS

4 slices bacon, cut into pieces
1 can (21 oz.) pork and beans
1/3 cup brown sugar, packed
1/4 cup chili sauce
1/2 cup onion, chopped
1/2 Tbsp. Worcestershire sauce

Preheat the oven to 325 degrees F. Brown
the bacon in a skillet, then drain and
crumble into a bowl. Add the pork and
beans, brown sugar, chili sauce, onion, and
Worcestershire sauce. Stir, then pour into a
baking dish. Bake for 1 1/2 hours.

EASY CHEESY BROWNIES

1 pkg. fudge brownie mix
8 oz. cream cheese
1/3 cup granulated sugar
1 tsp. vanilla extract
1 egg

Preheat the oven to 350 degrees F. Prepare the brownie mix according to the directions, then spread the brownie batter in a greased 9-by-12-inch pan and set aside. Beat the cream cheese with an electric mixer until smooth, then add the sugar and mix well. Add the vanilla and egg and stir until blended. Spread the cream cheese mixture over the brownie batter. Cut through the batter with a knife to achieve a marbled effect. Bake for 35 minutes. Cool and cut into squares.

DRUNKEN PECAN CHICKEN

1 chicken, cut into pieces
1/4 tsp. dried thyme
1/2 tsp. dried rosemary, crumbled
1/4 tsp. garlic powder
1/2 cup red wine
1 Tbsp. butter
1 cup chopped pecans

Preheat the oven to 375 degrees F. Arrange the chicken in a 9-by-12-inch baking dish.

Sprinkle with the thyme, rosemary, and garlic powder. Pour the wine over the chicken. Dot the chicken with pieces of butter. Sprinkle with the chopped pecans. Cover with foil and bake for 30 minutes. Remove the foil and continue to bake for another 30 minutes.

DELTA CORN PANCAKES

2 cups corn kernels (canned, frozen, or fresh)
1/3 cup red bell pepper, diced
1/3 cup onion, finely chopped
1/3 cup melted butter
1 1/2 cups flour
3 eggs
1 1/2 cups heavy cream
Sour cream (for topping)

Combine the corn kernels, bell pepper, and onion. Stir in the melted butter. Add the flour and mix until the vegetables are well coated. In a separate bowl, lightly beat the eggs, then add the heavy cream. Fold the egg-and-cream mixture into the vegetable mixture. Cook as dollar-sized pancakes until golden brown. Top with a dollop of sour cream. (Note: Bacon or sausage is the perfect accompaniment!)

CARMELA'S POPEYE PIZZA

1 grilled pizza crust
1 cup prepared spinach dip
1 cup shredded cheddar cheese
1 cup mozzarella cheese

Preheat the oven to 400 degrees F. Place the grilled pizza crust on a pizza pan. Spread on the spinach dip, then top with the cheddar cheese and mozzarella cheese. Bake for 8 to 10 minutes, or until the cheese is all melted and golden.

SOUTHERN CANDY BAR PIE

1 pkg. (8 oz.) cream cheese, softened
1 container (8 oz.) frozen whipped topping, thawed
4 (2.1 oz.) Butterfinger candy bars
9-inch graham cracker pie shell

Beat the cream cheese until smooth, then fold in the whipped topping. Crush the Butterfinger bars and fold them into the cream cheese mixture, reserving about 2 Tbsp. for topping. Spoon the mixture into the pie shell, then sprinkle with the remaining candy topping. Refrigerate for at least 2 hours before slicing. (Note: Kit Kat bars can also be used. Yum!)

ABOUT THE AUTHOR

Laura Childs is the *New York Times* best-selling author of the Tea Shop Mysteries, the Cackleberry Club Mysteries, and the Scrapbooking Mysteries. She is a consummate tea drinker, scrapbooker, and dog lover, and travels frequently to China and Japan with Dr. Bob, her professor husband. In her past life she was a Clio Award-winning advertising writer and CEO of her own marketing firm.